"Elizabeth Goddard [...] mantic suspense wi[...] you hooked from start to finish. Amnesia, a hero with dangerous ties, and a deadly storm all combine to create a thrilling ride, perfect for devouring in one sitting. Looking forward to the next one."

Lynette Eason, bestselling, award-winning author of the Lake City Heroes series

"Elizabeth Goddard's *Storm Warning* is perfectly named. This book takes readers by storm as her characters, photographer Remi Grant and former military pilot Hawk Beckett, face danger not only from outside forces but also from the deadly secrets that rage inside their souls. Secrets that could cost them . . . everything. Highly recommended."

Nancy Mehl, author of the Ryland and St. Clair series

Praise for the Novels of Elizabeth Goddard

"A fast-paced journey through beautiful yet isolated parts of the Last Frontier."

Booklist starred review on *Hidden in the Night*

"The author does a fabulous job of keeping the suspense level high, the danger coming, and readers like me on the edge of our seats!"

Reading Is My Superpower on *Shadows at Dusk*

"Close relationships, believable characters, danger, murders—*Shadows at Dusk* has it all."

Life Is Story on *Shadows at Dusk*

STORM
WARNING

Books by Elizabeth Goddard

UNCOMMON JUSTICE SERIES

Never Let Go
Always Look Twice
Don't Keep Silent

ROCKY MOUNTAIN COURAGE SERIES

Present Danger
Deadly Target
Critical Alliance

MISSING IN ALASKA SERIES

Cold Light of Day
Shadows at Dusk
Hidden in the Night

HIDDEN BAY SERIES

Storm Warning

STORM WARNING

ELIZABETH GODDARD

Revell

a division of Baker Publishing Group
Grand Rapids, Michigan

Published by Revell
a division of Baker Publishing Group
Grand Rapids, Michigan
RevellBooks.com

Printed in the United States of America

Library of Congress Cataloging-in-Publication Data
Names: Goddard, Elizabeth, author.
Title: Storm warning / Elizabeth Goddard.
Description: Grand Rapids, Michigan : Revell, a division of Baker Publishing
    Group, 2025. | Series: Hidden Bay ; 1
Identifiers: LCCN 2024026545 | ISBN 9780800746148 (paperback) | ISBN
    9780800746735 (casebound) | ISBN 9781493448630 (ebook)
Subjects: LCGFT: Christian fiction. | Thrillers (Fiction) | Novels.
Classification: LCC PS3607.O324 S76 2025 | DDC 813.6—dc23/eng/20240617
LC record available at https://lccn.loc.gov/2024026545

Scripture used in this book, whether quoted or paraphrased by the characters, is
taken from one of the following:

The NET Bible®. Copyright © 1996, 2019 by Biblical Studies Press, L.L.C. http://
netbible.com. Used by permission. All rights reserved.

The Holy Bible, New International Version®, NIV®. Copyright © 1973, 1978, 1984,
2011 by Biblica, Inc.® Used by permission of Zondervan. All rights reserved world-
wide. www.zondervan.com. The "NIV" and "New International Version" are trade-
marks registered in the United States Patent and Trademark Office by Biblica, Inc.®

Cover design by Mumtaz Mustafa

Baker Publishing Group publications use paper produced from sustainable forestry
practices and postconsumer waste whenever possible.

25 26 27 28 29 30 31   7 6 5 4 3 2 1

To Sharon.
I know how much you miss walking
the rocky beaches of the Pacific Northwest.
You're an inspiration to me
because you've always been
such a bright beacon of *His* light.

As memory may be a paradise from which we cannot be driven, it may also be a hell from which we cannot escape.

John Lancaster Spalding

———

The waves roar, O LORD,
the waves roar,
the waves roar and crash.
Above the sound of the surging water,
and the mighty waves of the sea,
the LORD sits enthroned in majesty.

Psalm 93:3–4 NET

Prologue

D *éjà vu.*
A premonition.
Call it whatever you want. But Jo Cattrel had always had a feeling it would come to this. Her job as a maintenance engineer required long hours and, at times—okay, yeah, most times—the worst conditions, and she had to work in a way that caused the least amount of inconvenience to guests and even other employees.

She wasn't so good at the inconvenient part, or rather, she was great at the inconvenient part, possessing a real knack for inconveniencing others.

Like right now. In the dim lighting of this rustic cabin, the guest emerged from the bedroom wearing a winter mask and coat, ready to head out into the storm.

"A face mask is a good idea." She smiled. "I've inconvenienced you. I'll come back another time."

And try not to act like I saw those disturbing images on your tablet.

She'd always feared this exact scenario—that she would

11

witness a crime or see evidence lying around. She spent too many nights reading crime fiction.

Retracing her steps to the door, she walked backward. Something—maybe her literary experience—told her not to turn her back. The guest had been informed she would be checking on that leaky sink and hadn't answered when she'd knocked, so she let herself in because the storm of the decade was moving in and she wouldn't be able to come back later.

She needed to finish all her tasks, eat dinner with Pop, and get back to her own quarters on the property, though she could expect to be called upon to answer some kind of maintenance emergency that kept her life exciting. She'd always had a knack for fixing things, just like Pop, and she loved her job.

She loved Pop too. Wanted to eat chili with him tonight like they'd planned.

The eyes behind the mask narrowed.

He knows.

He knew . . . that she'd seen too much.

She'd never been a good liar. People could read her emotions on her face, and that transparency came with a lot of negatives. Like now.

At least she had "Little Jo" in her back pocket if she needed protection, but a small handgun would have been better than her heavy wrench.

"I have to go now." She turned and rushed to the door like a fleeing coward, reaching in her pocket for the wrench.

Pain seared her shoulders as he gripped her and yanked her away from the door, throwing her to the floor. Little Jo rattled across the floor and slid under the bed, but she could reach it if she moved fast enough. Except he'd pinned her in place with the darkest eyes she'd ever seen. Her heart rate shot up as he studied her. Was he considering how best to silence her?

He held a knife at his side.

"Whatever you're planning, you're not going to get away with it," she said.

He approached, then dropped to one knee. Jo had the strangest sense of familiarity. *Do I know you?*

She wouldn't give up without a fight and twisted, scrambled toward her wrench, but her limbs failed to respond. At the prick in her neck, she jerked around, grasping at her throat. Realization dawned that she'd already lost. She glanced again toward the knife but saw a syringe instead.

And he'd already won.

Dizziness pressed her body against the hard floor. Darkness edged her vision. He was going to throw her into the ocean where she'd never be found.

"This can't be the end," she whispered.

I'm so sorry, Pop!

1

Time was short.

And Paco was missing.

The storm system of the decade bore down on the Washington coast, and Remi Grant was right in its path on a beach battered by waves during what was projected to be a dramatic king tide.

Oh, she knew better. But . . .

"Paco! Where are you?" She doubted her shouts could be heard over the breakers lashing the shore, crashing into the rocks.

The expected heavy rain hadn't started yet, but the wind remained cold, constant, and strong.

Sea stacks dotted the beach, and a rocky outcropping blocked her path as the tide rushed in, rising too quickly for comfort.

The only way around was to wait for the breakers to subside. Another wave crashed against the formation, then slinked back beneath the next one rolling in, building momentum.

Now!

She rushed around the mass of rocks, her efforts slowed by wet sand packed with rocks, barnacles, and shells. Beach Safety 101—never turn your back on the waves. But Remi did just that as she ran toward the bluff while simultaneously watching her steps along the rock-studded beach. Twisting her ankle or falling could be a death sentence.

Behind her, the roar of the sea resounded, filling her with fear. The ocean was closing in on her, and the beach would be gone in minutes.

The Pacific wouldn't take her today. Not if she had anything to do with it.

She made it to the dry beach—what was left of it—and that's when she heard the smallest of cries. Given the thunderous waves echoing against the cliff, she was surprised she'd heard anything else. Heavy sea spray doused her, but she expected no less from the approaching ferocious monster.

Heart pounding, she moved along the cliff, searching for the small pooch. *He must be frozen in terror.* Remi had to find him in time, for both their sakes.

She always expected the unexpected. And while she waited for the unexpected, she planned everything to the last detail. She'd prepared for the storm system of the decade, but she hadn't expected a guest from Texas to lose their lapdog on a dangerous beach as the storm moved in, eventually bringing mammoth twenty-foot-or-more waves.

"Paco! Come on, boy. Where are you?"

In response, she heard nothing but the angry surf, best enjoyed from a distance during a storm, which was just the setting her lodge on the bluff provided. She couldn't return without the Yorkshire terrier. Remi shouldn't be on the beach now—no one should—but here she was, headed north and away from the safety of the lodge.

Where could he be?

He probably would have hunkered as far away from the encroaching Pacific Ocean as he could get. She hurried along the cliff, looking into the crevices and around small piles of rocks and tumbles of driftwood. In this mess, she might never find him.

"Paco! Where are you?" Could he even hear her? If he did, would he trust a stranger with his fate? "Come on, boy . . ." she mumbled to herself.

Concern for the small creature chased her, but she wouldn't entertain the strong possibility that he might already have been swept out to sea.

And there . . .

Huddled in the smallest of alcoves at the base of the cliff face, Paco shivered. Though time was running out, she approached slowly so he wouldn't feel more threatened. If the dog ran away from her, escaping her efforts, then she wouldn't have enough time to find and save him.

Salt water rushed toward her, reaching farther with each crashing breaker.

God, help me. I'm out of time.

Crouching, she continued forward, wishing she'd brought a treat. "I know you're scared. I am too. But let me get us out of this."

Trembling, cold, and wet, he shrank against the porous bedrock, deeper into the small recess. Then Paco sprang from his hiding place and dashed between her and the rocks, his short legs carrying him faster than she would have thought. Except he was in survival mode, adrenaline fueling his doomed getaway.

But it also fueled Remi, and with everything in her, she reached out for Paco.

But he slipped away. "No!" She raced after him as more salty water rushed toward them. "Paco, come back." *You're going to die if you don't!*

17

He slowed, turning back in fear as the tide chased them. His hesitation gave her the chance she needed. She sprang forward and snatched him, careful not to crush his small body while still maintaining her grip. Barking and biting, he tried to wriggle free, his sharp little teeth sinking into her thumb, but she ignored the pain and held him against her. "I've got you. It's going to be okay."

Rushing forward out of the water's reach, she gently tucked Paco inside her heavy raincoat to keep him warm. The terrier seemed to finally trust her, or he succumbed to exhaustion, but either way, he settled against her inside the coat. His trembling form reminded her of her own predicament.

Their predicament.

Remi pressed her back against the cliff, then raced toward the rocky outcropping that could trap her and block her escape to the staircase up to Cedar Trails Lodge at the top of the bluff. Waves washed back out to the ocean, but she saw now what she'd feared. The tide had already come in, blocking her way to the steps to safety.

So she turned and headed north in search of a place on the cliff where she could find traction and climb higher. Rescue crews would be hard-pressed to reach her in time out here, and she couldn't afford to wait for help.

Her radio squawked. She fished it out of her pocket. "I got him. I just need a way out."

"Use Jo's ladder!" Erika's voice sounded garbled over the radio.

"Roger that."

Jo had secured a rope ladder at the end of the campsites in case of an emergency until they could build another set of actual steps, but Remi had never found a need to use it. They'd always been adamant about when the beach was safe and when it was not safe, especially in the winter months, during the storms that people came to the lodge to watch. Today, someone had violated those rules.

Paco squirmed inside her jacket, and she continued to speak to him in soothing tones. The cold wind knocked into her, bringing salty, cold spray along with it as she jogged forward. Polished rocks—large and small—made up most of the beach and were a tripping hazard if she didn't watch where she stepped. Half jogging, half slow-stepping, she made her way to a patch of wet, gray sand.

She should almost be near where the campsite ended on top of the bluff, and she paused to stare up the cliff face. Jagged edges melded with patches of dirt and bedrock, and at the top, loamy earth and thick evergreens. In places along the coast, the cliffs were as high as a hundred and fifty feet. Here, it was half that. Still . . .

Tidewater rushed around her ankles, reminding her that time was slipping away, along with her way out of this.

There . . .

She spotted the marine rope ladder that Jo had secured for the unfortunate scenario of getting trapped by the tide. Her heart jumped with hope.

But to get to the ladder, Remi had to traverse significant piles of driftwood stacked against the cliff. Sighing, she rushed forward, weaving her way around the large, pale tree trunks, some of them massive, which meant she'd have to climb over them. She stepped over one driftwood log after another, slid down between two larger ones, then crawled over the last log.

Once the water started rushing in, she'd have more to worry about than sneaker waves or breakers that could smash her against these rocks. She would be crushed by the driftwood.

She stood at the bottom of the cliff and looked up.

That Jo had assembled a rope ladder to span the distance

was impressive, but it didn't hang low enough for Remi to reach.

She peeked inside her coat. "I'm going to need you to stay still, okay?" He wasn't going to like it, but she had no choice. She secured him in the inside pocket of her coat, grateful he was small enough, zipped it closed, then tightened the bottom of her jacket. She fastened it completely up to her neck and secured the snap, then pulled her hood tighter—all of this just in case he clawed or chewed his way out of her pocket.

"Hold on, Paco." She jumped for the rope.

Jumped again.

Then she pulled a small chunk of driftwood over and balanced on it. Just one last jump. She reached with both hands and caught the bottom rung. Then pulled on it and walked along the rocks until she could gain traction with one foot, then the other.

Calisthenics. She'd done her share of them in the past, but clearly, she needed to beef up her exercise routine. Muscles straining, she climbed the ladder, which she realized didn't have anchor points. Once she got out of this, she and Jo would have a long talk.

"Hang in there. I'm climbing this ladder, Paco, and before you know it, you'll be safe in your momma's arms."

Despite the cold temps and buffeting winds, sweat trickled down the middle of her back. She was halfway there.

We're going to make it.

The ladder suddenly dropped a few inches. Her heart rate jumped.

Pulse soaring, eyes shut, she held on as the rope swung out and slapped against the bedrock. At least it had held.

Holding on tight, she stared up. What was going on? No time to ponder that question. This thing was slipping for some reason she couldn't fathom. She gripped the rope.

Stepped on another rung, pushing through the fear of falling and breaking her body against the rocks or driftwood.

Don't look down. Don't look down.

Remi looked down.

Mistake. Big mistake.

The tide had come in hard and fast, and seawater rushed against the cliff directly below her. Driftwood shifted and moved with the force of nature. Her heart clamored against her ribs. Remi once again squeezed her eyes shut, the sound of her pounding heart overpowering the waves.

You can do this. Just keep going.

One hand on the rope, she reached for the next rung, but it broke in half, leaving her pawing the air. Her palms slicked as she found the rope again and held on for dear life.

Caught her breath.

Paco whined. She could feel his body quivering in her pocket. "It's okay, buddy. I've got you."

The words came out breathy.

And you've got me, God.

She just had to focus and climb. She'd be up on top soon. Otherwise, she'd be swept away, lost forever.

Like the big hole in her life that left her unsure who she could trust, wary of everyone. And beyond this cliff, once she made it—and she would—she knew that time was running out for her. She could feel it.

But she could only worry about one crisis at a time as she continued climbing the failing ladder. She should be nearing the top. Ten feet.

Eight feet.

Five feet.

Four . . .

She looked at the last three rungs. Broken. She saw the crack in each of them. They wouldn't hold her weight. She'd just have to pull from all her past training and climb the rope instead. Hope for the best.

Remi glanced up, focusing on what must be done. She started climbing and realized that the rope had been shredded.

She literally hung by a thread.

Her chest constricted. All the air whooshed out of her. *What am I going to do?*

With the next crash of waves, she could have sworn she heard a voice. Had she imagined it? Desperation fooling her mind? But she glanced up again, searching, hoping.

Hands reached for her. A stranger with steel-blue eyes stared down at her.

"Grab my hands now before it's too late."

"What . . . ?" Her throat constricted.

"You're going to die if you don't take my hands now."

Images suddenly crashed into her mind, paralyzing her, blinding her, then she was somewhere . . . hot, dry . . . somewhere else.

A breaker lashed hard against the cliff, bringing her back to the present. The rope thrashed with the impact. The thread broke. Remi reached for his hands and missed. Once again, she pawed the air.

Fear paralyzed her.

I'm going to die!

But the man caught her wrist.

Below her, the rope ladder tumbled down the cliff, leaving her feet dangling.

Now a stranger held her life in his hands.

2

Adrenaline spiked through Hawk Beckett.

Lying flat to anchor his body, he gripped both her hands. In one momentous heave, he dragged her with him from the edge and hauled the woman up to safety from where she hung over a furious sea. He'd pulled her from the brink of death.

The angry ocean had boiled below her, stirring the driftwood into a soupy, deadly mess. For a minute there, he thought they were both done for. That she might pull him down with her and he'd drop right alongside her because no way would he release her hands.

He stared up at the thick green canopy and thanked his lucky stars. No. Not luck. He didn't believe in luck. But the trajectory he'd been on, he wasn't sure God wanted anything more to do with him. Sea spray coated his face, thanks to the gusting wind.

Lying next to him on a cluster of sword ferns, she gasped for breath. He climbed to his knees but didn't stand. Instead, he peered down at her, assessing.

How had she ended up on that beach?

23

Hazel, no wait, gray-blue eyes blinked up at him. He couldn't pin down the color, but her gaze held him. And just like that, he lost his train of thought. A small bark escaped from somewhere on her person, surprising him. He scrambled to his feet and offered his hand. She took it and stood, appearing to cradle the small creature she protected. Her rain hood had blown off, and she tugged it back on, but he'd glimpsed her long, auburn-brown hair. A smattering of freckles across her nose.

"Are you okay?" he asked.

"I think so. Thanks for your help." She unzipped her jacket and dug around in another compartment before pulling out a small pooch. Then held and comforted the barking ball of fur.

Two people hurried through the woods toward them, shouting over the wind.

"Remi! Remi!" A tall, blue-haired woman shouted from a distance. She looked stocky in her heavy raincoat as she weaved her way along a narrow trail that hedged the cliff.

Remi? He took another look at the woman he'd pulled from certain death. Must be Remi Grant—the Cedar Trails Lodge manager he'd planned to find and meet while here.

Holding the small dog against her with one hand, Remi swiped rain and sea spray from her face with the other. Then she looked at him, gratitude in her gaze. "I can't thank you enough. You saved our lives. You know that?"

While he believed that she was grateful, he hadn't missed the wariness that lingered in her eyes. Interesting. Saving her life wasn't reason enough to trust him. He understood that sentiment since he'd come to this wilderness coast, running from his own demons.

"You're welcome." A better response would have been to tell her that beach wasn't the safest place right now. But he'd come across as harsh and insensitive. Besides, he suspected she knew that. Or if she hadn't known that before, she knew it now.

"Paco!" Breathing hard, a mix of relief and fear twisted up in her demeanor, a plump older woman cut her way through the underbrush, making a beeline for her baby. "Did you find my Paco?"

Blue-Hair came up behind her. Remi handed Paco off to the plump woman. "Here you go, Mrs. Daley. He's perfectly fine, just a little wet and cold is all."

And scared, but Hawk suspected Remi wanted to comfort the woman rather than add more stress.

Mrs. Daley pulled Paco to her and squeezed so hard that Hawk thought she might end his life by accident, but then she held Paco up to her face and let him lick the moisture off her nose and mouth. When the dog was satisfied, she tucked him under her arm and looked at Remi again. "I'm so sorry this happened. I can't believe—"

A gust of wind rattled the treetops and cut her off. All eyes looked up at the canopy. Then Hawk glanced out at the dark Pacific . . . boiling out in the depths, waves building momentum as they chased the coast. They needed to get out of the weather.

"It's okay." Remi touched Mrs. Daley's arm. "You should get inside. We'll catch up later."

Blue-Hair hugged Remi to her, pure relief in her eyes. "You made it. Thank goodness for Jo's ladder."

"Yeah, thank goodness for Jo's ladder." Remi eyed Hawk. A look passed between them. They shared a secret about that ladder. No mention of his assistance, but he wasn't looking for recognition.

She avoided looking at the ground and the auger-style anchors to which the rope ladder had been affixed. The marine rope wasn't old or worn out, and the quick assessment, impression, he'd gotten was that it had been intentionally shredded. The cuts looked recent. But he kept it to himself for now.

Blue-Hair glanced around as if searching for the rope, her green contacts shifting in her eyes.

"Let's get inside out of the weather," Remi said. "The wind and rain are picking up." Remi looked at him, raising her voice over the wind. "I didn't get your name."

"Hawk Beckett. You must be Remi Grant."

"That I am." She scrunched up her face. "Your name sounds familiar. Come back to the lodge. I owe you more than a cup of coffee, but we can start with that."

"I'm Erika, by the way." Blue-Hair's eyes were sharp, and her smile was warm and friendly.

Erika turned and headed back toward the lodge. Mrs. Daley had left them behind in her rush to return Paco to a warm environment. Remi followed Erika, and Hawk followed Remi as they made their way along the trail that would lead them back to Cedar Trails Lodge. The trail was close enough to the cliff that he could look out over the rocky beach drowning in ocean waves. If anyone asked him, it wasn't safe.

An image of Remi climbing up the doomed ladder, then hanging by a thread flashed in his mind. He needed to talk to her about that rope, but in private.

They passed the area where the rental cabins were located, spread out and secluded enough in the trees to provide privacy. Then they walked through another patch of dense woods before stepping into a clearing on their approach to the main lodge, built from driftwood logs almost a century ago.

Remi slowed to walk next to him. "Where are you staying?"

"I'm in the Bluff Cabin."

"Wow, you landed the best one."

"A cancellation opened up at the last minute, so I took it."

Another cold gust urged him forward to shelter, but Remi stopped in her tracks, and he stopped too. Her big, beautiful eyes peered at him from the shadows of her raincoat hood.

"How did you happen to be in position to pull me up? I mean, just in the nick of time." That caution flickered again.

What was going on that she would question his reason for being in a position to save her? Her wariness kind of took him aback. "I recently came to town." *Rented a house temporarily.* "I was considering getting a camper and wanted to check out the campground."

"It's closed during the winter months."

"I got that. I was just making my way back."

Remi appeared satisfied and they continued forward. When they reached the lodge doors, a strong wind slammed them both with sideways rain. When he opened the door, he got a taste of the strength behind that approaching storm—it would only get worse. Inside the lodge, a few people were gathered at the panoramic windows.

"Please, order a coffee on me." Remi smiled. "Coffee *and* breakfast are on the house. Whatever you want."

Remi left his side, spoke to the blond barista behind the coffee bar, then moved to the window to speak with Mrs. Daley and Erika. Though she smiled and acted like a great hostess, Hawk could tell she was still shaken from nearly falling to her death. Who wouldn't be?

He stepped up to the coffee bar and looked up at the menu. In his peripheral vision, he tracked Remi until she disappeared down a hallway. Hawk frowned. Considering he needed to talk to her about the frayed ladder, he could have handled that so much better. He ordered the plain Americano with two shots, and while he waited, he moved closer to the wall of photos to get a better look at the amazing, framed images of breakers crashing against the rocky outcroppings and sea stacks.

A couple of them depicted faces in the waves. Seriously? One of them was a monster, his mouth wide, ready to chomp down on his prey. Disturbing. He walked along the wall, absorbing the images and looking for the photographer's signature, but found none. Hmm.

The image of rolling marine fog drew him closer. A ship was barely visible inside the fog. He couldn't put his finger on what was so special about the photo, but it was stunning. The barista approached and stood next to him.

"That's the *Specter's Bounty*."

"Huh?" He took the coffee she handed him. "Oh, I'm sorry. I could have—"

"No problem. That's my favorite picture. I've heard about the *Specter's Bounty,* but I've never actually seen the ghost ship."

"Who took these?"

But she had already turned to rush back to the coffee bar against the far wall. Had the photographer also drawn the sketches and caricatures on display?

A couple left a small table by the window, so Hawk sat while he had the chance. This place must have been built around this perfect view of the ocean and the rocky shore below because it was truly mesmerizing. The lodge itself was rustic and backwoodsy. Not many people chose to travel to a place with spotty if no cell coverage and no Wi-Fi.

To him those features, or lack thereof, were a big plus. Technology was neither good nor bad, but it had taken over people's lives. Sometimes a person needed to unplug. Literally. Humans had a way of taking something meant for good and using it for evil, but the difference between the good guys and the bad guys was often a matter of point of view. At least that's what his former commanding officer, retired Chief Warrant Officer John Marshall, often said.

He was glad he'd listened to John's advice—his urging, really—that Hawk visit Cedar Trails nestled at the edge of Hidden Bay. When the place had been booked up, Hawk rented the house in the nearby small town of Forestview. That's how much he trusted his former CO, the pilot with whom he'd flown over fifteen missions. John now worked in the private sector, but he remained Hawk's friend and mentor.

Finished with his coffee, Hawk debated heading back to his cabin before he had to face off with the blustery weather. He gave up hope that he'd have an opportunity to talk to Remi again, at least today. Hawk returned the mug to the counter and headed for the door.

"Leaving already?" Remi called.

He paused, turned, and smiled. "I finished the coffee." He closed the distance between them. "Honestly, I'd hoped to talk to you more."

The way he'd said the words came out entirely wrong and sounded like he was flirting, which he absolutely wasn't. But admittedly, her eyes kind of sucker punched him that first moment they'd stared up at him. He shoved those thoughts away, hoping she hadn't taken his words the wrong way.

She glanced at her watch and gestured to the table by the window where he'd been sitting. "I have a few minutes."

He sat in the same chair as before and gestured at the wall. "Who's responsible for the photographs and sketches?"

She shrugged. "The artists didn't want to be identified."

"Artists?"

"Someone took the pictures and someone else drew the sketches."

The way her cheeks warmed gave him a clue that she

was one of the someones but didn't want to talk about it. Just as well, he had a serious question. "Why'd you do it?"

"Do what?"

"Risk your safety like that."

"Come on. Don't tell me you wouldn't have tried to save the dog."

"All I'm saying is that it was risky." *You could have died.* "I've seen people swept away in lesser waves." He wished he could unsee it.

"Well, it's over and Paco's safe, thanks to you."

He hadn't known she'd been harboring an animal in her coat, and he'd been even more impressed with her skills to make that climb on a rope ladder that hadn't even been secured at the bottom.

She clasped her hands on the table. "I owe you more than coffee."

"You don't owe me anything. What was I going to do? Let you fall?"

In spite of his efforts, she'd almost done just that. "About that . . . did you happen to notice anything about the rope?"

Expression grim, his lips flattened. "Yes. I had hoped to talk to you about it."

Her expression turned serious, and she leaned forward. "I'm listening."

He didn't think she'd fully bought his explanation for being there at the right moment, so he'd start with that. "When you were on the beach, I didn't see you at first. I was looking at the storm brewing in the distance. Through the trees, I saw two women at the top of the steps, looking down and shouting. That's when I saw you and realized you were trapped by the tide. So I walked along the edge, trying to figure out what I could do to help. I saw the rope and figured you were heading there. I wanted to make sure it was secure, and that's when I got a closer look and saw it had been tampered with. Shredded . . . but not completely. I tried to get your attention, but you couldn't hear me over the waves, and even if you could, that rope ladder was your only chance. I didn't have time to grab something else, you know?"

She leaned back and blew out a breath. "I'm just . . . thank you. I don't want to think about what would have happened if you hadn't reached out for me."

"I'm glad everything turned out all right." Frowning, he crossed his arms. "But whoever is responsible for tampering with that ladder—knowing that someone would eventually use it and get hurt or die—needs to be caught."

She gave him a hard, questioning look. "You don't think it was kids?"

"I think that's for the local law to figure out. I can't call them without cell service, but *you* can." Or he could just drive into the county seat and talk to a deputy sheriff, which he wanted to avoid.

"I'll talk to them, but only a portion of the rope remains," she said. "I'll call the sheriff and let him know. He might want you to explain what you saw as well."

"And I'm willing to do that."

"Your help is appreciated." Remi's eyes held him again, as if she was studying, searching. Though she'd been congenial in this exchange, he still got the feeling she was wary and not just about the incident, but about *him*.

But she could think the same about Hawk because he was also on edge. And maybe he was only seeing himself reflected in her gaze, but he doubted it.

She shifted in her chair. "Hawk Beckett." Angling her head slightly, she squinted her eyes. "Why does your name sound familiar? I mean, yes, you're a guest here, but do I know you from somewhere else?"

Well, that was just great. Good thing he showed up in person. "Honestly, that kind of stings."

Her eyes widened. "I remember now. You left a message for me about running a helicopter tour package out of the lodge." She pressed a hand to her head. "I've had so much on my plate, making sure everything at the lodge is ready for the biggest series of storms in more than a decade."

A half-grin erupted. He shouldn't, he really shouldn't, but he would. "And like you said, you owe me."

"I said that, didn't I?" She quirked a grin.

Cute. But that was no answer.

"At least give me a chance. You've got nothing to lose." The idea had popped into his head only a couple of weeks ago. After all, he had his own bird, and it would give him the freedom to stay on top of his personal mission to search for answers.

"I tell you what." Her eyes met his. "I'll give you a chance to convince me."

Seriously? He hadn't thought it would be so difficult and figured she would jump on the opportunity. He'd heard a few complaints about the lodge experience—not that he would share that with her right now. But some complained that there wasn't much to do here other than walk on the beach. To his way of thinking, the beach should be enough—with the sea stacks and cliffs, driftwood. What more could a person want? Except maybe a helicopter tour of the region.

He scratched his temple. "Challenge accepted."

"Right. Well, the thing is, it's quiet here," she said. "The noisy rotors kind of ruin that."

Hmm. If noise was her only complaint, he could work with that.

"Obviously you're not flying during this storm, so let's meet again on this topic next week." She drew in a breath. Hesitated. "Plus, I need to know a little more about you."

Again, that guarded look in her eyes, and it increased his own questions about her.

Remi's radio squawked. "Remi?"

She gave Hawk an apologetic look. "Excuse me." Then spoke into the radio. "Go ahead, Dylan."

"Jo isn't responding on the radio and one of the doors on Cabin 10 is stuck."

"I'll find her. Thanks for letting me know." Remi stood and looked at Hawk. "I need to get back to work. Enjoy your cabin stay, and we'll talk more on the other side of the storms."

Then she left him sitting there, watching her walk away. She was as mesmerizing as the ocean tempests. Hawk shook his head. What had gotten into him? Nothing good, that's what. He pulled his gaze away and focused on nature's show through the window. Usually, the skies were flat and gray this time of year, but dark, angry clouds were rolling in fast. He stared out the window, taking his time to process everything she'd said.

She wanted to know a little more about him. Understandable. And that's what he could offer her—a *little* more. And with her guarded expression, maybe he needed to know more about *her*. But he wouldn't pry.

He left Cedar Trails Lodge and walked back to his cabin. The path was lined with the towering forest, including old-growth Pacific red cedars, the ground covered with a plethora of underbrush and sword ferns. The Bluff Cabin where he stayed was the last cabin along this trail, and four cabins away from the lodge. He'd lucked out getting the one right on the bluff so he could actually watch the storm. Others were tucked in the woods around him, but not close enough to actually see the forces of nature in action from the safety of their cozy dwelling.

Inside, the cabin shook and rattled with the gusts, and

Hawk began to question his decision to stay here, right over the bluff. He'd noticed signs of erosion. Years in the future, this cabin would probably be gone.

That was the perfect metaphor to describe his own slowly eroding life. He assumed that most everyone was already holed up. High wind warnings were in effect, and he should hunker down like the rest of the guests. Or should he drive into the county seat and report what he'd seen of the rope? But who was to say that he hadn't been the one to cause the trouble? It would be just his word.

And right now, he doubted his word was any good when it came to law enforcement.

3

Lodge guests gathered around the fireplace or lingered at the windows overlooking the ocean and the strengthening storm, and all was as it should be. She entered her office that was tucked down a long hallway, then closed the door behind her. Finally alone, she paused to catch her breath.

To think back.

Hawk Beckett had saved her life. Never mind that the situation could have been avoided. It happened. But those last few moments—he'd been reaching for her.

She'd seen . . . the desert? She'd had a flashback of the missing days. That had to be it.

Was that good or bad? Remembering should be a good thing.

She wanted to remember. She *needed* to remember.

Dr. Lindie Holcomb, the clinical neuropsychologist who specialized in memory disorders and brain trauma, had explained that causes of amnesia were either psychological or neurological. The mind versus the brain. In Remi's case, she had experienced a perfect storm—she had incurred a brain injury to go along with a traumatic event. Remi loved the acronyms—TBI and PTSD.

Well, in the two years since the incident, her brain had recovered from the injury, and now it appeared her mind was still trying to protect her from any psychological harm—something to do with memory subpaths created during a terrifying experience. Not all scientists, therapists, and doctors agreed, she'd been told. Okay. Whatever. She didn't understand all the science behind it, and she didn't have to. That's what Dr. Holcomb was for.

Dr. Holcomb had given her two possible outcomes. She could rest and relax and over time those memories would return. But if they didn't, Remi could intentionally expose herself to an extreme situation that would somehow cause her brain to access those same neurotransmitters used in the inciting incident, a happening she didn't even remember.

Thinking about it hurt her brain.

I just want to scream.

Six months ago, Remi had given up on retrieving what she'd lost. Trying to find the missing few days had left her feeling alone and defeated. Until she knew the truth, it wasn't like she could move on enough to ever fall in love, get married, and have 2.3 children—no, make that 4.5 children. If she was dreaming, she might as well dream big. Otherwise, those days that remained in the dark for her would hold danger and grief for those she might bring into her world and love. She couldn't take the risk. Couldn't have a simple life or her secret dream until she was whole again.

Emotion thickened in her throat. Regardless, she'd made a life here by throwing herself into managing the lodge. Taking photographs of the tumultuous Pacific had soothed her soul and helped her forget she'd lost a small part of her life.

I mean, who remembers everything anyway?

Maybe no one. But when the past threatened the present or the future, it mattered. Pressing her face into her palms, she rubbed her eyes. Now more than ever she needed to focus her attempts on recalling what she'd lost.

She was pretty sure someone had made an attempt on her life today, and even without that attempt, the flashback of a lost memory was motivation enough.

I should call Dr. Holcomb.

No, wait, I need to call the county sheriff first to report the incident. Remi used the landline and spoke with someone who took down the information and said a deputy would get back to her either in person or by phone.

That call out of the way, she turned her attention to calling Dr. Holcomb.

Would Dr. Holcomb even take her calls? After meeting with her once a month, Remi hadn't made any progress and stopped seeing the doctor six months ago. Dr. Holcomb had been the reason Remi was at Cedar Trails Lodge to begin with. The psychologist had reservations but suggested Remi could take her place, since, after a death in the family, she wouldn't be able to keep her two-week reservation at the cabin.

So, Remi had stayed here and taken the photographs and . . .

Fallen in love with the ferocity of the ocean, the rugged, rocky coastline and majestic sea stacks. After the two weeks were up, Remi didn't want to go.

Lucky for her there had been an opening, so the lodge owner had put her to work as a barista. With her bed-and-breakfast background, Remi made herself useful, and within six months she'd become the manager. Of course, there was much more to it. Turned out the lodge owner, Evelyn Monroe, was someone who focused on helping certain individuals who needed to stay hidden. Remi suspected she wasn't the only one working here who had wanted to be invisible to the outside world.

Considering she had a good life here, maybe remembering something her brain had fought so hard to protect her from wasn't a good idea. Dr. Holcomb had told her that she would remember when she was ready. What did it matter if she wasn't ready to face the past? It was becoming all too clear that she *must* remember.

Last week, she'd received an anonymous package containing a puzzle piece along with a cryptic note. The package had no return address, but the postmark was from Nevada.

And the cryptic note?

REMEMBER.

Had the puzzle piece—a partial image of treetops and a stone building behind them—been meant to jar her memory? Well, it hadn't. But for some reason Hawk's hand reaching for hers the moment she would have fallen to her death had been the catalyst for the brief flashback and all the emotions that came with it.

A gust of wind shook the walls and pulled her focus back to Cedar Trails Lodge. She shrugged off the unknown past that haunted her. She could deal with it later. Her staff needed her.

She called Jo on the radio again. Remi had seen her early this morning. She'd give Jo time to finish whatever task she'd gotten knee-deep in, but she might need to go check on that door and fix it herself. She shuffled through the mail someone had laid on her desk and picked up the landline to try Jo at home. She got no answer, not even an answering machine on which to leave a message.

Remi needed a few supplies, and if Jo hadn't picked those up earlier, she could be doing that right now, but Remi couldn't know if the woman didn't respond.

The last item of mail on her desk—a familiar small box. Oh no.

Remi froze. Her breath caught.

What . . . is . . . ?

No return address. No postmark this time. Did that mean someone had hand delivered it personally? She dropped into her chair and opened the box to find another puzzle piece of an image. More trees. More of the stone building. The cathedral in Zarovia? That would make sense. She'd been at the café across the street—the last thing she remembered before she'd woken up in the hospital.

She lifted the card in the box to read the words. The same message as before, with added words.

REMEMBER BEFORE IT'S TOO LATE.

Her heart might have stopped right there. Hadn't she already tried? Now someone was actively *stalking* her, prodding her. Lungs aching, Remi realized she wasn't breathing and sucked in a breath.

What should I do? Run again? Hide again?

A light knock on the door drew her attention. Erika opened the door and stepped inside, then frowned. "Are you okay?"

I don't know. "Yes."

Erika pursed her lips. Remi expected her friend and assistant to press her for the truth, but she didn't.

"A family in Cabin 8 is having issues with the woodstove. Dylan says he can't fix it and needs Jo. We can't find her."

"Are you sure she isn't on the property?" Remi asked. "Because I saw her this morning."

"Dylan says she's not here," Erika said. "I shouldn't have bothered you with this. I can look for her."

"If you find her, let me know. In the meantime, I need to get those supplies she was supposed to get. In fact, she could be in town right now, so I'll look for her while I'm there."

"That seems like an inefficient use of your time."

"It's fine." If a deputy was at the Timberbrook County Substation, then she could drop in and report the rope ladder incident. The substation was a new addition to the county services but was rarely staffed.

Erika stepped forward as if still concerned. "You seem upset. Is it because you got trapped on the beach chasing Paco?"

Remi tried to wash the distress from her features, but her efforts weren't working. "That wasn't a great start to my day." And she'd leave it at that.

Dylan's voice suddenly squawked over Erika's radio. "What's happening? Did you find her?"

"On my way," Erika replied into her radio. She shrugged at Remi. "I'll help Dylan. I've learned a thing or two in the time I've been here."

Remi couldn't help but smile. She appreciated the people she worked with. Dylan was a scrawny ranch hand from Wyoming who still wore his Lucchese cowboy boots and Stetson. He and Erika couldn't be more different. But everyone worked together.

"Keep me posted."

Erika nodded and left her alone. Remi shoved the two puzzle pieces into her drawer and locked it. Her office provided a door that opened directly outside so she wouldn't have to take the long way down the hall and through the lodge to her vehicle in the parking lot. She tugged on her coat and gloves and grabbed her rain boots just in case the deluge hit before she returned. Then exited her office and stepped out into the weather. She rushed around to the parking area and found her old, red four-wheel drive Ford Bronco and got in.

Buckled in, she grabbed the steering wheel and took a moment to catch her breath.

"Remember before it's too late."

In a rush to get to Forestview and back before nature's fury was unleashed, she drove too fast as she steered down the rutted path. That should have taken most of her attention, but that second puzzle piece filled her mind, which was already racing with a kazillion thoughts.

Puzzle pieces.

What image would all the pieces ultimately create? Would she remember once she saw it?

The fact that she'd received the puzzle pieces meant that someone had found her. The eerie feeling that she was in imminent danger crawled over her. She thought back to her first meeting with Dr. Holcomb.

The woman was small and thin, her blond hair chopped. She had sat in a plush chair in her office. Remi sat in the other.

"Tell me the last thing you remember before waking up in the hospital."

"It's kind of a blur, really. I was sitting outside at a small café. It's just so fuzzy. It's like I kind of have this sense of dread. And then when I woke up in the hospital, I didn't know why I was there. It was the most unsettling feeling."

"Understandable. People often can't remember the events surrounding a traumatic incident. Feeling disoriented and confused isn't unusual."

"I wish I could say that makes me feel better, but it doesn't."

"What were you told about what happened?" Dr. Holcomb asked.

"That I'd been pulled from the Baltic Sea and had barely survived due to hypothermia and a head injury. The Baltic Sea? I remember visiting the country of Zarovia, sitting at a small café in the capital city of Novograd. Sure, it's close to the Baltic in relative terms, but it still makes no sense."

"I suspect that your brain doesn't want you to relive those moments."

"Moments? I'm missing *days*, if you count the time I was unconscious in the hospital."

"This might seem strange, but in my practice, I find it's beneficial to determine *why* you need to remember. In other words, is it *important* that you remember?"

"Who wouldn't want to remember?"

"That's a fair point, especially with what you've just shared. Even so, many people who have gone through terrible traumatic events, some of which they never remember, go on and live fulfilling lives, leaving the dark or missing memories behind. Memories themselves can't hurt you."

Dr. Holcomb studied her, then continued. "Let me put it a different way. Sometimes by trying to remember, you can actually make things worse by creating an incorrect understanding of what happened. In my practice, I prefer to focus on moving forward. Usually whatever happened in the past—those lost memories—isn't what's hurting you today. What creates the pain is when you continue to think about the memories, lost or found. But we can live in the present and create a new trajectory for our lives."

"That makes sense, but for me, personally, it's important that I remember. Can you help me or not?"

"Yes. Of course. I wanted you to understand that you have a choice to remember or to put it behind you. And in trying to recall those events, you risk altering them." Dr. Holcomb offered a slight smile. "This is progress."

If you say so. Maybe she'd made a mistake in talking to someone. But she was here and she was doing this. She shared the rest of her story with Dr. Holcomb. Remi had overheard a phone call outside her hospital room that left her disturbed. Someone had come to see her twice and asked her questions and then on the phone had explained that Remi had no recollection of the events.

Despite her amnesia, Remi's instincts told her that something was very wrong.

"I made my way back to the States to visit my old stomping grounds in Nebraska and tried to make sense of my life. That's when I spotted the stranger who'd questioned me in Germany."

"Are you saying he followed you?"

Remi's gaze drilled into this doctor she was trusting entirely too much. "Yes. That's why I need to know what happened. I fled Nebraska and traveled all the way here. To lose him."

Dr. Holcomb moved around to the other side of her desk. "Who was he?"

"No idea. I should have gotten names. I should have faced him and asked him what was going on. But I was still so shaken that I just decided to run and hide."

"Did you change your name?"

"What? No." She lifted a shoulder. "I mean, not legally. I just used different names at motels where I stayed."

"But your real name is . . ."

"Remi Grant. This is a private conversation, so I'm not worried about someone tracking me here. Look, I'm driving around in an old Bronco I paid cash for in Nebraska. It's untraceable, especially on lone state highways and small towns. They don't have cameras on every corner to catch a license plate, right? Then I drove across the country, staying at motels where cash was accepted."

A bump in the road jarred Remi back to the present and to the lush forest on both sides of her. After Dr. Holcomb sent her to Cedar Trails Lodge, where she'd taken on a different persona, Remi had lived in a dream world, believing she was safe when she was not.

And here in the remoteness of Hidden Bay, nestled up

against federally designated coastal wilderness, she'd let that itch fester—that need to recall those missing days. Dr. Holcomb had told her to let it go, the memories would come when her mind was ready.

"Like in the middle of a life-and-death situation, hanging from a ladder?" she grumbled out loud. "That's when it came?" But it hadn't really been a full memory, just a moment . . . a burst of . . . images and emotions. A flashback.

Steering from the obscure forest road—the only way to get to her isolated lodge, which amazingly wasn't included on any global positioning maps—she turned onto Highway 101, then drove another three miles before turning toward Forestview, a small town nestled in the rainforest at the edge of the Quinault Reservation. Mist covered her windshield, and the streets were busier than she would have expected, but then again people were probably stocking up in case of a power outage.

While she steered down Main Street, she scanned the usual places Jo might visit. Though she didn't want to stalk the woman, it wasn't like Jo to be *this* unresponsive. Then she drove to Jo's tiny house at the back of an elderly woman's property. Jo was supposed to stay in her quarters at the lodge over the weekend to be on hand and was usually reliable.

Remi bounded up the two short steps and knocked on the door. The place was too small for Jo not to hear her outside. "Jo? You in there?"

She didn't want to unnecessarily worry Jo's father, but if Jo didn't respond, she'd stop at his shop. She sent Jo one more text, which she might not get, and that's why they relied so much on the radio.

Where are you?

Concern crawled through her.

A reply came almost immediately. Her heart jumped and relief filled her.

Send me the list. I'm in town.

> I'm here too. I'll get it. You're needed back at the lodge.

Okay.

That settled, Remi drove to Settlers General Store. They carried everything in small quantities, and the whole town had already been there and gone. Settlers was out of batteries, kerosene, matches, and bottled water. But they had plenty of what Remi needed. Supplies loaded, she headed back to the lodge. She exited off 101 and turned left onto the mud-rutted path. About a mile in, she slowed.

"Are you kidding me?"

A full-size tree trunk had fallen across the road. She wasn't getting by that.

Remi radioed Dylan to send help, then pulled her hood on. Zipped her heavy rain jacket up but decided against the rain boots. She hopped out and hiked around to the back of the Bronco to get the small chain saw. She'd found it in the back of the Bronco when she bought it and, living here, she'd had to use it twice already. She couldn't see around the hood but heard the slush of footsteps in the mud.

Good. Someone could help her with this.

Remi stepped back from the Bronco. Someone approached, wearing a black winter face mask. Her heart stuttered. A knife slashed toward her.

4

Hawk slammed on his brakes. His truck fishtailed before stopping on the muddy path. A large cedar trunk blocked his way. And on the other side sat an old Bronco. The door hung open.

He stepped out of his Ford F-150. Holstered his Colt M1911 handgun. He took in his surroundings as he hiked over to the fallen trunk and called out. "Hello?"

Weird. No one was around. Had someone walked all the way back into town for help? He skirted the length of the tree to get around it rather than climbing over—because it was huge—then approached the empty vehicle. Why leave the Bronco open? Rain could damage the interior. He closed the vehicle, marched around, and looked in the back of the Bronco. A chain saw rested inside just waiting to be used, along with plastic bins, a big bag of flour, and a few sacks from Settlers. Something wasn't right. Two sets of boot prints, one bigger than the other, drew his attention. The marks left in the muddy road could mean signs of a struggle.

Skin prickling, he readied the Colt and followed the

tracks that led him into the dense forest and thick underbrush, which made it easier to follow the trail. Moss grew on the rocks, the trees, and made the ground slick in places. After a few minutes of weaving between spruce and cedar trees, Hawk paused to listen. Water dripped in the rainforest, slightly blunting the effects of the approaching storm, and the tree canopy blocked much of the light.

Groans and grunts drew his attention to the right. Alert to the danger, and the fact time could be running out, he followed the recently trampled ferns. He couldn't see who fought, but sounds of a struggle warned him that he was getting close. He pressed his back against a tree. Then peered around, his gun ready.

His gut clenched when he saw Remi crouched against the tree about fifteen feet from him, clearly hiding. Relief swept through him that she was okay, but it was short-lived. Her reaction told him the danger was near, too near. He wanted to get her attention and let her know that he was here to help. She must have skills to have fought off an attacker. Hawk looked out from behind the tree and searched the woods for the imminent threat but saw no one.

A sudden gust of wind rippled through the evergreens, and rain dripped through the foliage. Hawk decided to make his move, except Remi suddenly stood as if bracing herself.

A darkly dressed figure in a balaclava or ski mask emerged from between the trees and stalked toward her, flashing a knife. Remi avoided the strikes like a pro, surprising Hawk.

He rushed forward. "Freeze or I'll shoot!" He aimed his weapon at her attacker and continued forward, stepping over a large branch, avoiding tree roots and dense foliage, never taking his eyes off her attacker, who then moved to stand behind Remi, using her as a shield. Hawk couldn't shoot without endangering Remi.

He fired a warning shot, but the fighting didn't stop. He rushed toward the struggle, ready to insert himself in the middle and stop the madness. Remi punched the assailant in the throat. He stumbled back, then slipped behind a tree before making a run for it. Hawk really wanted to go after the jerk, but he headed for Remi.

Leaning over her thighs, she gasped for breath.

"Are you hurt? Are you okay?" The question sounded ridiculous. Of course she wasn't okay. But had she been cut with the knife or injured any other way? He looked her up and down.

"I'm okay." She was still breathing hard too.

"You know how to fight," he said.

Moisture beaded her face. "A little."

He wanted to ask about her training, but she averted her gaze. Wary. Secretive. He understood. They had that in common. Don't share too much. Don't let anyone in. Defense was the best offense.

"We need to get out of here." Gritting his teeth, he looked deeper into the surrounding woods that were unbelievably dark in the middle of the day.

Hawk wanted to go after her attacker, but he wouldn't leave Remi.

Anger burning in her gaze, she took a step in the direction where the knife wielder had disappeared. "I can't just let him get away, but these woods go on forever. A person could get lost. We would need search dogs to find him."

She pressed her back against the tree, closed her eyes, and took a deep breath.

"You have a cut on your temple." He reached up and pushed the hair away.

Her eyes flew open at his touch, and he thought she might punch him in the throat too. "Whoa . . . I'm just taking inventory. Where else were you cut?"

She stepped to the side and out of his reach. "I don't need you to take inventory."

Served him right.

Maybe his surprise at her attitude showed in his expression, because she said, "I'm . . . I'm sorry. Thank you for your help. That's twice in one day." The look she gave him didn't give him any warm and fuzzy feelings.

And it sounded almost as if it had cost her to thank him. Not like before, when he'd pulled her from the cliffside.

"This cut was from a tree branch, that's all." She averted her gaze again. "I got the feeling . . ."

"The feeling what? Tell me, Remi."

"I don't know." She shrugged.

What had she been going to say? Maybe the man hadn't touched her with the knife and maybe she had skills, but this guy . . . he had more skills. Maybe the man was toying with her, but Hawk knew better than to vocalize that thought because it would be insinuating that she hadn't held her own. And she had until Hawk got there. Who knows what would have happened if he hadn't decided to venture out and away from his cozy cabin and into town in inclement weather.

Remi stared at him again, studying, searching, and mentally grilling. He could tell. "You keep showing up when I'm in trouble. Why is that?"

Why are you in trouble? "I can't help it that I saw a Bronco just sitting there, the door wide open. Signs of a struggle. I didn't know it was your vehicle. Okay? And why am I defending myself?" He wanted to turn and stalk off.

Branches above them clacked together with the rush of wind. Remi jumped and stared up. The attack had put her on edge.

"We need to call the sheriff," he said. "Get out of this

weather and somewhere safe. Whoever attacked you could be circling back."

He eyed the woods once more and then offered his hand—just in case she needed reassurance. She looked at his hand but didn't take it as she moved past him. Okay, then. She was upset and he would give her space.

He let Remi lead them to the vehicles while he watched their backs, secretly hoping her attacker would show up again and Hawk could take him down, or at least capture him.

That's not what you do anymore.

Because his last assignment had ended catastrophically.

Keeping alert to his surroundings, Hawk stalked behind her—there was no hiking next to her in these woods. "So, what happened anyway? Do you know who attacked you and why?"

"How should I know? And right now, my main concern is getting that tree cut up into pieces and moved off the road."

In other words, she didn't want to talk about it. Everyone responded differently, but Remi's reaction to being attacked baffled him.

"I'll help with the tree." He cut around her and stood in her path. "Tell me what's going on."

"I don't know."

In the distance, the sound of chain saws roared, bringing a small sense of relief, at least to him. Her face relaxed. Chain saws meant that someone else was here to help and had already started the process of removing the roadblock.

At the road, two additional vehicles were parked. A couple of guys had already started on the massive trunk that had blocked the path. Apparently, finding the two empty vehicles hadn't raised any alarms, and hearing gunfire in the woods hadn't disturbed them. Or maybe they had been curious, but what else could be done except move the fallen tree? And they'd already made quick work of opening up the road. He and Remi weren't even needed.

Still, he followed her to the back of her Bronco, where she stood under the open hatch and examined her supplies. Making sure they were all still there? Wind gusts picked up, and they might have to remove another fallen tree before this was over.

"Can you please stop and take a breath?" Rain had soaked his head, but he didn't care. "You were attacked. You're allowed a moment."

Like it was his business, but he'd been there and considered himself involved enough to ask questions.

Remi's hair was dripping wet. Her hood had fallen back, and she hadn't bothered to pull it on again. Beneath the hatch of the Bronco, they were somewhat protected from the downpour.

When she didn't respond, he took a different tack. "Did you call to report the ladder incident?" he asked. "Maybe what happened today is related."

She sighed and turned to face him. "Yes. I explained that we might have a problem. I'll call to report the attacker as soon as I get back to the lodge."

He reached up to move the hair back away from the cut so he could get a better look, and this time she didn't stop him. The blood had caked, even as raindrops beaded on her face. Living near a rainforest, standing out in the storm, a person had to just deal with it.

She was probably too exhausted to care that he was getting into her space. "You sure you don't need to go back to town and stop at the urgent care clinic to get that looked at and cleaned up?"

"I can manage." She peered at him.

He took that moment to try to decide on the color of her eyes, which seemed to change every time he looked.

Hazel one second, then blue-gray or silver another. But he decided they were blue-gray for the most part.

"You love it, don't you?" He had no business getting personal. "You love living here. Working here."

"Yeah, I guess . . . I haven't really thought much about it."

"I can hear it in your voice. See the way you care. Today has been stressful, but it's nothing you didn't handle well." Except for maybe the rope incident. And the attacker . . . who could know? This woman was tough, mysterious, and she intrigued him. Against his better judgment, he wanted to know more, and that could only lead to disaster.

Just back off, Beckett.

"You don't need to get on my good side, okay?" She angled her head. "No need to butter me up."

See? Even she was telling him to step away, except he'd already kind of stepped into this with her. He wasn't one to turn his back on a situation involving a bad guy. From what he'd seen today, she'd attracted one. "You think that's what I'm doing?"

"Isn't it?" She shut the hatch and moved to get into her Bronco, and he followed her.

Not like a puppy, but he wasn't finished with this conversation.

"No. I thought I was already on your good side." He quirked a grin.

That elicited a small chuckle and the hint of a smile. He'd love to see that full-on smile.

"You want on my good side, or think you need to get there, because you want to hear what happened. Understand why it happened. The truth is, I'm still processing things. I'd rather just share it once, if that's okay. You can be there when I do."

That was fair. "I'd appreciate that."

"You shouldn't. I don't know why you'd want to get involved."

"Well, like you said before, I saw the rope, and it's gone now. I mean, all of it. Even the ground stakes have been removed." Before leaving Cedar Trails, he'd gone back to look at what remained of the rope ladder one more time and to take a picture. That's when he discovered the stakes were gone. Someone had to have removed them. Someone with malicious intent was still around. "Then I saw you fighting a masked attacker. I can tell the deputy sheriff what I saw. I'm in this whether you like it or not."

She swiped the hair out of her eyes, then once again looked away from him.

"I'm going now." Remi got in and shut the door.

That's all she had to say? He stood in the rain where she'd left him. He wasn't getting anywhere with her, and he wasn't sure what he was even doing here, honestly, because his reasons for coming to Cedar Trails had taken on a whole new purpose.

In his own truck, he turned around and followed Remi's vehicle. With buffeting wind and lashing rain, getting back to the lodge and his rental cabin was best even though the thick forest of insanely tall trees protected against much of the storm. He turned up the windshield wipers and accelerated to follow Remi, causing his Ford to bounce even harder.

He had this habit—good or bad, depending on one's perspective—of seeing something through all the way to the end. He never ignored the gnawing in his gut when something was wrong, and he wouldn't ignore it now. He'd have to be blind not to see that trouble was brewing around Remi Grant.

He'd come here to take a break from his own troubles. Get some space between him and what happened—everything had gone wrong. Everything.

He needed some perspective on his own dark secrets—the treacherous self-imposed mission to find a rogue agent and assassin before it was too late—but shoot if he wasn't inexplicably drawn to someone else's trouble. Not just anyone either, but an intriguing auburn-haired beauty with blue-gray eyes.

5

Remi downed the mocha latte and closed the door to the small office. She felt exhausted to her bones. Like she was ten—no, maybe twenty or even thirty—years older than her twenty-nine years.

Behind her desk was a set of bookshelves, and then on the opposite wall, behind a couple of chairs that faced the desk, was a sleeper sofa. She stared at it now. Could she get away with a short nap? The county sheriff's office was sending a deputy to take her statement. So, she wouldn't take a catnap, but at the same time Remi wouldn't hold her breath about their arrival or their ability to solve her problems that had suddenly come back into focus in just a few short hours.

If only things could be simple again like this time last year. A lesser storm had come in, but she'd enjoyed it. Sat in the lodge by the fire with the guests and sipped hot cocoa and watched the beauty and the fury of God's creation.

She'd taken plenty of photographs over the time she'd been here, even capturing a couple of eerie faces in the waves—one a beautiful woman and the other the monster from nightmares. Those photographs were out in the lodge and also on the wall here in her office. She'd framed them and added snippets of Scripture.

"*. . . who stirs up the sea so that its waves roar . . .*"

God.

God stirred up the sea. He set the waves to roar.

Even now in her office at the back of the lodge she could listen to the cacophony. Waves roared so loudly that she could imagine sea spray on her face. The ocean battered the rocky coast. Breakers thundered and crashed. Though she felt safe here, the structure shuddered under the force of the wind. She'd been reassured by the powers that be that the structure was solid and would hold as it had in the past century. That erosion wouldn't take the lodge or her cabins anytime soon.

But she'd heard from the locals that over the last few seasons, the storms were getting stronger. At least over the past two years, she felt like the strengthening storms were a perfect metaphor for her life as a maelstrom was gathering energy in her heart and mind.

The slashed ladder should have killed her. Had an attacker armed only with a knife shown up because she'd survived? If he'd chosen to use a gun, would she be dead now? She reached to her belt and felt her small S&W handgun in the holster at her waist. She wouldn't carry anything too big that her guests could see. She didn't want to scare or disturb them. She'd keep it with her from now on. *Stupid, stupid.* She shouldn't have left it in her Bronco for even a moment. With these attacks, she knew she was running out of time.

They had to be related.

"*Remember before it's too late.*"

Who was warning her?

God, please help me figure out what happened before.

She had no idea why someone wanted to kill her. Still, one thing she knew she needed was Dr. Holcomb's help again. Remi found the psychologist's number and called it on the landline. Of course she got voicemail.

"This is Remi Grant. I . . . something's happened. I need to talk to you. It's urgent. Please call me." Remi couldn't have her psychologist leaving a message on the main voicemail at the lodge, so she left her cell number, but she wouldn't get that call with no service. She'd just have to check for voicemail or text messages, which sometimes would come through. Heart pounding, she hung up.

At least she'd left the message.

A knock came at the door. Erika peeked inside, looking more stressed than usual. Remi moved toward the door, intending to come out with her and get busy again. Sitting in her office, worrying, wouldn't solve anything.

"A county vehicle just drove up."

"Thanks. Can you find Hawk Beckett for me and bring him to my office?"

She opened the door and waved at the deputy so she would head toward her office instead of going through the main lobby. Wearing a coat, the stout deputy tromped from her vehicle and headed toward Remi, who remained under the awning outside her office.

The deputy stepped out of the rain and pulled her hood back, revealing long silver hair pulled into a ponytail. This side of the lodge, the wind gusts were prevented from sending the rain sideways. Remi thrust her hand out. "I'm Remi Grant."

"Deputy Carla Hunter."

Remi motioned the deputy inside. "Please, take off your coat."

Deputy Hunter removed her jacket, then hung it on a peg near the door.

"Thank you for coming all this way," Remi said. "I know it's messy out there."

"I've been out in it all day already. It's part of my job." Deputy Hunter softened her tone with her next words. "I wasn't that far, dealing with a domestic violence problem. So the sheriff sent me the rest of the way. Said you had some issues."

"You could say that. Can I offer you some coffee?"

"I'd prefer to get to it. I want to get home before it's dark and the driving's even worse."

"I'm just waiting on another witness, someone else you want to talk to. So, while we're waiting . . ." She picked up the phone and called Shawna. "Hey, can you please bring . . ."

She paused and stared at Deputy Hunter, who then responded, "Just a large cup of black coffee."

Remi relayed the order, then hung up.

"I don't usually take anything when offered," the deputy said.

"No, I don't suppose you usually do, but I'm glad you're making an exception today."

The door suddenly opened, and Hawk peered inside. "Am I interrupting?"

Remi waved him in. "Deputy Hunter, this is Hawk Beckett. He's a guest staying in one of the cabins. He was there to help me during both incidents." Saying it out loud made his appearances sound suspicious, or maybe it was just her take on things.

After she explained what happened in both scenarios, Hawk shared his perspective. Deputy Hunter took copious notes in addition to recording everything with her smartphone. Finally, she looked up at Hawk.

"And you believe the rope ladder was intentionally tampered with. Not worn out from exposure?"

"It looked relatively new and was marine rope, so it would last a while." He glanced at Remi. "I didn't have much time to think on it, but that was my first impression. Then there's the matter of stability stakes being completely removed, as if destroying all evidence a rope ever existed. That seems deliberate enough to me."

"And you believe the shredding, as you called it, happened recently."

"It's hard to say, but again, at first glance, yes, it looked recent."

"Mr. Beckett, do you have any special skills that would give you the expertise to look at a marine rope and determine at first glance—a brief glance—that it had been recently tampered with?"

Hawk raked a hand over his jaw and sat back, appearing far more uncomfortable with the question than Remi would have expected. She took in his appearance, the scruff on his face, the angle of his jaw, and the sharp, steel-blue eyes. He wasn't big like a lumberjack, but with the flannel shirt he wore and his broad shoulders, he had that look about him and didn't much look like a helicopter pilot, at least in his current state.

She wanted to know more about him because he had been there to save her twice in one day. She wanted to know more about him . . . just because. Despite her best effort to ignore his good looks and charm and heroism, he occupied her thoughts.

"I'm former military."

That made sense.

"What branch?" Deputy Hunter asked.

"Army."

Deputy Hunter nodded as if in approval as she made a note, and that was enough to make him an expert on the shredding of marine rope.

She then turned her attention to Remi. "I'll share the information with our detective. He'll decide if Mr. Beckett's assessment is correct and someone tampered with the rope ladder."

Remi wasn't sure how she could question the assessment, especially since the stakes were removed. Then again, she hadn't seen that for herself and had to take Hawk's word for it, just as the deputy was.

Driven by fear and paranoia about the past, she could be getting ahead of herself, seeing suspicious action where none existed, and appreciated Deputy Hunter's fresh look at it.

The deputy scanned her notes. "The tree on the road today, did anyone happen to look at the cause? I mean, was it natural or otherwise?"

"You're asking if someone felled it so it would stop traffic," Hawk said.

Deputy Hunter nodded.

Remi shared a look with Hawk. "I didn't think to look. Taking a log out isn't all that easy, so I can't imagine why someone would do that intentionally—especially with the storm bearing down on us."

"While I agree with you, that's why you stopped and then you were attacked," Deputy Hunter said. "Ms. Grant, is there any reason someone would want to harm *you*, specifically?"

"No." With the word and the look both Hawk and Deputy Hunter gave her, she realized that she had just lied. Except she hadn't. She didn't know the reason anyone would want to harm her. She could think of much easier ways to do it than trap her with a downed tree and attack her. As for the ladder on the beach, how could anyone have known she'd need to go up that ladder? Or need to go after Paco?

Hawk continued to look at her as if he could infiltrate her mind and learn the truth by sheer will alone. And with the guilt surging through her, the stares she got, Remi wanted to chew a hangnail when she didn't chew nails.

Should she bring up the two puzzle pieces? The lost memories? She'd come here to hide, and she didn't feel comfortable telling all her secrets to these two strangers. Without knowing who was behind the puzzle pieces, the demand to remember before it was too late, or the attacks, she couldn't trust anyone. Not yet.

Not even heroic lumberjack helicopter pilot Hawk Beckett.

And the worst part of it—she couldn't be one hundred percent sure that she hadn't, through no fault of her own, become involved in something terrible, something horrible, about which she would want no one to know, or at least strangers, until *she* knew. Her mind was blocking it for a reason. Nope. Not telling the deputy yet.

"And neither of you got a good look at this guy?" Deputy Hunter asked.

"He had a black mask and a hood, and it was dark in the woods. I can tell you he had brown eyes. I don't know . . . I . . ." Her throat constricted and she looked at Hawk.

"You said he tried to stab you with a knife at your Bronco," Hunter said.

"Yes, but I got away, and he was between me and the Bronco, so I couldn't get my gun. I ran into the woods, and he caught up with me. I was forced to fight him. He was strong and had more stamina, so I figured my only way to survive was to get away. I was able to knock him in the head with a branch, and that's when I started running back toward the road, but he was closing in on me, so I stopped at a tree to try to get my bearings. He attacked me again, and then Hawk showed up. The distraction was what allowed me to punch his throat. Plus, Hawk had a gun, and he fired a warning shot."

Deputy Hunter wrote more and lifted a brow. "Makes you wonder why he didn't have a gun too."

"I don't know." Remi was growing tired of this whole thing.

Deputy Hunter closed her notepad and stood. "Thanks for the coffee. That's going to hold me over on the drive."

"That's it?"

"Unless you have more to add. I think you should at least make sure your guests lock their doors. There's an assailant out there somewhere—unless, of course, you think that you're the target."

"I don't know why anyone would target me." There it was again. That half-lie. Holding back was the right thing, wasn't it? She'd bide her time and, worst case, she'd tell the county sheriff's department, but what could they do even if they learned she had amnesia?

Because what did she know, really? Nothing. She *didn't* know why someone would target her. Only that she might . . . she could be . . . a target for reasons unknown.

"Thanks again for coming out in the storm. Let me walk you out."

"No, don't bother. You stay inside. I can find my way to my vehicle."

Remi got the feeling the deputy was ready to be alone with her thoughts. She had that same feeling, but Hawk was still here. He had the demeanor of someone who intended to stay until he got answers. But she didn't know him and wouldn't be answering his questions. He could even be the person who had left her the puzzle pieces. He was former military. Army. Remi had been Army.

He'd shown up, and suddenly her world was crashing.

What was he doing here now, really? Though Remi would

remain on guard and wary of the man, Hawk had saved her twice, so the thought that he could have left her the warning puzzle pieces to remember before it was too late didn't feel right. Didn't ring true. Dr. Holcomb had told her that even if she remembered, she couldn't trust those memories. They could be inaccurate. A way her brain tried to fill in the gaps. If memories could be inaccurate, what made her think she could listen to her instincts or trust her gut?

Trust herself?

Remi had the sensation she wasn't tethered to anything solid and had no foundation. The wind blew hard enough in this storm that it might rip her away and carry her off into oblivion.

She caught Hawk staring, and her cheeks warmed. All this distrust of the man couldn't dampen the stirring inside when he looked at her like that. *Oh, come on, Remi. Get it together.*

"So, Army, huh? What did you do?" she asked.

His genuine smile warmed her up. "Would it surprise you that I flew helicopters?"

Even after the day she'd had, a small laugh erupted. "I guess not." She didn't know this guy at all, and she knew to be wary of all strangers, including Hawk. But . . .

I like you, Hawk Beckett.

She hadn't wanted him here, running a tour package, for more than the explanation she'd initially given him—too much noise. But though she couldn't remember those hidden days, she had the sense that she'd trusted the wrong person. And she wouldn't do that again.

6

Hawk could be reading it all wrong. But he didn't think he was.

Remi was holding back. Hiding something. And it was putting her in danger. He had to figure out how to get answers from her, but he could see in her eyes that she had made the decision to keep him uninformed. She had no idea who she was dealing with in him—and that could be part of the problem.

Hawk had been trained to find his way in the dark, so he had no doubt that he would learn the truth.

Remi pursed her lips, then lifted her cell, her eyes wide. "A text came through. I need to take this."

He could just stand there and wait for her to read it, but her eyes flashed with irritation and she gave him a look.

"I know when I'm being dismissed." He bit back any other words he might have said, like *we need to talk* or *I'll find you later*. No need to ramp up her determination to keep him ignorant of the truth.

He closed the door behind him, frustration pulsing through him. Now what?

A terrible feeling brewed in his chest, and he wanted to get a handle on what was going on. He'd love to believe the shredded rope ladder could have been some kids playing a practical joke, not realizing the danger. Maybe they'd been scared and had come back to remove the stakes and evidence. Sure. That was possible. And the tree could have fallen because that's what trees did, especially during storms.

In that case, the knife attack could have been random, and he was building a case out of nothing.

Except . . . for Remi's reaction. He needed to know more about the situation.

Not Remi herself. No, he didn't want to know about her at all. Her eyes didn't draw him in. Her determination and the mystery surrounding her didn't intrigue him in the least. He would keep telling himself that because he couldn't afford any kind of romantic entanglement, not until he finished his personal mission. No one deserved a guy like him.

Besides, Remi was giving him mixed signals with her suspicious looks. She had her own baggage, which prevented her from trusting, and he understood. Good for her. Trusting the wrong person could get her killed.

He moved into the great room feeling antsy and useless. Maybe he should back off and away from Remi's trouble. That would be the smart thing to do. Guests gathered at the window that Hawk assumed was made of some kind of impact-resistant glass. He secured a chair with a view while he waited to see if he'd get another chance to speak with Remi. He remained by the window and chatted with a few folks, learning about their backgrounds and what brought them to the lodge, while they watched the waves crashing and building. Some oohed and aahed and others projected a respectful level of fear.

When Remi didn't show up after half an hour, he decided he was done pestering her. Scratching his head, he stood and grabbed his jacket. He should get to his cabin or else he might have to spend the night in the chair. Best to be inside where he was warm and safe . . . and unfortunately alone. He didn't even have a dog to bring with him to keep him company.

No internet.

No television.

No cell signal.

Just Hawk all by his lonesome with his thoughts. Pulling his heavy rain jacket tight and his hood over his head, he exited the lodge and hiked to his cabin on the bluff.

Inside, he shrugged out of the coat and stoked the wood-stove.

Cedar Trails Lodge was supposed to be a restful place to get away from the busyness and chaos of the world and offer the kind of answers that came to a person out of doing nothing at all.

His former CO, John, had urged him to come here, especially after the failed mission—a catastrophe, really—that got him fired and left his copilot and friend, Jake, dead. But Hawk could focus on his own problems after he figured out what was going on with Remi and why someone had targeted her. John couldn't have foreseen this set of circumstances that would lead Hawk into solving a problem rather than getting rest.

The clock ticked as the storm's energy built and the wind howled around the cabin, shaking it. He stood at the window of his cabin—the best one for a view—and let the height of the waves keep him on edge.

By now, most everyone was already holed up in their cabins, preparing to see the spectacle they'd come here to see with the series of winter storms. Eventually, they could expect gale-force winds, and he would hunker down like the rest of them. The cabin rattled, and Hawk began to question his decision to stay here, right over the bluff.

But wait . . .

He angled his head. He'd heard something. A branch knocking against the roof? No.

That was a knock at the door. In two steps he was there and opened it, surprised to find anyone out in the weather.

A medium-height figure wrapped in a heavy overcoat waited, so he could barely make out her face, but he recognized those eyes that stared back at him from beneath the dark hood. His first instinct was to reach forward and pull her inside and out of the weather, but he thought better of it and opened the door wide for her to enter on her own.

Instead, she simply stood there.

"You want to come in?" he asked.

"You left early. I needed to talk to you." She sounded frustrated with him.

You could have fooled me. Their interaction felt like they'd known each other for years when they'd only met this morning.

"You could have just called," he said. Oh, wait a minute. No cell service.

"I tried."

"Well, either you come inside, or you go back without me talking to you because I'm not going back to the lodge in this."

She blew out a breath, then stepped inside but kept her distance. He closed the door, which barely muted the sounds of the wind and rain and trees and waves. Nature's wrath at its finest.

He held his hand out. "Coat?"

"I'm not staying long." She dropped her hood, so he got

to see her dark-auburn hair, partially wet after battling the rain on the hike to his cabin.

"This must be important for you to get out in this."

"You were former Army. A pilot. A warrant officer, then?" She remained rigid and questioned him like she was practiced in interrogations and he was a suspect.

He ran his hand around his jaw and chin, scratching the stubble there. "Yes. Why?" He wished he'd said nothing, but the deputy had wanted his background.

"And since then, before coming here, what did you do?"

He frowned. "Why the third degree?" Why not just look him up on the internet? Oh, right. That wasn't readily available here.

She stepped forward. "Hawk, I need to know."

He looked into those earnest eyes that had turned a deep, mesmerizing blue now. She was scared, but not of him. Or if she was, why was she standing here alone in his cabin, facing off with him?

"I'll tell you everything I can if you tell me why it's important."

Her hands shook as she fished something out of her pocket, then showed him two puzzle pieces. "Do you know anything about this?"

He took the two pieces from her. He couldn't make anything out of the partial image. "What's this? Part of a puzzle?" He handed the pieces back. "No idea."

She looked at him long and hard. "If you're the one who sent these to me—if you're behind this—I want to know and I want to know now. I don't have time for games."

"What does my background have to do with anything? Why would you think I had anything to do with this?"

"You first. You said you would tell me everything."

"Look, if I was the one to leave you the mysterious puzzle pieces, I could just lie about it."

68

"I'm good at seeing through lies. I would see holes in your story eventually."

This woman.

He didn't need this kind of drama. Or maybe he did—it occupied his mind so he couldn't think about himself and the crash and Jake. Oh, and the fact he didn't have a job.

"I was 160th SOAR. Special Operations Aviation Regiment (Airborne). Night Stalkers."

"And then what?"

He didn't see that his past had any bearing on her current dilemma over a puzzle. "I was a deputy for the King County Sheriff's Air Support Unit. Seattle's the county seat. You can check it out if you want." *But please don't.* "Look, Remi. I'm one of the good guys. Whatever has got you freaked out about those puzzle pieces has nothing to do with me. And I can't help if you don't tell me what's going on."

She bit her lip and frowned. "Then who left this for me? I wish I had cameras everywhere now, but that kind of defeats the 'no technology' theme going on at this place."

"Does the puzzle have to do with the attack today? And if so, then why have you been targeted?"

Remi stared at him as if she was some kind of mind reader, penetrating his brain to find out if she could trust him. Then she turned her attention to the window and looked out at the storm, but he could tell she wasn't seeing the display. The dark, furious clouds muted what remained of the fading sunlight anyway. She turned to open the door so she could walk back outside and into the storm. Hawk moved to stand in her path. He had to know.

"What's your story? Why are *you* here? What did *you* do before?"

Her face twisted as her frown deepened. "I came here to remember."

Funny, because Hawk had come here to forget.

"I shouldn't have come to your cabin." She tugged on her hood, moved past him to open the door, and stepped outside, then pressed into the chaos.

Hawk stood in the doorway and let the rain lash him as he watched her disappear into the woods, where nightfall had come quickly. Eventually the flashlight beam was lost in the darkness. Her determination reminded him of one of the 160th Airborne mottos. *Night Stalkers don't quit.*

Then there was . . . *Death waits in the dark.*

7

Along the dark path, wind buffeted and rain pelted. The sun had already dipped below the horizon, and the heavy clouds ushered darkness in much sooner. Pulling her hood forward, Remi pushed on.

Why had she told Hawk? Said anything at all? She'd wanted to ask him while he was in her office, but Dr. Holcomb had texted and insisted it was vital she meet with Remi as soon as possible.

Maybe she'd been rash, impatient, but she had to know if Hawk was to blame. He'd shown up on the very day she'd not only faced death twice but also received another puzzle piece—hand delivered—along with the warning to remember. Two years ago, she'd woken up in a military hospital, and deep inside, she had the strange feeling that everything was somehow related to the military. Hawk had been Army and she'd been Army, and so following that to a logical conclusion, she'd thought he could have been sent here by someone to pressure her to get her memories back. Like that would work.

But apparently that had been an illogical conclusion,

because she believed Hawk when he told her he had no clue what was going on. Then when Hawk had stared at her with an intensity that made her shudder all over—in a weirdly good way—she had to admit that, yes . . .

I need an ally in this.

And maybe part of her had wanted him to be the person who had sent the pieces, to help her remember, to warn her about the threat. That would mean that he knew what menace she faced. He knew what happened when she did not and could explain everything. But he wasn't the puzzle piece sender, and now he thought she was crazy. She didn't need to bring him into this with her. She shouldn't. Not when she didn't know the full scale of it.

She forced her mind to shut down the overwhelming thoughts to focus on getting to the lodge. Normally, she could walk this path blindfolded, but the wind and rain and crashing waves disoriented her.

I can do this.

Shining the flashlight along the path, she continued, heading back toward her own cabin where she could sit and wait out the storm and figure out what to do next. A branch blew past and nearly knocked into her, so she picked up the pace. This wasn't the first time she'd experienced storms here, but it would be the most intense, and yeah, okay, she'd been stupid to come out in it close to dark in the first place. But she'd needed answers and been impulsive. No way would she turn back and wait out the first of the storms with Hawk Beckett.

The sound of water rushing, flooding much too close, sent alarms through her. Cold water surged around her ankles. She wasn't on the beach, so what was going on? Her heart pounded. This shouldn't be happening. A practical river had formed, and she felt herself being tugged along. She had to get out of this.

Remi shined the flashlight at her feet at the same moment a hand gripped her arm and whirled her around.

Hawk stood in a soaking wet T-shirt. "You have to come back! It's too dangerous," he shouted as he pulled her with him toward his cabin.

Too stunned to argue, she let him lead her through the dark forest. Once inside the cabin, he shut the door and pressed his back against it as if his strong, broad shoulders were needed to hold down the fort.

She gasped, tried to calm her racing heart. In the low lighting, she caught his soaked form again. His chest rising and falling with his quickened breaths. He held her gaze.

"It was just rainwater flooding, rushing to the cliff to meet the ocean. You shouldn't have brought me back."

"The water is rushing toward the drop in elevation—I mean, a significant drop. Didn't you see it? Part of the cliff face eroded, falling right into the ocean." His voice was shaky.

Strong Hawk Beckett could get scared? Well, if that didn't shake her to her toes too.

He ran his hands through his wet hair before fisting them at his hips. Concern raked his features. "You almost stepped right off the new cliff."

"How did *you* see it?" He'd been watching her? To make sure she was safe?

"I saw the branch fly past and I thought you were hurt."

This guy never quit being a hero, did he? "Thank you."

His lips pressed into a thin line, and he pushed from the door. Remi had to absorb this news to understand. She removed her dripping jacket and hung it on a peg near the door, next to Hawk's jacket.

I don't understand. She had to get her mind around it, for her sake and for others.

"Scientists, geotechnical engineers, have already assessed the soil composition and stability. Eventually—in decades—even the lodge might become vulnerable." She paced the room, then moved to the woodstove to get warm. "This cabin would at some point be threatened. But not yet, Hawk." She looked at him. "I swear, I would never put anyone in danger. The evaluations, the powers that be, wouldn't allow me to rent the cabin out if it wasn't safe."

His mouth hung open before he slowly closed it, then said, "So, wait. You're saying you think this cabin isn't safe?"

"Are you seriously asking me that?" she asked. "You said you saw erosion a few yards away. That wasn't supposed to happen anytime in the near future. So how can we believe this cabin isn't going to slide right into the ocean tonight if water was flowing off the cliff? That just further destabilizes it. The other cabins, no. They're too far back. But this one? It's the closest to the edge. The best view of the beach, frankly, and the storm." Remi pressed her hands against her eyes.

God, what is happening? Cedar Trails Lodge is in danger on my watch? My life is falling apart all at once?

She dropped her hands. "I need to radio my staff. Let everyone know where I am and what's going on."

She fished in her pocket. Then both pockets. Reached into her jeans. *Are you kidding me?* Now that she thought about it, she'd been so intent on catching Hawk and getting answers, she hadn't grabbed the radio on her way out. She hadn't planned to stay long, so the thought hadn't pressed on her.

Hawk pulled off his wet shirt.

Great. Unfortunately, Remi took in his well-formed chest and ridiculously taut abs before she caught herself and looked away. *Work out much?* "Aren't you cold?"

He nodded and disappeared into the bedroom. When

74

he emerged, he was pulling a fleece hoodie over another T-shirt. Then he pulled on his heavy jacket and rain boots.

"Where are you going?" she asked.

He grabbed a flashlight. "I'm going to look around. We need to know what's happening before we make a decision."

As if he could look at the ground and predict what would happen next. "I'm coming too," she said.

Tugging her coat back on, she pulled her own flashlight from her pocket. "Let's go."

She followed him out into the stormy night. This close to the cliffside, the roar of the ocean was deafening.

"Stay close!" Hawk shouted.

Like she needed to be told they should stick together. The wind and rain were unforgiving, but reconnaissance had to be done. They each shined their lights around, searching for flooding and erosion in the middle of chaos. This wasn't how she imagined her day would end, but considering the way it started, maybe she should have expected this. Hawk led her around the back of the cabin and away from the cliff.

"Shouldn't we be looking closer to the edge?" she shouted against the wind.

"We will."

"What do you think you'll see? Are you an expert in coastal erosion?" And if so, he'd left that out of his already slim offerings on his verbal résumé.

"No. But I think it's worth looking, don't you?"

Remi and Hawk studied the ground that was visible in the ring of light as they moved around the cabin. Beneath the dense forest canopy, they were sheltered only slightly from the onslaught. Strong gusts blew the rain sideways as trees swayed and clacked around them. To think, this wasn't yet the true monster, which was predicted to come in last of the sequence of storms that were hitting during the king tides.

Behind the cabin, they stopped ten yards from the cliff's edge, which Remi figured should be a safe distance, but closer would have allowed them to see more. The light shone out into the cacophonous ocean. She saw nothing but gray and rain.

"Okay. We came. We saw. And we still don't know if it's safe. So let's get your things. I'll find you a place to stay for tonight."

"Just for tonight. We can check things out tomorrow in the light of day, but the issues with my cabin are the least of your worries, Remi." He gave her a look that, in the deep shadows cast by the flashlights, seemed dark and foreboding.

She followed him to the cabin, trying to figure out where she could move him. They were fully booked. She could let him stay in her cabin, and she could sleep on the extra sofa in her office. Or release him from the rental agreement to go home.

Inside the cabin, Hawk entered his room and less than a minute later came out again with his duffel. "I didn't bring much. Too bad we can't climb into my Ford and drive to the lodge." He smirked.

"Yeah, that. Campers and cabin stayers want a natural experience, which doesn't include cars parked so close. They have to hike in."

"You don't have to explain. Anyone who'd choose a place without internet and cell wants to leave civilization behind."

"Given the erosion and flooding, we'll have to walk straight east to be safe," she said. "We'll pass some of the other cabins. There's one cabin north of them, then we'll take the long path around to the lodge. That'll give us a chance to make sure they're intact and everything is all right. They have never been in danger of erosion."

"Only the cabin where I'm staying," he said. "Just my luck."

"I'm sorry. Are you good to go with me to check the others?"

"Of course."

She had to pick up her stride to keep up with Hawk. "I think looking around as we go is good. Thank you, Hawk."

After making their way around fifteen cabins, they checked on the last one, north of the rest, then went in search of the main trail back to the lodge.

Would she even have known until it was too late—until something more happened—if she hadn't been grappling with Hawk over those puzzle pieces meant to trigger her memory?

Though that strategy hadn't worked, Hawk's outstretched hand reaching for her, pulling her to safety, had done the trick. And maybe sticking with him, keeping him close, if possible, would help her remember more. She could figure out why he was the trigger later. But she didn't think he was dangerous . . . at least not to her.

The gusts died down along with the rain, giving a reprieve for who knew how long. She could actually hear the water dripping through the trees over the crashing waves. This storm would be great to watch in the daytime, nestled in a comfy chair by a fire in a *safe* cabin, in which there was no chance the cliff would give out beneath them. She'd love to take some photographs, and she could just imagine she might even have the good fortune to capture a face in the waves again.

She would put her photographs out there for the world to see—not just in this lodge—if she wasn't here to hide. But she hadn't done a great job, after all, and maybe subconsciously she'd wanted someone to find her.

And they had.

Two someones.

Someone to warn her.

Someone to kill her.

Remi waved the flashlight around, catching a couple of cabins in the distance. "The lights are off. The power must be out."

Movement in the trees caught her attention.

She gasped and grabbed Hawk's arm. "Did you see that?"

8

At the warning in her voice, the hair at the back of his neck lifted. "Down!"

He urged her to crouch with him behind a tree, then shined the flashlight in the direction she'd seen movement. He didn't see anything. Turning off his light, he leaned in close to whisper. "Turn off your flashlight. What did you see?"

She turned her light off, throwing them into complete darkness.

"Someone," she said. "I could have just panicked. Maybe someone else is lost. We should just call out."

"Keep still and quiet. You didn't call out because you instinctively sensed danger."

Or she was being paranoid, but after what had already happened, he would err on the side of caution. If someone was actually out in the storm intending to harm her, then Hawk and Remi weren't going to make it back to the lodge without fighting off another attack.

"Let's go back to the cabin," he said. "I need to think." At least they'd be protected from this new threat.

"What? No, we can't stay there. I don't want to hike all the way back. Let's just keep going to the lodge."

He ran his hand down his wet face. He would already be barreling through the forest but for the terrain and an unseen enemy. Maybe it was that lunatic who had attacked her on the road.

He palmed his Colt handgun, the sensation of being trapped unsettling him. They were in a forest, but a cliff's edge was at their back. Trees and the darkness closed in around them even as the threat of erosion pushed them toward the unseen threat.

"The risk at the cabin is less than the risk of hiking through the woods with someone out there waiting to pounce." Once they turned on their flashlights, they would be easy targets. Of course, the potential attacker could be wearing night vision goggles and watching them even now.

Remi leaned in close. "Hawk, if it's the attacker from earlier today, then I agree with you. The cabin is probably safer for now. But we can't know that."

"Wait here." He leaned closer to make sure she heard. "I was law enforcement before, remember, so let me do this."

Shining the beam of light would give him away. With no moon or lightning to guide the way, the night was pitch black. He stepped from the tree and found another one, then crouched. He could see candlelight or flashlights inside the other cabins, and that gave off faint light. His eyes adjusted and he searched the darkness, but he really needed to illuminate the deeper shadows, and he turned on his light.

"Watch out!" Remi shouted.

He ducked, then turned to engage an attacker, dropping the flashlight. The beam cast eerie shadows. Was this the same man who'd attacked Remi before? The attacker punched Hawk in the gut, then the mouth. He tasted blood but didn't miss a beat as he responded with thrusts and parries.

He could pull out his gun and stop this, but he didn't want it to turn deadly. The assailant brandished a knife and threw it. Hawk shifted away.

Thunk.

The knife pierced the bark and stuck next to Hawk's head. Too close. His stomach lurched.

Why was he holding back? Hawk was so done with this and reached for his gun, but the man rammed him into the tree trunk.

Grunt.

Pain ignited as bark bit into him. Hawk shoved back and slid to the side, out of the assailant's grasp, then turned the tables on the guy, forcing his back to the tree now.

Then he pressed his arm against the masked attacker's throat. "Who. Are. You? What do you want?"

He tried to rip the mask away, but the man jabbed another knife at Hawk's gut, drawing fire and blood. Hawk backed away, releasing him. Pulling his gun out, he aimed, but the man disappeared in the darkness. Hawk took off after him, racing through the underbrush and between the trees, but he lost him in the night. He'd gone south, in the direction of the lodge. Great. The attacker stood between them and escape.

Breathing hard, Hawk slowly lowered his gun. He opened his coat and lifted his T-shirt and hoodie to find a short, shallow graze. Fortunately, the knife hadn't made it through all the layers, and he had only been nicked. He pressed his hand against his side and felt the sting. It could have been so much worse.

He gave up his pursuit and turned, intending to go back for Remi, but she'd followed him and stood in a ring of light, watching, holding the duffel he'd dropped.

"You're hurt," she said.

"It's nothing."

She shivered, her lips blue. He didn't think he fared any better. The wind picked up again, and this storm he'd come here to watch in fascination, to enjoy, was bringing him down.

"This guy stands between us and the lodge." Hawk couldn't count on making it without risking more danger to her. "I'm not sure I want to go to the lodge and draw him there."

Remi spoke, but he couldn't hear her over the crashing waves.

"What?" he asked.

She leaned in, shouting in his ear. "I know where we can go. It's not the cabin. And it's close. Come on. I can lead you a short distance without the light, then we'll have to risk it. But unless the jerk has scoped out the details already, he won't be able to find it."

"Lead the way." He took his duffel from her.

She nodded.

He agreed with her in that he really didn't want to draw trouble to anyone here, but at the moment, he wanted to get her some place warm and dry and safe. They could try to call the sheriff's department, though he doubted help would arrive soon enough. She rushed between the trees, heading west toward the ocean. They were so far north in the woods that he could no longer see light from the cabins.

He hoped she knew where she was going because he was lost. But this was her place. If anyone knew, it was Remi. He remained vigilant in case the attacker came back.

Hawk wished he'd brought his gear. Night vision goggles would make all the difference. He could get Remi back to the lodge safely and then hunt down her attacker.

As they got closer to the cliff and the ocean, the sounds

of breakers crashing were jarring. "You're sure this place is close," he shouted.

"Yes. Almost there."

Ah. He got it. Why hadn't he thought of this before? "Please tell me you're not talking about those old war bunkers."

She kept going and he followed. Sea spray lashed them both, they were that close. But she caught a protective rail as he stepped onto concrete.

"And you have a way inside?" he asked.

"I do. Come on." She headed into a tunnel and kept going until a metal door stopped her. Hawk figured that an old military bunker would be locked to keep intruders out, but she pushed the metal door open, and the rusty hinges squeaked loudly, echoing against the concrete floor. Once inside, the raucous sound of the storm grew louder, bouncing off the walls.

"Wait." He touched her arm. "Get behind me." He held the Colt ready. No walking into the dark, supposedly abandoned World War II bunkers without clearing them first.

They could be ambushed if someone else had taken up space here during the storm. If that jerk had found his way here first or even made this his home base of operation. Hawk really just wanted to get his hands on this guy and find out what was going on. He'd almost had him before. He could kick himself.

Not tonight.

But tomorrow. Tomorrow he could kick himself.

She entered with him and stuck close behind with her own gun out and ready.

I don't like this. It wasn't the first time he'd found himself in an untenable predicament.

Remi shut the door and put a rock against it. Okay. She knew her way around this old bunker, then.

He shined his flashlight around their temporary shelter. "So, they just let people come inside, roam around on their own?"

"Some of the old bunkers are accessible to explorers. But this one had been locked up until someone busted it open, and sure, I looked around inside. And now here we are."

A scuffling noise drew Remi around, and she shined her flashlight into the inky blackness, revealing more concrete. "What was that?"

"A forest creature, maybe. A rat. Hopefully not a bear."

"It's like a labyrinth down there, and you keep going until you're deep underground. It was a bomb shelter. But we're not going deeper than this." She put her gun away.

Hawk wasn't exactly keen on the idea of not clearing the entire place, but neither did he want to stir up trouble. They wouldn't stay long. Just catch their breath and get warm, if possible, while they figured things out and made a plan.

She shrugged out of her drenched coat. He dropped his duffel bag, unzipped it, and tugged a blanket out, then spread it on the floor.

"You carry a blanket in your duffel?"

"Not usually, no. But I didn't know that I wouldn't end up sleeping in my truck or some hollowed-out tree, given the way this day has gone, so I snagged it from the bed. It's always smart to be prepared. And now here we are, like you said, and in this cold bunker, which is a step up from a hollowed-out tree." For which he was woefully unprepared, but he wouldn't say that out loud.

"I thought it looked familiar," she said.

"So, charge me for it. In the meantime, if we sit close enough, we can wrap the edges around us."

She scrunched her nose.

"You don't like the idea of getting close to me? You didn't

really think this through, did you?" He couldn't help but grin and maybe feel a little bit hurt.

"My only thought was to get out of the storm for a few minutes. We're here now. Let's make the most of it before we go outside to find our way back to the lodge."

Hawk blew out a breath. He didn't want to traverse through a pitch-black forest during a monster storm with a maniac out to get them. The man had attacked Hawk this time because he wanted to eliminate the man standing between him and Remi. And he almost had.

"As soon as there's a break in the storm," Hawk said, "let's get out of here. We need to keep a quick pace. Do you know the shortest and safest path back to the lodge from here?"

Remi sat on the blanket and leaned against the wall. "Nothing short about it, but I know the way."

"We should probably turn at least one flashlight off to save the batteries," he said. "I'm not going to sit here in the dark, though."

He slid onto the floor next to her and leaned his head against the frigid, hard concrete. She was cold and wet. He was cold and wet. He scooted closer and tugged what was left of the blanket over them. Yep. This was a predicament.

He was seriously unprepared for sitting out a storm in a cold, dank military bunker with a woman who had trouble brewing around her. "Now would be a good time for you to tell me what's really going on."

9

With Hawk next to her—*close* to her—this was panning out to be the tempest of the decade in multiple ways. But she had to admit she appreciated the warmth his body provided in addition to the blanket. Exhaustion threatened—tromping through the woods in the raging wind and rain really took it out of her, and she fought the need to lean her head against his very broad and adequate shoulder and close her eyes. Soak up even more heat. But he'd asked a question, and she owed an explanation, didn't she?

Except Remi didn't have the answers.

What. Is. Going. On?

I wish I knew.

Squeezing her eyes shut, she sighed. How did she tell this complete stranger that for some inexplicable reason he had triggered something forgotten in her? She needed time and space to think, which was hard to do when she was taking refuge with Hawk, cozying up to him. For survival reasons, of course, and nothing more. Nestled so close she could practically feel the strength and power contained in those muscles, which should have felt awkward but instead made her feel safe and comfortable. Maybe she was too tired to care about the proximity. But she really should care because she needed to know if she could trust him.

She opened her eyes and angled toward him. "To be honest, I kind of hoped you were the one to leave the puzzle pieces, then I'd have answers because you would tell *me* what was going on."

He huffed a laugh. "And why would you even think I had anything to do with it?"

She lifted one shoulder, though he probably couldn't see. "I don't know. I guess because you showed up at the same time as the attacks, and on the same day as a puzzle piece had been hand delivered."

"Anything else going on that you haven't told me? I need context. For one thing, you mentioned you came here to remember. What did you mean?"

Oh, Lord . . . what if me being here with him is not a good thing? How would she know? But shoot if she didn't want to trust this guy. He'd shown himself trustworthy, if that counted for anything. And maybe God was watching out for her by sending Hawk just when she needed a little help.

Because with missing days lost to her, days surrounding something vitally important, she was all alone in this, and she didn't feel like she could even trust herself. Her own mind had betrayed her.

"The night isn't getting any younger," he said. "And as soon as the storm dies down to catch its breath, we need to try to make it back to the lodge and hope Masked Man isn't so stupid to sit out there and wait for us. You might not get another chance to tell me—at least one in which we can be sure no one else is going to hear."

Hawk was a man of reason. And she desperately wanted

to talk to someone. She'd hoped to meet with Dr. Holcomb again, but that wasn't happening anytime soon.

Lord, let him be one of the good guys, please.

"The two pieces of a puzzle came separately. The first one was mailed and included a card that simply said, 'remember.' The second one was hand delivered and also included a small card that told me to remember before it's too late."

She waited a few breaths to let that sink in.

"Go on," Hawk said.

"When you pulled me from that cliff, your hand triggered a flashback. A memory."

"So, you lost some memories? See, I didn't know. I'm sorry. What *do* you remember?"

"Nothing. I lost almost a week. Five days, really."

"What were you doing at the time?" he asked. "I need a lot more details here."

Where did she even start. The details felt so convoluted. She shared about being a former military photographer and then deciding against reenlisting and traveling instead. Being at a café, then waking up in the hospital. About the man questioning her at the hospital and then following her back to the States.

"So, did you go to the police, the FBI?"

"What would I say, exactly, that wouldn't make me sound paranoid and make myself a target? I didn't feel comfortable talking to anyone else."

"I wasn't questioning your decision. I completely understand it. How did you end up here at Cedar Trails Lodge?"

She snorted a laugh. "I had to disappear. Get lost. It's almost impossible anymore. I withdrew as much money as I could from the bank. Bought the old Bronco and then went on a long road trip. I took the back roads and did my best to avoid being tracked. I used a different name, an alias, everywhere I went and paid cash. I found my way to the Puget Sound region. Mom and I had always wanted to see it, and so, with no place to go, that's where I headed. I knew I needed to talk to someone. Get some help, and I found Dr. Holcomb because she accepted cash patients. I told her everything, well, because she's a doctor and our conversations are private. I needed her help if I was going to find out what was going on."

"And?"

"And I met with her for a year and a half, but nothing was resolved, and so about six months ago, I just stopped going."

"What did she say about your amnesia?"

Remi shared everything Dr. Holcomb had said, adding, "She said that usually, our brains will block out memories to protect us when something simply too horrible to comprehend has happened." Her words echoed off the concrete walls and made her story sound even more ominous. "She said that it could be that I know something, and someone doesn't want me to remember."

Hawk said nothing for a while, and Remi figured he might be thinking the same things she wondered. Why not just kill her in the hospital? Why let her walk out and walk free? Maybe he had those thoughts, but he didn't say them out loud.

"But how did you end up here?"

"You mean Cedar Trails Lodge?"

"Yes."

"Dr. Holcomb had a reservation for two weeks and something came up, so she gave it to me. Said maybe the time spent in peace and quiet would help me to heal. Now that I know more about the place, I see that she thought I could find refuge here. And she was right. The woman who owns the place—Evelyn Monroe—she offers a safe place for a few of us."

"Us? There's more?"

"Yeah. Please don't ask me who else because I don't know. I only suspect."

"And you're running the place after only a short time."

"Well, I have experience running a bed-and-breakfast. I grew up on a small farm in Nebraska. When Dad died, Mom sold the farm to pay the agriculture loans he took out to maintain the farm. I know that sounds so cliché, but it happens. She had just enough money left over to invest in a new business—one she'd always wanted to try. She put a down payment on a home on the outskirts of Omaha. We turned it into a bed-and-breakfast. It was fun for a while, and we got to meet a lot of interesting people. In fact, that's kind of how I ended up in Zarovia."

"Zarovia, as in the Eastern European country?"

She laughed. "Yes. An older couple from Zarovia had stayed with us and shared all their stories. They invited Mom and me to come and visit them. What a pipe dream, but they obviously planted a seed. So, when Mom died, I failed to keep the place going and decided I wanted to do something else. I was lost, really."

"I'm sorry this happened to you, Remi."

"I'd always pass the Army recruiter office when I went in to grab groceries, and one day he was standing outside and caught me. We talked a bit, and he asked what I wanted to do in life. I told him I wanted to travel the world. I'd never seen anything but Nebraska, but I wanted to see much more, and that's when he talked me into joining the Army. Said I could see the world. With no one to keep me in Nebraska, I enlisted that day. I eventually served as a military photographer, and I wanted to be a combat photographer, but I ended up taking staged photos for public relations purposes when I'd wanted to be on the front lines. I decided once my time was up, I'd see the world on my own and maybe start a travel blog."

Those memories were bright in her mind, clear as a bell, as if they happened just yesterday. "So, when I came to Cedar Trails and stayed at the lodge, I don't know. I started taking photographs. Losing myself in the beauty. The ocean waves reminded me of the amber waves of grain in Nebraska—like in the song. I've seen those waves. Mom had a Scripture plaque on the wall at our bed-and-breakfast— 'For I am the LORD your God, who stirs up the sea so that its waves roar,' Isaiah 51:15. It would always make people ask because we weren't anywhere near the ocean. Those waves of grain were so mesmerizing. Anyway, an opening for a barista came up and I was experienced, so I took that job and made myself useful."

Those had actually been such good times. She'd been happy at Cedar Trails, pretending that she belonged and that the shadows of the past weren't chasing her.

"Eventually, Mrs. Monroe decided that she wanted me to run the place. But right now, I feel like I'm failing her. Some guests come to stay at the lodge, but a few come here looking for refuge, sent by others who know it can be a place to hide. There's no internet or Wi-Fi or cell, and it's just so remote. Probably the closest thing to a deserted island."

Guilt surged through her for telling him so much and possibly compromising others hiding at Cedar Trails Lodge.

Her flashlight flickered. Shoot, they were running out of batteries.

"So, someone has found you now," he said. "How did that happen?"

"I don't know. But I figured that it was just a matter of time."

The wind rattled the door, jarring her. When would the storm give them a reprieve? Let them escape the bunker?

"I'm in this with you now, Remi. I'll see you through it, if you'll let me."

Unless she was imagining it, his voice sounded tender, caring in a much deeper way than she would expect from a man she had known for a day. But she craved that connection. Remi reached for his hand and squeezed.

Blustery gusts swooped under the cracks, hitting her in the face. A cold slap in the face—that's exactly what she'd needed. She had to get out of this immediate proximity to Hawk Beckett. She released his hand and threw off the blanket.

Standing, she stretched her legs and immediately missed the warmth of his nearness. "We should get going soon, even if the storm doesn't quit."

"What is it, a mile to the lodge from here?"

"Give or take." A mile sounded so far at this moment.

"Okay. We can do it. We have to." He stood too and switched on his flashlight. "One more question, Remi, before we get going." Frown lines deepened in his face. He knelt to pick up the blanket, then stuffed it in his duffel. "Do you think the attacks on you earlier today were related? Someone doesn't want you to remember?"

"I wish I knew."

"You were right to disappear, but now that you've been found, what do you want to do next?"

"Go see Dr. Holcomb."

He sent her a half-grin. "We have to get out of this bunker first."

She wanted to trust him, but she wasn't doing him any favors bringing him along into what was looking like a dangerous situation. She'd had time to prepare for this day. She should have expected some kind of physical threat, but she hadn't understood the level of danger that she was in since she had no idea what had taken place during those lost days.

She would give this guy an out—his chance to be free and clear of her troubles. "Look, Hawk, I appreciate your help today, really, but this isn't your battle, and you don't have to help me."

"Sure I do."

"Why would you go to all this trouble for me? You don't even know me. Forget that I don't even know you."

He took a step closer and gazed down at her. "You know me, Remi. I'm the guy who's going to help you get your memories back."

10

Inside this place built to protect from bombs, Hawk stared down at Remi. In the shadows he couldn't see the shifting colors of her eyes, but the pure determination and fire that defined her flickered there and stirred something inside him. His heart pounded. He was getting too close too fast. He'd met her this morning. Known her for all of twelve hours, but the events of the day made it feel much longer than that.

Still, Hawk needed to take a step back—physically and metaphorically—but, oh, it was difficult. He wanted to wrap her in that blanket again. Cocoon her in his arms. A woman he barely knew.

But somehow . . . he *did* know her. She was a kindred spirit, running from demons. Knowing that time was running out before she had to face them. Her story could be his story.

Hawk forced himself to step back. Again. He sucked in a breath.

"I'm the guy who's going to help you get your memories back." Seriously?

What was he doing making that promise when he had no idea if he could keep it? He shouldn't have said it, but the hope flickering in her eyes bound him to this mission and he had better come through. Still, he hadn't actually promised as much as tried to reassure her that he would somehow help her finally connect the neurotransmitters in her brain to find what was lost—and he had no idea how to make that happen or truly help her, other than by protecting her.

Whether either of them liked it or not, he'd been thrown into her chaos.

Was it possible the man who had attacked her hadn't really wanted to kill her? Was he using a tactic he believed would trigger the memories again? Was he the same person to deliver the puzzle pieces? Hawk was only assuming that her attacker had anything to do with those missing days. With so little to go on, he couldn't know, and she could still be holding back information from him.

They put on their coats and prepared to face the cold, dark, stormy night. He wished they were back in the blanket together—as awkward as that seemed—with him putting his arm around her to keep them warm, but they were not there yet.

Not there yet? As if they were traveling down that relationship road. The idea startled him. While he one day hoped to forge a future with the right person, he was a man on a mission and had only come here to clear his head after the catastrophe that cost him his job and Jake's life, and his adversary was still out there at large. Now, of course, he had two missions, but neither of those included actually getting close and personal with Remi.

So he absolutely couldn't let himself go there with her. He needed to focus on keeping her safe and finding answers.

The door clanked and buckled with the wind gusts.

"Come on. Let's get out of here." He started forward.

"I know the property and the woods," she said. "I'll lead us back. We'll hike east and find the trail. Once we're on the path, we can move quickly." She donned her gloves. "But what about the guy who attacked us?"

"Let's hope he's taken shelter from the storm, but we'll remain on guard."

He needed to expect the unexpected. Whoever was out there, he planned to take down and get answers. He grabbed his gun. He left his gloves off since they weren't fingerless and he needed to stay ready to defend against their attacker, and this time he wouldn't bother engaging him physically if he came at either of them with a knife. Hawk had been caught off guard before, and he wouldn't let that happen again. Maybe the assailant was thinking the same thing and would bring a gun to the fight, but Hawk really hoped he wouldn't be waiting for them in the woods.

He opened the door to let the wind fully blast them.

"Wait!" Remi put all her strength into shoving the door shut again and then she moved deeper into the bunker.

"What's wrong?"

"I thought I heard something."

"Over the storm?"

"Yes. Coming from . . ." She pointed into the dark tunnel that led deeper into the bunker.

He waited and listened. Remi was right. The ruckus sounded like someone was banging on a pipe. Or chains clanking. He couldn't decide which, but the sound was eerie. "Maybe it's just the wind."

"Maybe." She kept going deeper, shining her flickering light around.

She wasn't going to give it up.

He didn't have much power left in his flashlight either.

"Maybe that's all the more reason we should get out of here." Frustration boiled up inside. This could be a mistake. He waved her forward and together they moved deeper into the labyrinth of the bunker.

This was the worst idea, but the banging persisted. Another sound met his ears. The muffled sound of someone crying out for help. A chill crawled up his spine.

Pulse racing, he accelerated his pace, Remi by his side.

God, please let this not be a trap.

They turned right and then left, down a set of stairs. His breaths quickened as he grew more claustrophobic. Finally, he stopped in his tracks.

His light beam landed on a woman bound and chained to the wall. His heart jumped to his throat. *What in the world?*

Next to him, Remi gasped, then yelped before rushing forward.

"Jo! Oh my goodness." Remi dropped to her knees next to the chained woman.

Adrenaline surging, Hawk shined the flashlight around to make sure Jo's abductor wasn't waiting in the shadows to nab both Hawk and Remi and chain them to the wall like animals. This was pure unadulterated evil, and Hawk remained wary of their surroundings.

Jo gasped, then sobbed. "What took you so long?"

The woman's anguish cut right through Hawk's gut. He moved to the wall to figure out how to free her so they could all get out of here with their lives.

"I mean . . . we didn't know you were missing." Remi's voice shook, her tone loud and anxious. "How long have you been here?"

"Since early this morning." Her voice cracked. "Now get me out of this prison."

Hawk examined the heavy chains looped through a hook sealed into the concrete. "The only way I can get you out without tools is to shoot the chain. Cover your face, eyes, and ears. I don't want any shards to hurt you."

"Wait." Remi unzipped his duffel, tugged the blanket out, then covered Jo. "This will help protect you."

"Ready?"

"Just do it!" Jo shouted.

He fired once, twice, and then the restraints fell loose. He quickly unraveled the chain from the wall and then pulled it through the link on the cuff on her ankle. "You'll have to wear that until we get the right tools to remove it."

"I don't care. I'm free now." She whimpered.

Stiff from being chained to a wall, Jo rose slowly as she climbed to her feet. Hawk and Remi assisted her. At least she had her own blanket on the floor and a bottle of water, but her lips were blue. She could be suffering from hypothermia. Fierce anger burned in his chest. She had only started calling for help when they were about to leave. Had she been asleep and then suddenly woken up? Whatever had happened, he was relieved she got their attention, otherwise she could have died in here alone. Or worse—at the hand of her abductor.

"Who did this?" Remi asked.

"Can we just get out of here before he comes back?" Jo asked. "He was supposed to come back tonight."

Remi shared a look with Hawk, who nodded. Was the man who'd chained Jo to the bunker wall the same man who had attacked Remi twice, and then Hawk tonight? The chances that two different villains were committing such heinous crimes in this remote place were minuscule.

"Can you walk?" Remi asked.

"What? You didn't drive here?"

"It's a long story," Hawk said.

"How did you find me, then?"

"We weren't even looking for you." Remi pursed her lips

as if trying to bite back the fury. "He was using your phone to text everyone that you were okay. I'm sorry. I . . . I feel so bad about this. I kept wondering about you, and I looked for you in town. I even went to your tiny house. But I got a response, a text from you that you were okay. And then . . . well, things have been kind of crazy today. I'll tell you all about it later. Let's get back to the lodge."

"Are you ready?" Hawk asked. "We need all our energy to fight the storm and watch out for the jerk who did this to you. We'll sort it out once you're safe."

Another small sob escaped, and Jo nearly collapsed. Hawk held her up. They stumbled their way through the labyrinth, back up the stairs. Hawk wasn't sure how they were going to make it through the woods once their flashlights went out because the batteries wouldn't last much longer.

Remi had talked about Scripture tonight, and he suspected she was a believer. She sounded like she loved Jesus, whereas Hawk had let himself believe that God was done with him.

He hadn't prayed in a very long time, but if he was ever going to start again, tonight was the night.

Please don't be done with me, God. Please, light our path. Show us the way.

Finally, they made it to the exit, where the storm bucked against the door, warning them of what was to come.

11

Lord, we need some relief . . .

Remi said the prayer over and over in her heart as they trudged through the onslaught, making their way back to shelter and safety. Finally, in the distance through the trees . . . her refuge. Relief filled her and she almost lost her footing. Cold gripped her bones and exhaustion weighed her down, but they'd made it this far without running into the man who'd stalked Remi and abducted Jo.

There it was—Cedar Trails Lodge—in all its century-old glory, just calling to her. The lodge had never looked more beautiful, and Remi could almost be glad for the rain to hide the tears streaming down her face.

"We have to enter through my office. I don't want to scare people." She urged them toward the awning at the back.

At her office door, Remi relinquished her hold on Jo, giving her over to Hawk. Jo was strong and had made it this far, but she was trembling. Remi feared for her friend. She'd been through psychological and physical trauma today. Remi searched her pockets, then found keys. They jangled in her shaking hands as she felt her way to the keyhole.

Finally, she unlocked the door and shoved it open. Quietly, they entered and felt the rush of warm air. The power was out everywhere, but fortunately the lodge and all the cabins had fireplaces, and guests understood power outages were possible and that generators would be used as needed.

Inside, Hawk assisted Jo onto the sofa against the wall. They shed their dripping jackets and rain boots. Remi threw a fleece blanket over Jo. "You're safe now."

Jo shivered and curled into the blanket and rested on the sofa. "I need my tool kit so I can get rid of this ankle cuff."

"I'm on it just as soon as I get some light in this place." Remi lit a couple of candles. To Hawk, she said, "More batteries for our flashlights are in the drawer over in the credenza."

Hawk hurried to open it and grabbed batteries, then refilled both their flashlights. Surprisingly, Hawk's had remained alive and well for most of their hike back and had died only moments before reaching the lodge.

"I need to call the sheriff and get an ambulance for Jo." Hawk lifted the receiver of the landline, then looked at Remi. "There's no dial tone."

Oh no. Had their stalker cut the phone line into the lodge? The landline was a fail-safe, working when the power was out. "I have a satellite phone. Give that a try."

He turned and found it on a bookshelf against the wall. "As soon as I make the call, we need to warn the others. I'll do my best to clear and secure the lodge. Let's make sure the doors and windows are locked. Then I need to head out." He set his pistol on the desk.

"Head out? Where are you going?"

"I'm going to find him."

"Hawk, no, please. Wait until daylight at least. Wait for the sheriff's department."

"I just want to make sure he isn't lingering near any of the cabins."

"They've already been advised to keep the doors locked," Remi said. The guests had been informed about her attack earlier in the day, and no one had left. No one wanted to get out in the storm, except, well, her attacker.

"Honestly, I don't think he's going to show up again tonight," Remi said.

"But the phone line? Come on, Remi." Hawk scraped a hand down his face.

"So, he delays our call to the sheriff to give him more time to try again," she said.

Hawk had thwarted the assailant's attempts, maybe because he'd come armed with a knife and not a handgun. In fact, he could have shredded the ladder with that knife.

Wait a minute. "So far, all his attacks have been with a knife. What does that mean?"

He rubbed his chin. "I'm still thinking on it."

"Lots of people in Washington have concealed carry permits, so it probably isn't a matter of a knife being more innocuous. Or maybe it is." She was getting nowhere.

I really need coffee.

"Both of you . . ." Jo coughed. "Listen. He's not after any of the guests."

She sat up.

Remi rushed to sit next to her and wrapped an arm around her. She needed to get them all something warm to drink, but especially Jo. They hadn't even gotten her story yet. "What do you mean?"

"I went to check on the cabin with the leaky faucet this morning. I . . . I knocked, and when no one answered, I walked in."

Jo shivered. "I announced myself again, and since it seemed like the place was empty, I headed for the sink in the kitchenette to fix that leak. While there, I couldn't help but notice the pictures on a tablet that was open." Jo lifted her eyes to Remi. "Pictures of you."

Terror streaked through Remi. "Me?"

"Yeah. Then a masked man came out of the bedroom, and I knew I wasn't supposed to see those pictures. Shoot, I knew the moment I saw them that I'd stepped into a bad situation. I tried to escape, but he had a knife. As bad as it seemed that I was chained up in the bunker, I . . . I thought he was going to kill me and throw me on the rocks. I'd get washed away and no one would ever know. He injected me with something. I woke up in chains. Maybe what he had planned for me was worse than death." Jo pressed her face into her hands.

"I'm heading outside to get a signal." Hawk sounded shaken. Angry.

Remi barely acknowledged that he'd exited. "Oh, Jo. I'm so sorry."

Did this happen because of me? Remi pulled her into a hug, and furious tears rushed down her face.

Jo pushed her away to look at her. "Why would he be after you, Remi? You act like you're not that surprised."

12

Outside, he stood in the frosty, inclement weather and moved around until he got a signal.

Even the satellite phone gave him trouble. The thick trees and heavy clouds hampered the signal. Hawk called the emergency services number and was put on hold, which wasn't unexpected. He'd put on his coat and prepared to stay until he talked to someone.

He secured the phone under his hood as rain poured over the edges.

Ah, this is the life.

He thought back to another windy, rainy day in the Cascades when he'd chased down a fugitive terrorist—in the Bell 206B-3 helicopter for King County—along with Deputy Jake Scott. He hadn't felt that alive since leaving what he'd long thought was his calling as a Night Stalker.

Flying through the rain, chasing a criminal, he'd thought he was doing the right thing, stopping a terrorist from fulfilling his destructive plan. Hawk had his own flaws—like not following orders when they were wrong. He knew all about working for the county as a deputy, the ins and outs, the politics, following some orders and disregarding others. Not everyone in the head role was suited to make good decisions.

Sometimes a person could believe he was making all the right choices for the right reasons, only to learn that he had made a fatal mistake.

Hawk had been dead wrong.

But Jake had been dead.

And so had the terrorist.

The price had been too high, and the ends had not justified the means.

He'd gone to John, not for the first time, to rant and rave, and his old friend had simply commiserated with him. Then given him a good kick in the rear. Told him he needed to get his head on straight. He needed a good dose of nature. Fresh air would do him good, John had said.

Hawk could still see the expression on his face when he'd added, "I know just the place. You'll find answers there, trust me."

And just like that, Hawk had gotten in his Ford and driven around the Olympic Peninsula loop until he got to the Hidden Bay region, and then he stopped in Forestview. Cedar Trails Lodge had been all booked up—which made sense because this was their busy season and reservations were made well ahead of time—so he thought he could just stay in town. He passed a house for rent and leased it on a monthly basis right off the bat. That was a week ago. No year lease for him until he knew he wanted to stay. The owner was willing to accept his terms because he hadn't been able to rent the place out.

It was a win-win.

Hawk had thought about what more he could do with his life, since he had failed as a county air deputy for the only helicopter law enforcement aviation unit in the state.

So maybe he could start up a helicopter tour business using his project bird. Genius.

He'd contacted Cedar Trails Lodge and tried to talk to the manager about offering the tour package to her guests, but he never reached her. Still, he'd left a message. She'd never called him back. But he'd gotten a call that a vacancy had opened up, and he took it.

And here he was, suffering out in the storm series of the decade, coupled with king tide season, as if he hadn't already endured enough tonight. But really, he hadn't suffered at all compared to Remi, or especially Jo. The thought of her chained to a wall ignited a rage he hadn't experienced in a long time.

He growled and kicked the puddles. He wanted to lift his fist and rage at the storm, but he wouldn't waste the energy. No, he needed to save his strength for that someone special who remained in the shadows of Cedar Trails Lodge and was after Remi.

He remained aware of his surroundings. Hawk hoped and . . . he prayed . . . the man had gone back to his hidey-hole. He'd stayed in a cabin, so that meant they could get some information, but that information would surely prove to be false. To be an alias. But possibly they could get DNA and find him in a military database, despite the attacker being a professional who would avoid leaving fingerprints or evidence behind. Criminals made mistakes.

Hawk was both surprised and relieved when he reached dispatch, though his call could drop before he relayed important information. Hawk did his best to concisely explain their emergency. He reported the attacker and Jo's abduction and that he believed the phone lines had been cut.

"Please hurry!"

As he suspected, emergency calls had been made all over the county, and the sheriff's department was out answering each emergency as fast as possible. The female dispatcher told him a deputy would come to the lodge, but it would be a while. To stay on the line while he waited.

What? "I'm standing out in the storm to get a signal, and I'm exposed to the elements and the attacker. I'm going inside now. Send someone as soon as you can. We need an ambulance too."

"Sir, we're calling in resources from other counties."

"In other words, your response time is slow." They might do better to take Jo in to the nearest hospital themselves, and that would get Remi out of this dangerous environment too.

He palmed his gun and stared at the lodge. It was barely discernible in the darkness. He wasn't the one in danger. The attacker was after Remi. Still, Jo had been put in danger because of proximity. Anyone at the lodge could face that same danger. Hawk might have been fired from the King County Sheriff's Department, but he could still defend and protect. He went back inside and found Remi still sitting next to Jo, trying to reassure and comfort her. She glanced up at him, expectantly.

"They'll send someone as soon as they can." He saw the disappointment in Jo's eyes.

Remi looked deflated but not surprised. He paced the small space. Not like he could return to his cabin and think in peace and quiet.

Jo mentioned the attacker had used a syringe and drugged her. Why hadn't he killed her and thrown her out to the ocean to be lost forever? Maybe the man was a hired assassin and had some weird moral code only to kill for pay. As for his penchant for knives, that particular weapon could be hidden, and he could more easily blend in. He wouldn't be noticeable. Hawk believed it was important to know why the guy had used a knife instead of a gun so he could be prepared. Maybe there was something in the psychology of it, his personal signature in his kills, that could give them clues about who this man was. But he could think about that much later. The details could be vital.

And for that matter, how did they even know it was a man? The assailant could be a well-trained, muscular female for all he knew. He needed to stop making assumptions and figure out how to keep Remi safe.

"Hawk." Jo's voice pulled his thoughts back to the room.

He stopped pacing and leaned against the desk to listen.

"Take her and get out of here." Jo gestured at Remi, but he had no doubt who she meant.

"She told you everything?" he asked Jo.

"She told me about the amnesia and the puzzle pieces, if that's what you mean."

"As much as I know, which isn't much. But I'm not leaving the lodge. I'm not leaving you," Remi protested. "Hawk called the sheriff. They'll be here sooner or later."

Later, probably.

And maybe then Remi would tell them about her lost memories. Without more details, it was hard to tell whom to trust. Still, the sheriff's department needed to understand what they were potentially up against, and now Hawk realized it was best to encourage her to share her story with the local authorities. She'd run to hide and was trying to do the right thing—but it was hard to distinguish exactly what that was. Even when a person did the right thing, everything could still go completely wrong.

Remi shouldn't carry this burden alone, and maybe she'd unloaded on Hawk, but he could admit when he wasn't enough.

13

The hard look of determination on Hawk's face took her fear to the next level. He was her self-proclaimed protector, at least until someone else took the job. The weight of it pressed down on her.

They'd send someone as soon as they could? Didn't they understand?

Remi rubbed her arms. She'd never really shaken off the chill of their time out in the storm. But she hadn't been chained to a wall in a dark bunker, so she wasn't going to complain. She glanced at her friend. How did a person recover from something like that?

"Remi." He leveled his gaze on her. "We made the call, and now while we wait, we do the next thing."

Remi had a feeling she knew where he was headed, and she didn't like it. "The next thing, as in, checking the lodge to make sure everyone is accounted for and safe?"

"Yes. I need to make sure the lodge is as safe as it can be. You can come along and make sure your guests are informed and comfortable. Then I'll check the cabins."

"We already checked them, remember?" They hiked around every one of them.

"Well, I'm checking them again. I'll make sure everyone is okay and knows what's going on."

Remi pursed her lips. She knew what he was up to. He was going to try to find the attacker while he was out there. In fact, he probably *hoped* to find him. But they'd made it back to the lodge without incident, and the guy was only human. Well, maybe he had been a Navy SEAL and had turned rogue, and in that case, he might suffer through the cold and rain, lying in wait for her or Hawk. She didn't want to think of Hawk out there alone, facing off with this evil, but she was familiar with the sort of determination that drove him because she felt it herself. She wanted to go back out and search for him too after she got her second wind.

But she wasn't going to leave Jo.

Hawk put the satellite phone back in the charging station for when the power came back on. "And then I think you and I should get out of here so we can take Jo to the hospital."

"No. I'm fine!" Jo said. "I'm not injured. I'm warming up now, and I need to work. Sitting in a hospital will only make things worse. If I'm working, I'll get this experience out of my head faster."

Jo didn't look fine, but for that matter, neither did Hawk. Remi could only guess at her own appearance.

"You need me here, Remi," Jo pleaded. "I can't go to the hospital."

"You've been training Dylan. He'll do in this situation," Remi said.

Jo hung her head, then lifted it. Tears streamed and she swiped at them as if furious they'd appeared. "If anything, I just want to go to Pop's. I kept thinking about how I missed dinner. We'd had an argument, and I was going to make it

110

up to him. And I didn't show up. He probably thinks I didn't show because—"

"He probably thinks you got caught up doing your job and you're stuck here for a few days."

Remi shared a look with Hawk. "Let Hawk make sure the place is secure. I'll speak to the other staff, and then we'll take you to get you checked out and then to your father's. Okay?"

"That's a plan," Hawk said. "You two stick together. Stay here."

"No, I'll get Jo out by the fireplace where it's warmer. She'll be safe with others, and then I'll find Dylan, Erika, and Shawna. I'll let them know what's going on. It's all hands on deck."

"That isn't a good idea. In fact . . ." He scratched the back of his neck. "This jerk could be inside the lodge, and I wouldn't even know it. Who is this guy? What name is he using for that cabin, Jo? Do you happen to know?"

"Right," Remi said. "He was a guest staying here, so he could be—" Chills crawled over her.

"He could be inside, getting warm. Blending in," Hawk said. "We have no idea who he is because he wore a mask. And if he doesn't know we have Jo . . . he might not realize that we're onto the fact that he's a guest." His brows furrowed. "Am I making sense?"

"Perfect. If we take Jo out into the common room and he's there, he could react. Take a hostage. Put everyone in danger."

"Let me think." Jo squeezed her eyes shut and snapped her fingers repeatedly. "He was in Cabin 12." She opened her eyes wide. "Collin Barclay."

Remi considered the name. "I didn't check him in, so I don't know what he looks like. Erika would recognize him."

"The name is probably an alias," Hawk said.

"He's after you, Remi," Jo said. "You go out there and you're the one in danger."

Remi rubbed her temple. "If I don't show up, then he's going to get suspicious and think we know he's here. Besides, we need to know if he is inside the lodge or not. I'll be very discreet and ask Erika to show me who he is."

Hawk's lips pressed into a tight line. "Or you could just wait here for law enforcement while everyone is out there. If that knife-wielding creep is here, I want him. I'm not waiting. I'll be discreet when I scrutinize everyone who has the same build." Moving to the door, Hawk checked his gun, then slid it into the holster. She appreciated that he didn't want to scare her guests.

"Hawk, you don't know what he looks like. I'll go too and talk to Erika. She'll know if he's here."

She turned her attention to Jo. "Stay in this room with the doors locked. I'll bring you something warm to drink, then I'll check on the guests. I'll be back soon." She pressed a radio into Jo's hand. "Call me if you need anything before I get back."

She shared a look with Hawk and nodded. They were doing this. Going on the offensive felt right. She would go crazy if she just sat in this room and waited for a deputy. Being in such a remote area had its benefits, and also its risks—they were without law enforcement, and it could take hours before anyone arrived. As for Collin Barclay, she couldn't decide if she wanted him here so they could trap him, catch him, or if she wanted him to be long gone from this place. Regardless, his time roaming free at Cedar Trails Lodge was done.

"Remember that he's here for you," Hawk said. "Let's get this over with."

Remi thrust her S&W into the small holster at the side of her waist. "Let's go."

After she dead-bolted the door to the outside, she moved to the office door that led out into the lodge. He stepped in her path, and he was the one to open the door, letting her know he would face the danger head-on and still intended to protect her.

She couldn't breathe.

Couldn't swallow.

This was real. As former military and a former deputy, Hawk had the necessary skills, which she appreciated. This had been a grueling day and looked to be an even rougher night. Telling her guests about the potential threat wasn't the first thing she wanted to do, or even the last. But this was no ghost story told over a campfire.

Unshed tears blurred her vision, and pain erupted in her already tight throat. "Has it come to this, really?"

"Would you prefer we sit here and wait for the attacker, who cut the phone lines and who may or may not have cut the power, to come after you?"

She slid her hand up to her throat. *I can't believe this is happening.* "I don't want to scare anyone. This will be the worst experience of their lives. They'll never come back."

Compassion flooded his expression—compassion and wariness—as he stepped forward and pressed his palm on her shoulder. "We're just cautioning everyone to keep an eye out."

She nodded. This was happening and there was nothing she could do . . . except remember.

Hawk secured the door, keeping Jo's presence a secret and protecting her, then moved down the hallway. The fire raging in the huge fireplace lit up the big room. A crowd gathered around the flames for the warmth and light. Darkness prevented them from seeing the storm outside, but tomorrow would give them stunning views and memories to last a lifetime—that is, if danger didn't rear its head in the lodge tonight. In the meantime, guests could hear the ferocity of the storm and feel the structure shuddering.

Erika moved to stand next to Remi, her eyes wide at first and then narrow. "What's going on?"

"Is this everyone in the lodge?" Remi kept her voice low. She remembered many of the guests and spotted Mrs. Daley and Paco sitting in a plush chair at the corner of the fireplace.

Erika recounted each family, singles and couples, by name. Dylan and Shawna, along with kitchen staff, lingered in the great room, sitting on the sofas and cushioned chairs and at the tables by the windows.

Maybe they should invest in some sort of indoor firepit for roasting marshmallows or cooking hot dogs when the power went out. She'd add that to her mental checklist of things to change at the lodge.

"Everyone is here," Erika said. "It's only eight. Still early in the evening."

"How long have they been here?"

"A couple hours, maybe. Most were eating dinner when the lights went out. Dylan checked the generators. We would have waited for the go-ahead, which usually comes from Jo, but she isn't here, after all. No sign of her. I went ahead and made that call, but they only power a few lights and the freezer and fridges. We want to conserve the fuel. As for Jo, I'm worried about—"

"She's okay. I know where Jo is. Just answer the questions."

Relief lodged in Erika's eyes.

"Don't look," Remi said. "Don't telegraph what I'm asking you. Looks like some cabin guests are here too. Do you know their names?"

Erika stared at Remi, then glanced at the floor. Back at Remi. Anywhere but at the guests.

Good.

"Yes. Tom and Katy Mason and their kids . . . sorry, I just can't think of their names at the moment."

"It's okay." Remi wasn't doing well either.

"I'm not sure how they're going to get back to their cabin tonight. And one other guest is here alone. A man."

"Mr. Barclay?"

"I . . . don't know his name."

Remi studied Erika, who wasn't looking at her. "Did you check Collin Barclay in?"

"I didn't. No."

Shoot. Who checked him in, then? "So, you wouldn't recognize him?"

"No."

"Where is the man from the cabin now? Is he here?"

"He's just there on the sofa, talking to a family."

Remi glanced that way at him. Was he the one she fought this afternoon? Remi couldn't tell. She wasn't sure what to say and she glanced at Hawk, who frowned. He left her side and crept through the rest of the lodge. Had he decided the guy wasn't the right build?

"Are you going to tell me what's going on?" Erika asked.

"I was attacked again tonight. Jo was abducted—she's okay. Don't freak out. Her abductor is a guest, we think. I don't know if the guy is here in the lodge," Remi whispered. "Just act normal. Calm. Can you do that?"

"Asking me that question doesn't make it easier."

"I know. Try smiling."

Erika's smile appeared unnatural.

"So, forget what I said. Don't smile."

Erika's lips flattened, then she frowned. Remi glanced away. Raked her gaze over the others, who seemed relaxed, unaware of the possible danger. The danger wasn't directed at her guests, but still, she wasn't sure if she shouldn't just tell everyone to load up their vehicles and go home. But that would be sending them out in the danger of the storm.

She squeezed Erika's shoulders and smiled, trying to act natural. "I'll keep you informed. In the meantime, could you get Shawna to make up three cups of hot chocolate without drawing attention? Set them at the back and I'll grab them."

Erika nodded.

Hawk had disappeared up the stairs. It wasn't like he could look inside the rooms with all the guests downstairs, but it made her feel better that he was up there looking around all the same. But when he was done with the lodge, he would head outside into the night to check the cabins again and then she could worry. Remi was concerned about that aspect of his plan, and maybe she should go with him. Have his back. The guests were her responsibility, after all, and not his.

Hawk was already making his way down the stairs. Erika was over talking to Shawna, and by the look on the barista's face, Erika was spilling everything. Her features grim, Shawna glanced at Remi. Remi slowly edged away from the gathering and toward the side door that led out to the stairway to the beach to make sure it was locked.

The door was barely closed.

Water and debris remained on the rug and then the wood floor leading into the lodge. Heart pounding, Remi followed the footprints back into the great room and then eyed each of the people there. One of her guests was the attacker and Jo's abductor. Had come here to Cedar Trails Lodge, the place she thought she'd found refuge until she could remember.

Her breathing turned shallow, and she needed to calm down.

She had to get out of here, put some distance between

her and the lodge. She'd put her heart into this place and almost forgotten her need to find what was lost.

Someone had found her and reminded her. She slowly moved around the group, making her way to the fire. Watching all the shadowed corners where the light flickered. She tried to act natural as she glanced around, looking at each of the guests, and then her eyes caught his.

He was staring at her.

For a moment, her heart might have stopped. Then her lungs screamed, and she sucked in a breath.

He wasn't the man who'd attacked her. The eyes were different somehow, and this man looked at her with interest, not a death wish. Still, memories could trick a person. She couldn't be sure.

Suddenly she couldn't move. Fear gripped her. The gathering and the fireplace faded. Other images bombarded her mind. Pulse roaring, sweat bloomed on her palms as she was transported to a different time and place.

A man. Dark hair and equally dark eyes, dressed in military fatigues, stared at her from inside a helicopter. He leaned out the open door and reached for her.

He was like a ghost stepping out of the hidden places in her mind.

14

awk stood at the door of Remi's office—the one that would let him outside into the turbulent, dark night. He bundled up and tugged his hood on. Extra ammo and a knife were stowed in his truck, and he'd grab those before going into the forest.

Remi stepped close and snapped the top button of his jacket as she looked up into his face—her action came across as personal. Intimate. Concern filled her soft, warm eyes. An image skittered across his mind—he was holding her, looking down at her, and leaned in to kiss her. Hawk shook off the outrageous thought. What had gotten into him? He must have been so completely exhausted that his mind was playing tricks. He didn't have time for an emotional connection. Once Remi was safe and in the clear, her attacker behind bars, he could take time to clear his head and then get back on track with his own personal mission to find an assassin he'd been hunting for far too long.

Remi stepped even closer and looked at him long and hard. A knot lodged in his throat, and for a split second he had the strange feeling she might lean in and kiss him goodbye. And even weirder—he would have let her. He really had to stop having these thoughts.

"Be careful out there." She squeezed his hands around the radio she pressed into them. "I want updates, Hawk. If I don't hear from you, I'll come out there and find you. Do you understand?"

"I believe you." He almost smiled at the idea of someone coming to his rescue. "But don't you dare. I'll be fine."

Before he got in deeper with this conversation—or, God forbid, *he* kissed *her* because he was losing his way in this pressure-cooker situation—he opened the door and stepped out into the violence of nature. That was the good, hard slap in the face Hawk needed.

He didn't know Remi.

She didn't know him.

The wind tried to take off his hood. Hawk tugged it forward and shined the flashlight around. He'd memorized the brochure map of the Cedar Trails Lodge layout, including the cabins, the trails, and the currently empty campground behind them. But he also kept it in his pocket in case he needed to refer back to it, though it would get soaked if he tried.

After grabbing the supplies from his truck, Hawk set out, heading into those forbidding woods.

God, please hide me in the shadow of your wings.

"Don't let this jerk sneak up on me," he mumbled to the air. That made twice he'd prayed in one day, as if he believed God had not already written him off.

After what seemed like hours but was probably less than an hour, he'd checked every cabin again. Though he didn't want people to open their doors to a stranger, he'd knocked lightly to do what he called a "cabin check" and informed them the sheriff's department was on the way and not to open their doors for anyone, despite the fact they had opened the door to him.

Exhaustion pulled at him as he pushed forward to the last cabin that he planned to visit. He couldn't forget they'd already done this earlier in the evening, checking each of them.

But this last one. This was Cabin 12. Collin Barclay, a.k.a. Jo's abductor and Remi's likely attacker, had stayed there. Hawk doubted he would find the criminal inside. He would be an idiot to return after what he'd done to Jo.

Hawk hid near a tree and watched for movement inside. He might have already given himself away long ago as he checked other cabins. After a few minutes he decided it was time to go for it. He should wait for the sheriff's department to arrive and let them do their job and gather evidence, but if Collin decided to come back, he could scrape all the evidence. Though he could already be too late, Hawk wanted a piece of that for himself.

He stalked up to the cabin and banged on the door. It creaked open because it hadn't been fully shut. Perfect. Too perfect. A trap? He didn't care as he stepped inside and shined the light into the darkness. He sensed no one was here. It was unoccupied. Completely empty. The place had been cleared out.

No iPad with Remi's image rested on the desk. He hadn't thought he would find it. Collin would probably have cleared out the moment he took Jo and hid her in the bunker.

Hawk searched the bedroom, the bathroom, and the closet. Nothing. Unfortunately, that familiar churning in his gut started up. He couldn't explain it, but something was off here. John had suggested Hawk come to Cedar Trails Lodge, insisting that he would find the answers he sought. Hawk had thought he meant that by getting rest he would get peace of mind. And that clarity would help him find his way in the mess he'd created.

But now he got the sense that John hadn't meant that at all. Hawk wasn't sure he was ready to face the storm—metaphorical or otherwise—but he stepped out of the empty cabin into the darkness. He turned on his flashlight.

Pain ignited in his head as he slumped to the ground.

Stunned, he couldn't move. He blinked a few times, wondering if he was dead already. Water pricked at his face and eyes as he looked up. He'd dropped his flashlight, and the beam lit up the woods around him.

A shadow filled his vision.

The ghost of his past that he'd been chasing stood over him.

"What are you doing?" the man asked.

Hawk struggled to respond as a million thoughts slammed into his mind. John had been right. Hawk found answers and what he'd been looking for at Cedar Trails Lodge.

"I'm . . . protecting her." He finally ground out the words.

The man shifted closer, taking in Hawk's face. "You're in the wrong place. Back out of this."

"I can't do that." Hawk started to climb to his feet but struggled with dizziness.

"You get up, and I'll end you."

He didn't doubt the man who had long evaded him.

15

Hawk hadn't reported in on the radio. Furious, Remi rubbed her arms. She thought he understood that if he didn't, she would come looking for him. And he didn't want her out there, did he? So, why in the world hadn't he responded to his radio when she tried him?

Jo paced the small space, also eager to be free of the office prison, while they waited on law enforcement to arrive.

"I need to go look for him." Going out into the storm meant leaving Jo, and it meant that something hadn't gone right. Hawk could be hurt.

Or worse.

Remi had to help him if he was in trouble. She yanked her coat from the rack.

"If you go, then I'm going," Jo said.

"You're not in any condition to keep up."

"I'm fine! Don't treat me like an invalid. You think that I'm going to let being chained to a wall all day in that cold, dank bunker debilitate me? Put me out of commission? I'm not that mentally fragile. I've been through things . . . before."

Before what? Had Jo come to Cedar Trails to hide? To feel safe?

Jo shook her head as if shrugging it off. "Remi, you can't look for Hawk. You're the one that jerk is after. Just wait, okay? Hawk Beckett looks like a big boy who can take care of himself. Don't you think?" She stared at Remi like she should know about Hawk.

And she did, sort of. "I guess so. I mean, if you count that he was a helicopter pilot in the Army and then a deputy who flew a helicopter for the King County Sheriff's Department. If you count his background, then sure, he can take care of himself. On the other hand, Jo, skilled people still die, and he could be hurt out there and need help." Remi hated that she'd just gone off on Jo. "Look, I'm sorry. I shouldn't have—"

"No, it's okay. You're worried about him and I get it." Jo's brown eyes grew huge. "Oh. Now I know where I've seen him before." She snapped her fingers. "He's that deputy who got fired. Something to do with a crash and someone died. It was all over the news a few weeks ago. You didn't see it?"

For once, Remi regretted not watching the news. "No. Hawk Beckett was fired? Are you sure?"

"Yes. But I think . . . I think—"

Remi snatched her gun from the desk and holstered it, then grabbed her coat. She wouldn't wait to hear more. It didn't matter.

"Remi, no." Jo stepped forward.

A knock came at the door. Remi's heart pounded and she pulled her handgun out, then waved Jo back. Jo moved over by the other door, and Remi pressed against the wall. She was about to peer through the window.

"It's me."

Hawk! Relief rushed through her as she unlocked then opened the door.

"Where have you been?" Maybe she sounded a little too demanding. "I was worried about you."

He stepped inside and closed the door behind him. Tugged off his coat and dripped water on the entry mat. He turned to hang the jacket up, looking unsteady on his feet. His movements were slow. His hands shook. And . . .

Remi gasped. *What in the world?* "Hawk? Why do you have blood on your head?"

When he faced her, his eyes were dark and grave. She'd never seen him like this. She didn't know him all that well, but the look on his face scared her.

He stared into space. Stunned? He was hurt. *Oh . . . Lord . . .*

"What happened?" Had he fallen? Or had a branch hit him in the head? Or worse . . . "He was out there again. He attacked you, didn't he?"

Hawk nodded, his face crinkling into severe distress. "Yeah."

"You need to sit down for a minute while I grab my stuff. I'm driving both you and Jo to the hospital." She tried to usher him to the sofa, but he was granite, just standing there.

Lord, what do I do? Remi's heart palpitated, beating fast and irregular. Her limbs shook. This was no time to be weak. Before she could try again to persuade Hawk to at least sit down, another knock came at the door. Without hesitation, Hawk opened it as though he knew who was on the other side. Maybe that's why he hadn't moved from the door.

Deputy Hunter entered the office. Hawk closed the door.

"Who else is with you?" Remi asked.

"You're looking at it." The deputy had come alone.

"Ambulances have been called out to other locations. We have to prioritize those who are in life-threatening situations."

Hunter's eyes scanned the room, then she scrutinized each of them until her gaze landed on Jo and softened. "Are you the one who was abducted?"

"Yes," both Hawk and Remi said.

"I'm Jo Cattrel, yes."

"Do you need medical attention? If so, I can drive you to the hospital."

Hello. Remi and Hawk could have done that, but Jo refused.

She shook her head. Lifted her hands, showing her palms. "I'm good. I promise. Even got the cuff off my ankle. I just got a little cold in that bunker, but I'm all warm now. Glad you didn't waste an ambulance on me."

"In the bunker?" The deputy's eyes widened.

Someone knocked on the office door that led into the lodge.

"I'll get it." Hawk held his handgun to his side and opened the door.

A disheveled man wearing coveralls under his coat stepped inside. "Jo?"

"Pop!" Jo shouted and ran into his arms, then sobbed on his shoulder.

Deputy Hunter eyed Hawk, her gaze zeroing in on his head wound. "What happened to you?"

Hawk touched the wound, then winced. "It's a long story."

If the deputy was unhappy with Hawk's answer, her expression gave nothing away. "*You* need medical attention, and I'll get you that as soon as possible. Looks like all the gang is here, so I'll get right to the point. Without going into the details, I'll just say we're stretched real thin tonight. Let me get your statements. We'll put out the warnings and whatnot and search for this guy as the weather permits. Now, we'll get your statements and be quick about it."

Over the next few minutes Remi, Hawk, and Jo gave their statements. Hunter made them all wait just outside the door, so she could take the statements in private, as if she thought she might catch someone telling a different story.

Deputy Hunter got her coat back on. "I'll take Mr. Beckett to get his head examined."

"I can drive myself." He sent Remi a pleading look.

"I'll take him," Remi said. "The storm's dying down a bit."

"The break will only last a few hours until the next one blows in, so you'd better get to it," Jo's dad said. "I'll hang out here at the lodge and help with whatever tasks are needed." He glanced at his daughter with a protective look. "We'll take care of the lodge, Remi."

"But Jo should see a doctor too," Remi insisted. "If for no other reason than she was drugged."

"Okay, here's what we'll do," Jo said. "Pop and I will square things away with Dylan and the remaining staff, and then he'll take me to the clinic. If it's crowded, we're coming back. I don't want to waste anyone's time."

"I'd advise you to go to the hospital instead," Deputy Hunter said. "Tell them you want a toxicology report. I'll check in with the hospital and follow up with you. You should go as soon as possible. Besides, at this hour, the clinic in Forestview is closed."

Jo nodded at the deputy. "Works for me."

Her father smiled at her, but Remi could see the severe pain he tried to hide, pain and anger at what had been done to his daughter, and from the sounds of it, not for the first time, though her previous experience could have been entirely different.

"Deputy Hunter, what about the guests and making sure they're safe?" Remi asked. "I was expecting you to come with more deputies."

"Deputy Carlson is en route. We'll check things out."

"Not if you're taking Hawk to the hospital. Plus you'd have to give him a ride back," Remi said. "I'll make sure he gets the attention he needs."

Deputy Hunter's radio squawked with an indecipherable message, but she seemed to understand. "Carlson's outside. I'm heading out and we'll search the area, starting with the lodge. None of you had a description of him, except you, Hawk. He's about five eleven, has thick brown hair, and brown eyes. Thirty-five."

That news surprised Remi. So, he'd gotten the man's mask off. Finally, a description.

"After we either apprehend him or make sure he's out of the area, one of us will stick around until morning," Deputy Hunter said.

Remi prayed it would be enough. It was all they could do.

"Come on, Hawk," she said. "Let's get you to the hospital." Since the clinic was closed now, they'd have to drive to Woodhaven, almost an hour away.

Shawna entered with a tray of coffees to go.

"You're working late." Remi glanced at the clock on the wall. It was nearing ten thirty.

"It's been a long night. The guests are back in their rooms, and I was going home," Shawna said. "But Erika sent me in with the coffee and to get an update. What's happening?"

Remi gave Shawna the long-story-short version and took the coffees. Honestly, Remi hated sharing the traumatic events with Shawna, who'd already been through too much. She'd killed her husband in self-defense, and now she was here, on the other side of the country, escaping the pain and serving up coffee.

"Are you sure you're up for the drive?" Hawk asked her, pulling her attention back.

No. She wasn't sure of anything right now. "We'll keep each other awake."

Coffee cups in hand, raincoats donned, they made their way to her Bronco and climbed in. After cranking the heat and stripping off her rain jacket, she pulled out of the parking lot and steered along the slippery, muddy road out of Cedar Trails Lodge and Resort—so said the sign. Every time she saw it, she almost snorted a laugh. Backwoods and rustic and *boasting* no amenities, the lodge didn't live up to the image of a resort.

Once she finally got onto the main highway, she headed south. On the road like this and away from the immediate threat, she could almost breathe. When she'd given her statement, she'd come clean and told Deputy Hunter about her amnesia. The deputy thought it might be a stretch until Remi told her about the puzzle pieces, which added substance to her conclusion. No more puzzle pieces had come to her yet, as far as she knew. Even if she had all the puzzle pieces put together to complete the picture, she wasn't sure if it would help her remember or if she would recognize the place.

Hawk grunted as if in pain. "I don't have time for this."

He was moving and talking okay, so maybe he was all right, but she was glad he agreed to see a doctor at all. She couldn't shake the sense that something was bothering him.

"Look, I know this has been a trying day," she said. "I don't know you all that well, but I can tell something is eating at you. What happened tonight? I mean, other than the obvious stuff that happened. Don't forget, Hawk, you're the guy who's going to help me remember." She hoped her not-so-subtle reminder would prompt him to open up about what he was keeping to himself.

"And have you remembered anything more?" He practically grunted out the question. "Because I think you have and you're not telling me. Maybe you told the deputy."

"I didn't have a chance to tell you, all right? I had a flashback. It was like reliving the moment. I was told this is how the memories could come back to me. Like someone who has PTSD. A guy was hanging out of a helicopter, looking at me. He was reaching for me, to pull me up inside. We were already in the air." Nausea threatened with the memory. The rush of contrasting emotions. Terror. Hope. Confusion. "It just seems crazy. I don't know what I was doing there, but it's in my head. It's a memory, I'm sure of it."

Remi's throat tightened. "Hawk, you don't think—he sounds like the man you described."

"No. It could be anyone. Lots of people fit that description."

"But it could make some sort of sense that the man who attacked me was with me during that missing week. I can't be one hundred percent sure I'm remembering correctly. Repressed memories are a complex issue. Memories can't really be trusted. Not completely. Your brain fills in the gaps, the holes. Fixes things, and sometimes it lies to you."

Hawk shifted in the seat. "Do you remember his name? Anything else about him?"

"He was a soldier."

Hawk's expression tightened.

"Now that the door has opened, the memories of that time should start coming back to me. I need to see Dr. Holcomb as soon as possible. I've been a little busy tonight, though." She accelerated on the lonely highway. The sooner they got to the hospital, the faster they could leave and she could get to Seattle. "You never told me what happened tonight. You obviously got his mask off."

"He wasn't wearing a mask. You already know he hit me in the head."

"And that's it? What else? I know you must have fought with him. But what *aren't* you telling me?"

Remi risked a glance his way when she should have really

been watching the road. In the dim light of the cab, she could make out the determined set to his jaw. Apprehension gripped her. Hawk had learned something vital. She could see it in his face.

"I don't know how to tell you this," he said.

"Just spit it out." *For crying out loud!*

"I know him."

"Wait. Just so we're talking about the same guy—you know who?"

"The man who attacked you."

Oh. She'd been hoping for a different answer. "Who is he, Hawk?"

For a few heartbeats, excruciating silence filled the cab. Then . . . "He's my brother."

Remi slammed on the brakes.

16

Hawk held on for dear life as the Bronco spun along the wet road and edged off into the ditch. "Are you trying to get us killed?"

He couldn't hold back his complete frustration. With himself, not Remi.

"I'm sorry." She stared at him. "Maybe you could have told me sooner. What do you *mean* he's your brother?"

Anger flashed in her eyes. That and a lot of confusion. She reached for her gun, slid it out, and gripped it, keeping it ready. Well, that was just great. His dreams were finally coming true. She was looking at him like he was a bad guy now.

Hawk lifted his hands in surrender, palms up. "I didn't know my brother was the guy behind your attacks, I swear. But now that we know the truth, please believe me that I have nothing to do with what happened to you."

"Do you even hear yourself? It cannot be a coincidence that your brother is here at the *same time* you are. He attacked me. Abducted Jo. You probably know about my missing days. You lied to me, didn't you?" She shook her head.

She wasn't wrong about the coincidence.

"Listen—"

"I don't believe this." Beyond willing to listen, she cut him off, and then she stared at him, a long, mean, scrutinizing stare that left him wondering if he should fear for his life. After huffing a few times, her face relaxed a little, and a hint of warmth replaced the cold in her eyes. "I would tell you to get out of my Bronco, but I'm supposed to take you to the hospital."

She shifted into four-wheel drive. The tires spun as she floored it, and finally the old Bronco gained traction. The back end fishtailed as she sped back onto the road. How did he make her understand when he was still trying to figure it out?

"Start talking, Hawk. Tell me right now what's going on."

Oh, I'd love to, but . . . "You need to let me get a word in for that to happen."

"I—" She glanced his way, then closed her mouth.

He might have smiled at that on a better day, but he wasn't going to comment. Hawk just wanted to close his eyes and rest in a nice, soft bed for maybe a thousand years, but he knew he wouldn't be able to sleep even if he was cozied up under a bunch of heavy, warm blankets.

She was waiting.

"His name is Cole Mercer."

"Wait, not Beckett?"

"He changed his name."

"But why?"

"Just . . . didn't want to be part of the family anymore. We were competitive growing up. Too competitive. I hadn't seen him in person for eight years." That didn't mean he hadn't been searching, especially when he'd heard that Cole had shifted to the dark side, working for the wrong people. Hawk needed to weigh just how much to share at this juncture. He needed to find solid footing. "At times I've even wondered if he was still alive. Tonight, he was the one to hit me over the head and tell me to stay out of it."

"It. Stay out of what?"

"You. It's all about you."

My brother even threatened to end me if I got up. Hawk had been shocked to his core. He'd tried to find him and then received the news from John eighteen months ago that Cole was a gun for hire. He and Cole were close growing up but, at the same time, at odds their entire lives. Hawk would take back everything he'd ever said to get his brother back. His words might have been the catalyst to send his brother away.

Regardless, Cole was lost.

He glanced at Remi, unsure what he would see in her eyes. Compassion? Understanding? But she didn't look at him. Instead, she remained focused on the road, her lips pressed into a thin line. Her hands squeezing the steering wheel too tightly.

And he couldn't stand the silence filling the cab. "I get it. You don't know what to believe. You don't know if you can trust me."

"Did you tell Deputy Hunter more than just his description? Did you tell her that Cole is your brother?"

"I told her his name and that he's a hired gunman. Though maybe that was a mistake. Telling her could just make things worse and put you in more danger."

"I can't believe she didn't tell us everything that you shared. And she knew this information and let you walk out of there. She has to know that you're connected somehow." Remi's voice shook.

"She doesn't. I didn't tell her that I'm connected, but she'll find out soon enough." Man, he was digging his own grave here. The deputy might have detained Hawk, and then what would happen to Remi? This conversation wasn't going well, but there was no good way to break this news to her.

"And how is telling law enforcement who to look for going to put me in more danger?"

"Because he's a ghost. They won't find him." He didn't want to scare her, but he needed to get it all out there, and now was the moment. "And don't you see? If there's a manhunt for Cole Mercer, that could move up the timeline on his hunt for you, or whatever it is he's planning." He shook his head and stared out the window.

He should have recognized the man by his tactics, his movements, if nothing else. But Cole had never been much for using knives. Maybe that tactic, along with the relentless storm, had been enough that Hawk had not recognized or felt any sense of familiarity. Then again, maybe no one would recognize a masked assailant, even if they knew the person well, and Hawk was blaming himself, being too hard on himself.

It didn't matter who the masked man was, or that the man had turned out to be Hawk's brother. Right now, he needed to keep Remi safe. *If* she would let him, and that was a big *if*.

God, please help me keep Remi safe!

For too long he believed God wouldn't hear his prayers anyway, so why bother? But that was all on Hawk. Holding on to his past mistakes, Hawk had been the one to pull away. Funny how desperation changed everything. He was ready to reach out and close the distance he'd created. Move past his own insecurities . . . for Remi. He needed to win this time. And he couldn't do that alone.

I need you, God. I need your help.

Seeing Cole tonight, seeing the contempt in his eyes, had stripped Hawk to the marrow.

"You could have told me this sooner," she said again.

"Sooner? I just found out tonight, then the deputy

showed up. I'm finding my way through this mess, and believe it or not, I planned to tell you tonight. As for Deputy Hunter, she's processing through the facts, and those wheels don't move as fast as we would like. We already know he's dangerous. I want him caught. Incarcerated. But there's something I want more than that. I want you to live."

"And you think you're the one to protect me. That you're also the one to find your brother because no one else can do it."

He wasn't going to argue with her until she calmed down. No point until she was ready to listen. She was visibly shaking now, and maybe he needed to drive. But she was in no frame of mind for him to suggest it.

"I think . . ." She growled. "Let's see how you are. If your head is good. If you're going to be okay. Then I'll bring you back to the lodge, and you're going to check out. You should leave now, Hawk. There's not going to be any helicopter tour package either, in case you were wondering."

Oh man. She was kicking him hard, and the pain radiated out of his heart through his body. Between finding Cole tonight, learning he was the man after Remi, and her complete rejection of Hawk, her utter distrust of him, Hawk had never been this down and out. Not even after feeling responsible for Jake's death, then being fired.

But he couldn't let any of that keep him down for long. He had to get up and keep going, at least until he handed Remi's protection off to someone else. He just didn't know who that was. She'd done fine on her own, but everything had changed and she needed serious help now.

How could Hawk convince her? "Look, that's not a good idea."

"You can leave after you tell me everything. Why are

you here, really? What does Cole Mercer have to do with me, and what happened that week in my life that is now gone?"

Hawk's head was really starting to hurt now. Remi was piling the stress on, but he didn't blame her. He was upset too. Unfortunately, he didn't think he could convince her to let him stick around to make sure she was safe. So, he would get his head checked. They would go back to the lodge where he would pack up and . . . go where? He shoved off those concerns. Remi was his priority, whether she believed him or not, whether she wanted his help or not.

"I don't know why he's here for you, but I intend to find out. As for the reason *I'm* here, someone said I'd find answers at the lodge. I thought he meant I would clear my head and find perspective. Now . . . I know differently." John had sent Hawk here because he suspected . . . or he *knew* that Cole would show up. There was no other explanation. Somewhere in Hawk's list of next steps, he needed to find his former CO who must have intel. Hawk would get answers from him. But first, Remi needed protection. She had no idea who she was up against. Hawk wished he didn't.

Major Cole Mercer.

Cole. *My brother.* Anguish squeezed Hawk's chest.

He'd been special forces. A Green Beret. He could blend in anywhere. And now that he'd gone rogue . . . "He's a trained killer, Remi. An assassin." Hawk had hoped to find Cole and save him, pull him back from the edge, but he'd been caught completely off guard. As if that excuse would remove the weight on Hawk's shoulders.

Finally at the hospital, she swerved into the parking lot, going much too fast. "What does it say about you that you have an assassin for a brother?"

"The bigger question is what does it say about *you* that an assassin is after you? And I promise you, he's only been toying with you or you'd already be dead." That must be his modus operandi. "Next time, you won't see death coming."

17

Remi paced the waiting room.

"You won't see death coming."

She got it now. Dangerous forces were closing in. And Hawk Beckett—the stranger who'd stepped into her life, pulling her from certain death, sending her attacker fleeing twice now—was connected. Just how connected was he exactly? Because he'd been the one to trigger her memories.

He'd explained that someone had suggested he would find the answers at Cedar Trails Lodge. And now he realized the answers had to do with Cole Mercer? There was so much more to that story. Whoever had sent him here could very well know what Remi had forgotten.

Whatever was going on, Remi was freaking out.

Lots of people sat around, waiting for care. A hurt wrist, a twisted ankle, bruises and cuts, and who knew what else. A few people wore masks and coughed. The flu? The place was busting at the seams, and they could be here all night. At least Hawk had already been taken back.

God, what am I going to do? Help me find a way out of this.

Besides the sheriff's department, who else could she call? The FBI or some other government agency? The only person she had trusted with her limited knowledge of events was Dr. Holcomb. She'd trusted Hawk. Briefly and on and off. And she still *wanted* to trust him.

She had to steel herself against the lumberjack with the stormy blue eyes, ignore his protective demeanor and how it warmed her insides. Maybe he affected her like this because she'd been alone far too long. But it was hard to forget that he'd been a helicopter pilot in the Army and then an aviation county deputy. He'd been a hero. No doubt about it. And then he'd stepped into her life and been her *personal* hero. She couldn't forget that either, but maybe she should. If she were checking things off a list, well, Hawk would be a stand-up citizen. But he showed up at a suspicious time, and now his reasons for being here were also suspicious.

She kept pacing. Chewed her thumbnail. She stopped and stared at the nail. Since when did she bite her nails? So, things had finally come to this.

I have to figure this out.

She'd told him he had to check out of the lodge and leave. She needed space from him, even though he'd triggered memories, but he brought his own brand of trouble with him, and did she really need more?

Once she rid herself of Hawk, she'd head to see Dr. Holcomb. What could be so bad that she'd hidden it from herself? So bad that an assassin had been sent to kill her?

He wasn't all that good or she would already be dead. Then again, maybe Hawk was right and he liked to play with his victims. But why? That could send them into hiding or into protection. That could warn them they were in danger and make his job that much more difficult or challenging. Maybe Cole Mercer liked the game. He wanted to up the ante because killing Remi was no challenge for him at all.

Hawk had been wrong. Cole wanted her to see death coming. He wanted her to expect it, to fear it and brace for it, and that would make her murder that much more satisfying for him.

What was with all the morbid thoughts? *What do I do? Where do I go?*

Lord, shine the light in the hidden places of my heart. What could be so bad that I've hidden it from myself? You know. You can see it. Help me to see it before it's too late.

Remi kept her eyes closed and tried to calm her heart and thoughts. So, they now knew who had attacked her and maybe had an inkling of the why. But had the attacker also sent the puzzle pieces, as if two pieces of an image she couldn't decipher would make her remember before it was too late? No. More pieces had to be on the way. Once she had the whole picture, then maybe she would know what this was about. What if the attacks on her were a sordid effort to jog her memory? No. She doubted Cole the assassin would bother.

She was overthinking it.

Exhausted was too weak a description for how she felt as she rubbed her eyes.

She opened them to see Hawk emerging through the swinging doors. He strode toward her, then paused before approaching. Hesitating, he held her gaze. Fearing what she might do or say?

Maybe he didn't deserve the glare she gave him. He'd been there to help her, after all, and that alone could come across as suspicious. As if he deliberately inserted himself into those situations so she would trust him. With that, she knew she was reaching far and deep to try to push him away.

I don't know what to think, Lord.

With a resigned look, he closed the distance, and she stood, bracing herself. He said nothing. Waiting for her?

Sure, she could start this awkward conversation. "I guess you're okay if they're letting you go."

"I'm good. Thank you for bringing me all this way. I know you probably don't feel like taking me back."

She shrugged. "My feelings are the least of my worries. Our worries. I don't understand your role in all this. It seems . . ."

"Fishy. I get it. I wouldn't trust me either." He glanced behind him at the hospital staffer clicking away at the computer to check in another patient. A woman with a young boy had come into the emergency department.

Hawk leaned closer. "Can we get out of here? We can hash through next steps while we drive."

Remi said nothing but instead headed out the doors. "Did they give you a prescription or anything we need to get filled?"

"They gave me a prescription, but I don't want to be fuzzy, so I'm not getting it filled."

"Suit yourself." She unlocked the Bronco, yawning. She'd need to grab coffee at a drive-through. Before they could get into the Bronco, a county SUV drove up and parked next to them. Sheriff Thatcher and Deputy Hunter both got out and faced them. She'd seen the sheriff's picture on the county website, so she easily recognized him.

Remi's heart rate spiked. "What's wrong? What's happened?"

Deputy Hunter held her hand over her weapon as she approached, striking a chord of terror through Remi. She sensed the moment Hawk stiffened behind her.

"What is this?" he asked.

"Ms. Grant." The sheriff nodded. "Deputy Hunter told me what's happened. I came to see you myself. Knew you'd be at the Woodhaven emergency department and called to check. Seems you're in danger and we need to offer you protective custody until this is resolved."

"Protective . . ." She glanced at Hawk. "Uh. I don't know if that's necessary."

What would that look like exactly? The only way to end this was to find answers, to remember, and to talk to Dr. Holcomb. Now she had to admit, she needed to keep Hawk close because he was connected. She doubted being hidden away at a safe house was going to get her anywhere. She'd already gone into hiding at Cedar Trails Lodge. She wasn't going to run anymore.

"Maybe we can talk at the county offices." The sheriff eyed Hawk. Was that dislike and suspicion in his eyes? Or was Remi imagining it? Was that recognition too? "And you too, Mr. Beckett."

"Uh, okay," she said. "We'll follow you." The county seat was about a half hour from Woodhaven.

No harm in finding out what Sheriff Thatcher had in mind. She stifled a yawn again. She might not be thinking clearly enough right now to handle this. Her exhaustion could be adding to her paranoia, but this didn't feel right. It felt like much more than the sheriff and his deputy simply wanting to put her in protective custody at three thirty in the morning. They were working around the clock apparently. But assumptions and conjecture would get her nowhere.

"You look exhausted. Both of you. You can ride with me," the sheriff said. "Deputy Hunter will drive your Bronco." He spoke in a tone that brooked no argument.

A chill crawled over Remi that had nothing to do with the cold and rain.

She reached for her keys and fingered them in her coat pocket as she took a step forward. "Have you learned something about Cole Mercer?"

Sheriff Thatcher looked like he'd been working straight through since the storms started. "We're working on it. As soon as Deputy Hunter shared the information with me, I decided we needed to talk more. I have questions, and I'd like to work out protection for you."

Remi had caught a glimpse of Hawk, but she wouldn't look at him more than that. His expression told her nothing, and that was unusual for him, at least what she knew of him.

Sheriff Thatcher opened the door to the back seat. "Please, get in."

The sheriff wasn't asking.

18

Sitting in the back of the county SUV, Hawk tried to remain nonchalant, but he knew his expression came across as grim. He had half expected Deputy Hunter to cuff him just for having a connection to an assassin, but she hadn't, so that could mean they didn't know yet.

Everything would hit the fan when they found out.

Timberbrook County law wasn't prepared to face this adversary. Once Hawk was back at their offices, he would try to convey that message as best he could without insulting anyone. As he'd been informed, the sheriff was already overtaxed as it was. But it wasn't really the sheriff and his intentions that worried Hawk.

Remi hadn't looked at him. She didn't trust him. He couldn't really blame her for wanting to get far away from him, but they needed to stick together.

Cole would come for her again, and God willing, Hawk would be the man standing in his way.

Again.

As he sat in the back of the vehicle, he looked out the

window at utter darkness and let himself imagine the thick, moss-covered ground and the evergreens of the Olympic National Forest swaying in the wind. The sheriff steered them along the two-lane highway, through the woods, toward the county seat. Though Hawk wasn't driving, he could still feel the wind buffeting the vehicle, meaning the next storm was moving in already.

If he wasn't so exhausted, he might press the sheriff for answers, but he didn't trust himself to speak right now. At least they had a few minutes before they would arrive, and maybe by then Hawk would know what to say.

And what *not* to say.

Sheriff Thatcher cleared his throat.

Hawk lifted his gaze to the rearview mirror, where he locked eyes with the sheriff. Sheriff Thatcher focused back on the road. Hawk waited for what he would say.

"What happened back in King County, Beckett, I read about it. I contacted a buddy of mine. I won't say his name, but I know that you took the blame for all that went down. You made the hard choice, the hard call. No one can know what they would do if faced with that kind of moral dilemma."

Moral dilemma. Save thousands or save one. He could have saved Jake, but the terrorist would have gotten away. He hadn't known that Jake would die, and Jake had been the one to nudge Hawk farther in a direction he'd already been leaning. So he went full throttle. He took the terrorist down, but Jake died.

Hawk's chest constricted. He hadn't expected those words or that perspective from the sheriff, given the way the man had looked at him, but clearly he'd been misreading the situation, and now he remained unsure of what to say. Maybe he should have gone to the other side of the country to flee the story following him, but in this digital age, it was impossible to escape. And besides, John had sent him to Cedar Trails Lodge.

The sheriff kept eyeing him through the rearview mirror. The least Hawk could do was respond. "Glad to have your vote of confidence." He hadn't meant that to sound sarcastic, but he wasn't sure that's not how it came across. "But now you're having doubts?" Because he knew Cole was Hawk's brother? Hawk wouldn't bring it up. Not yet. Timing was everything.

Sheriff Thatcher worked his jaw. "Let's put that conversation off for now. I just wanted to lay the cards on the table, as the saying goes, and let you know where I stand. I'm on your side."

Hawk wasn't sure the sheriff believed his own words, and only time would tell. A churning grew in his gut, that sense of complete wrongness.

Thatcher glanced in his rearview mirror again, only this time he wasn't looking at Hawk. Then he jerked his gaze to look out the driver's side window. "What—"

The county SUV bucked. Metal twisted and crunched as another vehicle slammed into them. The seat belt kept Hawk in place. Screams of terror erupted. Hawk pressed his hands against the cab as Remi's scream filled his ears. Sheriff Thatcher's curse-laced shouts of anger drowned out her screams.

The vehicle spun, then slid down an embankment before slowly rolling onto its side and then rolling once more before resting upside down. Heart pounding, Hawk caught his breath. The cab hadn't been crushed and remained intact. They were still alive. He hoped. He believed.

He slowly got his bearings, pulled himself together, and turned to Remi. "Are you okay?"

Face pale, she looked at him, stunned, disoriented like him, but she nodded. Held his gaze.

Hawk unbuckled. "Sheriff Thatcher?"

"My leg . . . it's stuck. I'm not sure it isn't broken." He groaned, then got on his radio and called for emergency services.

Deputy Hunter's face appeared in the sheriff's window.

"Get them out," Thatcher said.

She shifted to assist Remi and Hawk and spoke to her boss. "Sheriff, more deputies are coming from around the county."

Hawk was able to kick the door open after a few tries, and then he crawled out onto the soaking wet grass and pushed off from a moss-covered rock to stand. This could have been so much worse. He scrambled to the other side, where Remi stood looking around.

The county vehicle lights illuminated a portion of the road. Her Bronco was parked on the shoulder near where they'd gone over the embankment. Down the street, an engine idled, one headlight on bright, the other missing— the offending vehicle.

"How did they hit us?" Remi asked.

"It was intentional," Deputy Hunter said. "Get down. Crouch on the other side of the SUV. I'll help the sheriff."

"What?" She looked dazed but then nodded.

A burst of gunfire filled Hawk's ears. "Down! Get down!" He dropped to the ground next to Remi. The sheriff was trapped in his vehicle and couldn't escape the bullets. They had to protect him until help arrived.

Deputy Hunter had also dropped to the ground. "I'm shot." Her voice sounded shaky.

"How bad?" Hawk crawled over to her and assisted her behind a thick-trunked red cedar and set her in a patch of ferns.

She grunted in pain and pressed her hands against the wound at her side. "I can stop the bleeding. I'll be okay until help arrives. But the sheriff. We have to protect the sheriff."

Hawk had already pulled his gun and in that moment realized the sheriff had never asked for their weapons, even when transporting them, so he really had trusted Hawk. He got into position to protect the others.

The shots had come from across the street. He got a better look at the vehicle that had sent them into the ditch. The massive front-end grille appeared only slightly affected. The truck had come at the SUV from a forest road, ramming into them from the left, sending them down the embankment. That's all that had been needed to disable them.

"You're going to be okay," Remi said to Hunter. "Help will be here before you know it."

He'd had a bad feeling about this entire ride to the county sheriff's offices, but he hadn't expected this.

"Are you sure you're okay?" He gave Remi another quick once-over. She didn't appear injured.

"I'm good. Just a little shaken. What about you?" Fear swam in her eyes. Fear for the deputy and fear for their lives.

"We need to protect the sheriff," Deputy Hunter said again.

Hawk wanted to go after the aggressor. Cole. It had to be.

The sheriff suddenly appeared, crawling forward to the deputy. He grimaced, then held his leg. "The impact jammed my ankle. Feels like something's broken."

"And you didn't wait for help?"

At Hawk's surprised look he shrugged. "I was a sitting duck. Sometimes you just have to push through the pain to save your own hide."

Sirens resounded in the distance, growing closer.

Using a small flashlight, Sheriff Thatcher checked his deputy. "Hang in there, Carla. You'll be okay."

"I can't die before my retirement next week. I'll survive," she said, though her voice was still shaky.

Remi started to push up. "I can get the medical supplies—"

"No." Hawk and Sheriff Thatcher said the word at the same time.

"You'll expose yourself."

"*I'll* get the supplies and then go after him," Hawk said.

"No. Beckett, get Ms. Grant—Remi—get her out of here," Sheriff Thatcher said. "You can get her to the county offices. Our deputies can protect her. Carla and I are both injured."

Hawk eyed the woods around them, ready to defend them. Cole would make his move soon. In the meantime, he had to make the sheriff understand what he was up against. "An assassin who would attack law enforcement isn't going to let a building with a few deputies stand in his way. I don't want to see you or more of your deputies hurt or killed. I don't want to see Remi die. Now, you told me you were on my side, and you understood the hard choice I made before. I hope you'll be as understanding now when I tell you I know how this guy works and thinks. I know how to keep Remi safe, and I know where to get answers. So once backup arrives to protect you, Remi and I are going to disappear."

"Now, you listen—"

"He's right." Remi cut off the sheriff. "You want me safe, Sheriff, then let me go with Hawk. You don't want my blood on your hands, do you? You don't want more of our deputies shot. Thank you for your offer of protective custody, but I choose Hawk to be my private security."

Deputy Hunter groaned and cried out, pulling all their attention to her. Sheriff Thatcher shined his flashlight on her blood-soaked hands and, grimacing with his own pain, added his hand to hers to put pressure on the wound.

"Hang in there, Carla." Fear for his deputy and friend edged Sheriff Thatcher's voice.

Hawk got it. He understood what was going through the sheriff's mind. Fear and anger that his deputy, his partner, had been shot. His vehicle was mangled. His authority challenged. He didn't like the choices he was forced to make.

As far as Hawk was concerned, Thatcher had no choice. He must have realized it too and gave Hawk a subtle nod. "We'll keep working the investigation from our end. I can arrange a safe house too, if needed, just let me know. Get out of here if you're going."

"I won't leave you." He couldn't abandon them to defend themselves. This was a whole new level of attack. It was crystal clear that Cole didn't want Remi in police custody to reveal her secrets. Her memories.

"We'll be all right," Thatcher said. "Help is on the way."

Hawk understood. Thatcher hadn't said the words. Remi was the target. Getting her away meant giving them a chance. How messed up was that? But it was true.

"Fine. I'll take her, but first I need to try something." He had a long-buried bone to pick with Cole. He didn't wait for the sheriff's permission and left them, pressing forward into the woods toward where the big truck idled in the road. Hawk was battle ready, military trained, but a little rusty compared to Cole, who'd taken his own road down a dark, fatalistic path.

Standing behind a tree near the road, Hawk fired one shot into the ground. "Come on, Cole. What happened to you?" He shouted the question, knowing he wouldn't get an answer, but he needed to reach the man—if his brother still remained somewhere inside that assassin's head.

He didn't get an answer. Cole didn't want to give away his position.

"I won't let you get to her," Hawk said. "You'll have to go through me."

Potentially lethal words, those, but he spoke truth. His pulse raced in his ears as he waited for Cole to make a move.

Sirens resounded, and not only did an ambulance show up but also a fire truck as well as two other county vehicles. More law enforcement. They could arrive quickly if the situation was dire enough, close enough, and threatened their sheriff and fellow deputy.

Surprising Hawk, Cole responded with gunfire, bullets hitting the tree. If he wanted Hawk dead, Hawk would be dead. He ducked, knowing that Cole was making his escape. Wheels squealed as the truck sped away.

Hawk jogged back to the rolled county vehicle, where medics were already attending to the deputy and the sheriff as well as doctoring the scrape on Remi's forehead near the cut she'd endured yesterday fighting with an assassin. Hawk's head didn't feel all that good, especially since he already had a mild concussion—probably, the ED physician's assistant had told him—but he didn't have time to give in to the pain.

He shrugged off assistance and zeroed his focus in on Remi. She had a strange look on her face. She searched the woods and then found him coming toward her.

"Hawk." Her voice was oddly strong. "Did you see him? Did you see . . . Cole?" Remi hadn't said "your brother." Was she actually trying to protect Hawk in case the sheriff didn't know yet?

Actually, no. Hawk hadn't seen their attacker, but who else could it be? Who else had pursued her since yesterday morning?

"Do what you said you were doing. Get out of here. Remi, Hawk is the man of the hour." The sheriff's forehead beaded with sweat as the medics attended his ankle in the back of the ambulance. "Go. Get out of here."

Apparently, the sheriff had resigned himself to Hawk and Remi's decision, and maybe he was a little out of his head with pain at the moment too. Hawk had hoped someone else, someone more competent than himself, would take this on, but right now, he was the one invested. The man of the hour, as the sheriff put it.

He had to get to Cole and end this before someone else was hurt.

Or Remi was killed.

Remi, however, shook her head, unshed tears in her eyes. "This is because of me. All because of me. I can't hurt another person."

Hawk gently grabbed her arm and urged her toward her Bronco. The keys were still inside. He assisted her into the passenger seat. His mild concussion wasn't a foregone conclusion, and Remi didn't appear to be in the frame of mind to drive.

Steering them up the highway in the opposite direction that Cole had gone, Hawk said nothing. He needed time to think. He might have spoken with too much confidence when he told the sheriff he knew how this guy worked and how he thought and that he knew how to keep Remi safe. That was all partially true. But he *did* know where to get answers.

John had sent Hawk here for one reason, and that meant he knew details about Cole's whereabouts or where he was suspected to show up. John was in the intelligence business, after all, so Hawk shouldn't be surprised. He would know why Cole was after Remi.

"Where are we going?"

"To talk to the man who knows more than we do about what's going on."

Her breath suddenly quickened. "Not yet. If you're in this with me, then help me, Hawk. Take me to Dr. Holcomb. I need to see her as soon as possible."

Hawk didn't know how to tell her that could be a mistake.

19

Heart pounding, Remi had let Hawk take the wheel of her Bronco, and it felt like she was letting him take charge of her life too. She remained unsure if that was a good decision or not, but this entire situation was unfolding on her faster than she could keep up. Her life was at the mercy of this fierce storm blowing through her.

He sped around the curvy two-lane road so fast she thought her Bronco might fly right off the road, and after the experience they'd just had, her anxiety was sky-high. She should say something to him. Tell him to slow down, but his expression was intense as he squeezed the steering wheel. Breaking his concentration could be a bad move. In Remi's opinion, Hawk drove entirely too fast for a man running on no sleep, who'd been hit in the head. To be fair, he was trying to get her as far away from Cole as he could. She should be grateful.

The events of the last many hours seemed to have infused him with adrenaline, the same as her, only now she was crashing. She couldn't seem to let go of the intense fear and shock of the county vehicle rolling, and those same gripping emotions mingled with the intensity of the flashback she'd had earlier that night.

The image of the man reaching for her from the helicopter, the darkness surrounding her, kept flashing in and out of her mind, fuzzy one moment and clear the next, but then gone so fast she couldn't wrap her thoughts around it. She'd give anything to lose the gut-wrenching sensations that came with the flickers of memory.

Anything.

Lord, can I just remember without reliving it?

Memories can't hurt you. Memories can't hurt you.

That's what Dr. Holcomb had told her. True enough. Those events themselves couldn't harm Remi now. They were over. Done. But she still faced an unknown danger stemming from what had happened.

"I know it's almost four thirty in the morning, but I don't care. I'm going to call my doctor and tell her I'm coming. She'll understand. I have a signal here, but in about three miles, as we get deeper into the Olympic National Forest, I'll have zero bars."

Hawk said nothing. She got on her cell, but she didn't want to make the call until—"I'm telling you this to confirm that's where we're going. Because if not, let me off at the lodge. I'll do this myself."

He glanced her way intermittently while driving. What was he thinking? Why wouldn't he say something?

"Can you please slow down?" she asked.

"No. I want to get us off this road as fast as I can."

"I understand that, but what good is it if we're killed while doing it?"

"The longer we're on this road, the more danger we're in. We have to get somewhere that he isn't watching and can't follow us. I'll take you to see your doctor if you believe it's important, but how well do you know her? Can you trust her?"

Her pulse skyrocketed. Seriously? Incredulous, Remi looked at him while she used her cell to contact Dr. Holcomb. "I know her better than I know you. Of course I trust her. What kind of question is that? And I need you to pull over before the signal's lost."

Hawk grumbled under his breath but found a turnout and slowed to a stop. Mr. Lumberjack and his blue eyes and broad shoulders reassured her that she was in good hands. It felt good to have someone at her back, someone she could trust—at least, in Hawk's case, wanted to trust.

God, please help me trust him if I should. Show me the way out if I shouldn't.

As they sat on the turnout, exposed if Cole should show back up, she was well aware of the seconds that ticked by as she waited for the call to finally connect with voicemail. "This is Remi. I'm on my way to Seattle. Call me back. I won't have cell service for a while. I need to see you, or at least talk to you, immediately. Someone's trying to kill me." What more could she say? Those words had to get Dr. Holcomb's attention and hopefully a quick response. It was Remi's greatest fear come true.

Hawk pulled from the turnout and back onto 101.

"Please just text—" The call dropped. "Wait. What are you doing? I wasn't finished."

"Time's up. We've been here too long and so we're leaving now." He stared at the road, his brows deeply furrowed.

"It'll take us four or five hours to get to Seattle," she said. "Let's stop at the lodge and rest first. I need to make sure everything's running smoothly. Check on Jo."

"No. Jo, Erika, Dylan—your whole gang is trained to take care of things. You've made sure of that. Going back there just puts not only you in danger but your staff and your guests. So we're not going to the lodge."

But . . .

He was right. She was stupid to suggest it. "Where are you taking me, then?"

"To switch vehicles."

She let that soak in. At least Hawk was thinking things through.

"I never could have imagined this scenario. I wish I knew why someone wants me dead."

"You do. By now you must realize that you witnessed something, know something that someone is willing to kill you for and someone else wants you to remember."

"You're right, but I meant details. I don't know the details behind why." She rubbed her temples. "I think we both need sustenance and sleep." She'd been going strong for close to twenty-four hours. Hawk too. They had the training to keep going. "I want to be fully coherent, given what I might face. What's coming."

"I agree."

He steered through Forestview, then to the outskirts, where he pulled up to a small clapboard house probably built in the seventies, but a few renovations gave it an updated look.

"Where are we?" she asked.

"This is the place I rented before the cabin became available." He pulled right into the garage, then got out and heaved the door shut.

She hopped out of the Bronco and glanced around the old, musty garage. "I thought you said we were switching vehicles."

"We are. But you're right. We need a few hours of sleep. I don't know if the power went off, but it's on now. I have stuff to make sandwiches, and even if the power went off, it's probably still good."

He clomped up the steps and unlocked the door into the house, and she followed him inside.

"And you're not worried about Cole following or finding us here?"

"He didn't follow, and he wouldn't know about this house."

She wished she had a duffel bag with clothes. She should have planned ahead and stashed a go bag at the bus station like they did in the movies. Forget clothes. Her priority now was the sandwich he mentioned, then crashing on a sofa. Shoot, she'd even take the cold hardwood floor.

The place was old and musty like the garage. "Oh, it's cute."

"Nothing is mine. Nothing is fancy. Just an old sofa, couple of chairs, and a bed. Not much." He washed his hands in the kitchen sink. "Make yourself comfortable."

Then he peered inside the fridge. "We have Black Forest ham or smoked turkey."

"Turkey."

"Mustard or mayo?"

"Plain?"

"That's kind of boring, isn't it?"

"Maybe. Just surprise me."

She settled on the sofa and sank right in. It was old and well-worn but comfortable. She'd almost drifted off to sleep when Hawk offered her a plate with two loaded sandwiches. "Eat now, sleep later."

She lifted the bread to peek inside. "Mayo and mustard on both."

"Ah, now you know my secret sauce."

"Whatever. I'm hungry."

"You get the bed. I'll take the sofa."

"I couldn't," she said around a bite. In her stupor, the explosion of flavors was lost on her.

"No, really you can." Had he eaten that entire sandwich in two bites?

She hadn't finished the first one. "Because you're a gentleman?"

With his mouth full of sandwich, he only shrugged in response. Remi guzzled the bottled water he handed off. "Okay, I'm heading to the bed. I'm going to crash, and even with a bad guy like Cole Mercer trying to kill me, I'll probably sleep like the dead." Maybe she wouldn't dream or have nightmares about the terror that chased her. The clock read 4:52, but it was winter and still dark outside.

A few hours later, she woke to the aroma of bacon and eggs. After rubbing her eyes, she took in her surroundings. The musty smell reminded her she was in Hawk's rental house. The clock read 8:30 a.m. She'd gotten just over three hours, so she'd be running on a deficit, but she was glad Hawk woke her with breakfast smells.

She scrambled out of bed and cleaned up as best she could in the bathroom. Finger-combed her hair and rinsed out her mouth. If she was going to meet Dr. Holcomb, she really wanted to clean up first.

"Remi, you awake?" Hawk's voice sounded gentle.

And comforting. What would it be like to wake up to that voice every day? Remi pinched her face. She had to knock those thoughts into oblivion.

"I'm coming." She exited the restroom. "I wish we could stop at the lodge. I need clothes if I'm going to meet Dr. Holcomb."

"We've been here too long. Cole could be in town searching for you even now. We're leaving the vicinity after we finish breakfast. You look fine."

Focused on eating quickly, they ate in silence. He put the dishes in the sink and didn't even bother washing them out. "Time to get out of here."

"You wish we hadn't stopped, don't you?"

"Yeah."

"You brought us here for me? So I could rest and eat? I could have kept going."

"Like you said, we need to be coherent and have the energy to face the day. So here we are." He stood at the back door and opened it for her.

She was curious about the ride. A monster truck? *Lord, I hope it's a Hummer built like a tank.*

She stepped through the door and into the cold, wet, rainy day.

Remi couldn't move.

Her gut clenched. *No.* "I can't."

20

Trudging ahead of Remi, he opened the door of his helicopter for her. He got the Agusta 109 series bird for a steal at a salvage yard—where helicopters go to die—though it had still cost a pretty penny. Great for flying in weather like this, so he had no regrets. "This will get us out of Cole's grip faster so we can lose him for the time being. You need time to figure this out."

When she still hesitated, he urged her on, waving her over. "Let's go."

He didn't want to be a jerk, but neither did he want her to remain in danger needlessly when he had the power to get her to safety, even if it was short-lived. They had a slim window before another wind and rainstorm moved in, and a stormy flight would make Remi even more uncomfortable. He wanted her experience with him to be a good one for reasons that had nothing at all to do with running from his rogue brother.

But she might not experience a helicopter flight with Hawk as the pilot because Remi hadn't budged, she hadn't followed him. He grunted under his breath. She was going to need some strong nudging.

Remi stared at the helicopter, a battle raging in her eyes.

And Hawk stared too, like an idiot, but for a different reason. The thick, lush greenery behind her framed her. Her auburn hair hung long and tangled. Even exhausted, her eyes were bright, but torment lurked in her gaze.

He couldn't put it into words, even in his own mind, but on some deeper level, he understood. Hawk didn't know Remi's favorite color or what sauce she dipped her French fries in, but in the way that counted right now, he *knew* her. Or he was just a fool desperate enough to play games with himself.

He closed the distance and gently gripped her arms, unsure of how she would react. Hawk couldn't force her, and maybe he shouldn't act like he was the one running the show. But this was a good plan.

Why couldn't Remi see that? "You're one of the strongest people I know."

And he meant it. She'd been through something so horrible that her mind had shut off the memories, and her mind needed to get with the program or whatever stayed in the shadows could get her killed.

If they didn't act.

He intended to do everything in his power to keep her safe and end Cole's pursuit.

"This is our fastest way out of here. Did you forget that your life is in danger?"

He was surprised she wasn't already dead. And that scared him the most—once Cole was done playing games, he would end her. Could Hawk stand in his way and save her? Would he lose his life in that effort? He was willing to die, but he wanted to save them all. Save Remi and stay alive too, long enough to bring Cole back to the light.

Say something!

Finally, Remi's expression shifted. She sucked in a breath. "And my life won't be in danger in *that* thing? It looks old. I'm sorry, Hawk, no offense, but frankly, it looks like a piece of junk." She bit her lip.

He pressed a hand over his heart. "You wound me, Remi Grant." This was what he could afford on his slim salary plus some of his inheritance. "This is my baby. My project."

"I'm not sure I want to go up in stormy weather in your project helicopter."

"You don't get it, do you? She might not be beautiful, but everything bad that could happen has already happened to her. She's solid." He blinked the raindrops from his eyes. He couldn't hold back anymore if he was going to get her in his bird. "Listen, you know I flew a helicopter for the Army as a Night Stalker. The pilots who fly special ops units—think Navy SEALs—to their covert missions. That means I can fly anything, anytime, anywhere in the world."

He'd said it with conviction, bringing that emotion all the way from deep in his core. *And, like my baby right here, everything bad that could happen has already happened.* Except, well, he hadn't died. "I can get us where we need to go."

An icy wind slapped at his back, and that meant he was running out of time. He could fly this bird in a storm, but every helicopter and every pilot had a limit. Nor did he want to make this experience worse for Remi. If the storm picked up too much, she would never fly again.

Please.

Shrugging out of his grip, she stomped to the chopper.

"No, Remi. Get in on the left side. Helicopter pilots sit on the right." She'd been a photographer and probably had flown in helicopters with two pilots, so this wasn't something he would expect her to know. Though even in that case, the PIC—pilot in command—sat on the right. Usually but not always.

After she sent a handful of dagger stares his way, she slowly got in. Not like he wanted her going into this with a bad attitude, already deciding she hated it, but her safety was what mattered now. He'd gotten her inside his project bird, and that was enough for now.

He did a quick preflight check—rotors were clear of debris. Plenty of space to fly out of here. After finishing the mental list, he did a final walk-around and then jumped inside before Remi changed her mind.

He got in and put on his headset. Handed her one too so they could talk. Then he powered up, reviewed the weather, and focused on getting them in the air while he still could. With the inclement weather, he'd have to fly IFR—instrument flight rules—and he filed a verbal flight plan since he had no time for anything else. If something happened to them, someone needed to know where to find them. He wanted to get in the air before the wind became too much—and before Cole tracked them.

When the helicopter lifted off the ground, she sucked in a breath.

Then she did it again, and again.

Much too fast.

"You're going to hyperventilate. Close your eyes. Think about something else." He steadied the bird, focusing on lifting out of the trees. He had to get high before Remi entertained thoughts of jumping out.

Grinding his molars, he mentally berated himself for being much too hard on her. She was suffering from PTSD on multiple levels of which he couldn't begin to understand, even with his own struggles. She'd experienced such trauma that her mind had shut it away from her.

As for his experiences? His memories?

If only he could forget them.

What is it about some minds that hide the horror, bury it away, and other minds turn the memories into a living nightmare?

The helicopter lifted high and hovered over the house and woods.

Remi yelped. She gripped his forearm and squeezed. "Hawk! I can't . . . I can't, I can't!"

"You *can.*"

Yeah, he was a complete jerk. But sometimes a person had no choice but to go through the fire. In this case, the storm.

She fell silent, for which he was grateful. It was hard ignoring her pleas, and he hoped that she knew she could do this. She would be better for it on the other side. Maybe she would even remember the past. And if he was wrong about it all, and putting her through grueling torture was a mistake, then he'd own that on the other side.

He angled toward the Olympic Mountains—the shortest route to Seattle—planning to skirt around them. Heavy gray clouds threatened to completely hide the frosted peaks.

"Remember when you said you would give me the chance to convince you to run my tour package out of your lodge? Well, this doesn't count. Sure, you'll get the grand tour at some point, but I want you to give me the chance to show you my world *after* the storm."

With this flight, he could be blowing those chances. Right here and right now. He doubted his words would convince her not to count this experience against him, but he had to try. As for being a jerk to get her into this chopper, if it meant saving Remi's life, then there was no question he was doing the right thing. He would take that hit like a champ.

She groaned and covered her eyes. Was she going to pass out on him? The wind gusted, pushing and shoving the helicopter more than was comfortable, even for him, because this was a lesser helicopter than he'd flown for the Night Stalkers. But she was his, all his.

"Focus on the beauty of God's creation. The Hoh Rainforest is just below us. You're a photographer, so you should appreciate the view." Stupid line. *Everyone* could appreciate the view. Another time, another place, she'd fly with him and bring her camera and capture the most fantastic shots, just like she had with the waves. He hoped.

And, yeah, he was turning into a praying man.

You hear that, God? I'm a praying man now. And I want to ask for safety for this flight. And if you could offer a little hope for my brother, that'd be nice too.

She dropped her hands. In his peripheral vision, he saw her chest rising and falling dramatically and then, finally, slowing. Calming. She blew out a breath, lifted her chin, and looked out the window. "It's beautiful."

Progress. He inhaled deeply. Now he could focus on flying. Remi was a big distraction.

"Oh." Remi fished her cell from her pocket. "I got a text." She read it. "Wow. Okay."

"What is it?" he asked.

"From Dr. Holcomb. She said not to come to Seattle. That I'm in danger." Her voice shook on the last words. "I already know that. I told her that someone was trying to kill me."

Well, that wasn't good. Remi was counting on seeing Dr. Holcomb. "Anything else?"

"No. Wait. Yes. More came through. She says to meet her in Port Angeles. She'll be at Downriggers on the Water at eleven thirty a.m." He got on the radio and adjusted his flight plan. Port Angeles was on the Strait of Juan de Fuca and part of the Olympic Peninsula.

"Squatchcon is going on now," she said.

"Squatch what?"

"Con. Like a Sasquatch convention. You know, Bigfoot."

"Yeah, I know. We had Bigfoot sightings in Kentucky too. What does that have to do with meeting your doctor?"

"Nothing. It's on a flyer back at the lodge in case someone wants to go. Jo had wanted to go. Usually it's in March."

Remi fiddled with her phone.

"What else did she say?"

"She said to turn off my cell phone so I won't be tracked."

Interesting. "You could still be tracked depending on who is doing the tracking and how sophisticated they are. Cell phones can still give off signals, even when turned off. Like, you can still locate your iPhone with Apple's locator app when it's turned off." He pulled out his cell and handed it over. "There's no cell service here, but we'll have it in Port Angeles. We don't need our phones pinging the cell towers if someone is searching or tracking the GPS. Mine never allows tracking, but turn it off for me anyway. We'll get burner phones."

He viewed the map, reviewed the weather alerts, and set course for William R. Fairchild International Airport in Port Angeles.

"To the right is Mount Olympus. We can't see the peak. The clouds are too low."

"But I can still see that it's covered in snow. It's breathtaking from this view. I've never actually seen it since you can't see it from Seattle. It sits in the middle of the range. I've heard you have to go to Hurricane Ridge, and you can view it from there. No roads go in or out of the Olympic range. Just around it." She glanced his way. "Maybe that's why people want a helicopter tour of the mountains."

A warm zing filled his chest. She was getting it. Showing someone the wonders of the world always made him happy, but for some reason, Remi's reaction dipped much deeper into his heart.

He couldn't explain it.

Maybe it was her big blue-gray eyes that had snagged him from the beginning. Or the small intake of breath she'd taken just then. He shouldn't be thinking about her like this, not while they were both in survival mode.

He couldn't have imagined he would be on the cusp of finding his brother while caught up in trying to save a woman's life. A woman he wished hadn't caught his attention, hadn't intrigued him.

"Oh . . . maybe someday I could get used to this. Maybe someday you can take me back up when there aren't any clouds."

"I'm counting on it."

Her words drew him back to the moment, the present, where he very much needed to remain focused. He'd been flying on his own personal autopilot. Remi sounded somewhat relaxed. Maybe this would be a good experience for her, after all—well, not counting that she was running for her life. And despite the fact that he wanted her to love this as much as he did—even with his own horrific memories—he should really focus on why they were here.

They knew who was after her, but Cole was a hired man, and they needed to know more. And why.

"Besides what you've told me, have you remembered anything else?" he asked.

"No. It's all still blurry. The feelings. It's almost as if I'm reliving it, and right now I need to think about something else. Talk about something else. Let's talk about you. Tell me what happened back in King County."

He cringed. Wanted to know what she knew, what she'd heard, what she'd read or seen on television. But he had no intention of talking about it if he didn't have to. Not yet anyway. But he did get her strategy. If she was going to share with Hawk, then she'd want something from him.

"How about I tell you about the Night Stalkers." Then he wouldn't have to tell her about what happened in King County, the part that wasn't in the news.

Sure, he could fly anything, anywhere . . . until he couldn't.

21

awk landed and powered down the bird. As soon as the rotors started slowing, Remi hopped out, glad to plant her feet on the ground. That and, well, she had to give herself some space from Hawk Beckett, the former Night Stalker who could fly anything, anywhere, at any time. And being so close to a guy who had already acted as her personal hero a few times—and no doubt he was a hero to many others—threatened to turn her insides to mush. She admired him. Now was absolutely not the time to let the blue-eyed former Night Stalker get under her skin. Was he trying to do just that? She couldn't quite figure him out.

She lifted her face to welcome the harsh slap of cold wind on her cheeks. She looked out over the angry waters of the Pacific Ocean, more specifically, the Strait of Juan de Fuca. Across the way, low-lying clouds almost completely shrouded the mountains of Victoria, British Columbia.

She'd gotten to Port Angeles and quickly, thanks to Hawk, who had basically forced her to get on his ride. At first, when he'd taken off into the escalating wind and rain, she thought she would have a heart attack. Either that or lose the contents of her stomach.

But she listened to Hawk and forced herself to relax. Once they were in the air, she listened to his stories—the heroics he shared of his team after he changed the names to protect the innocent. He was counted among the best pilots in the world, which begged the question—Why was he here at this moment with her instead of flying VIPs to private island summits? Regardless, if she couldn't trust Hawk Beckett to get her to her destination, then she couldn't trust anyone. No point in fearing death by helicopter when she already had a killer bearing down on her.

The rain felt like tiny pricks of ice stabbing her face. She glanced around for Hawk. Ah. Of course. He was still sitting in the cockpit. She peeked inside. He flipped switches on the dashboard.

She opened the door and climbed back inside. "Brr. No point in me standing out there until you're ready."

Hawk looked at her. "I had hoped the helicopter ride would also help jog your memory. Anything?"

She slowly shook her head.

"Nothing at all?" His lips flattened in disappointment.

"Nothing." She chewed on her lip.

"Time to get a cab. Come on." Hawk led her to the airport terminal, acting as if he came to Port Angeles all the time.

A few minutes later, Remi and Hawk stepped onto the sidewalk in front of a mall-type structure called the Wharf. "We just need to meet her at a place called Downriggers on the Water."

His brows furrowed, and his gaze took in their surroundings as if he was ready to pounce or protect at any moment. "Doesn't this feel a little weird, Remi?"

Had he really just asked that question? "Which part exactly?"

"Meeting your doctor like this? I've never seen a doctor, a specialist like a neurologist, neuropsychologist, therapist, or psychiatrist, whatever she is—or let's even throw in a gastroenterologist—meet a patient at a restaurant."

"Given she said that I'm in danger, it *is* weird and yet not surprising. It feels about right."

"Fair point."

The wind blew cold and hard, and Remi tugged her hood up and over her head until they got into the building. Once inside, they walked by shops selling T-shirts, rocks and shells, ice cream, and taffy on their way to the restaurant.

"We're here." He stood next to her and stared up at the sign.

Remi glanced at her watch. "And right on time."

She had to prepare her thoughts. What would she say? Everything was scrambling together in her mind, and she was going to sound completely incoherent if she didn't think this through. She should have written it all out ahead of time.

She started forward, but Hawk suddenly ushered her into an alcove.

"Let's wait a few moments," he whispered. "Watch. Make sure it's safe."

"She wouldn't lead me into a trap, and now you're making us late."

"You don't know that this isn't a ruse."

"I think if she wanted to trap us, she would have met me at her office." Remi hadn't left the Hidden Bay area since the last time she'd gone to Seattle to see Dr. Holcomb, and then, with no progress in recovering those missing days, she found excuses to stop going. Still, she'd spoken to her at times over videoconferencing.

"Come on, let's go find your doctor."

"It's safe?" She frowned up at him. "How can you tell?"

"I can't, but I think it's best to get this over with."

She led him into the restaurant, where a hostess met them at the foyer.

"We're meeting someone," Remi said.

"You're welcome to look around."

Remi led Hawk through the packed restaurant, conversations buzzing and waitstaff shuffling about. After searching the restaurant and coming up empty, her heart rate kicked up, as if she wasn't already on edge.

"I don't understand," she said. "We're not that late. We should try to get a table and wait for her."

"No," he said. "I don't like this."

"I'm hungry again."

"Already?"

"I worked up an appetite trying to survive that helicopter ride. Let's sit here and eat. This is as safe as any place, and I don't want to miss seeing Dr. Holcomb."

Hawk's features were granite. "We'll get food somewhere else and watch for her."

This man was infuriating. "Fine. After this, I want to hear everything about your brother. You owe me an explanation." She knew that his assassin brother, Cole Mercer, was a sensitive topic, and she wanted that conversation to be at the right time in the right way. But she should have demanded answers the moment she'd learned the truth.

A brief scowl flashed on his face and then it was gone. He led them out the side door of the restaurant.

A flash across the parking lot caught her attention. Remi slowed . . . and stared. *What in the world?*

Hawk continued to walk ahead, but he turned to find she hadn't followed. "What's wrong?"

"That was her. I saw her," she said.

"Where?"

"She just went into the convention center through the

side door." Remi rushed across the packed parking lot, leaving Hawk to chase after her.

"Where are you going?" He caught up.

"After Dr. Holcomb, what do you think? She could be in danger. We have to help her."

Remi opened the side door and entered a wide corridor outside of the main attraction of the Field Arts and Events Hall. Signs everywhere reminded her about Squatchcon. Remi wanted to follow Dr. Holcomb, but to get into the event she would need to pay, and that meant that Dr. Holcomb would have also paid. Would she have exited somewhere else, then?

Remi continued forward. Behind her, Hawk grumbled something she couldn't make out as they approached the guy standing at a side entrance.

"Hey, you need a pass if you want inside."

"I'm looking for a woman wearing gray slacks and a navy coat. Did you see where she went?"

He narrowed his eyes. "No. Lots of people coming and going today, lady."

Remi didn't believe him. "Look, we're her friends. I think she's in trouble. She just came through that door." Remi pointed to the exit outside. "You couldn't have missed her."

"You want inside, you need a pass." Great. This guy wasn't budging or being the least bit compassionate.

She wanted to roll her eyes. "So, where do we get a pass?"

"Up front."

Remi huffed and turned to head to the front, unsure if Dr. Holcomb already had a pass or would have gone into the convention center. But if she was trying to hide, she might have.

Hawk grunted and stepped closer to the guy. "Here's our passes." He stuffed something into the guy's hand.

"You're good to go," the guy said.

Remi eyed Hawk briefly but said nothing when he held the door open for her. She stepped inside and Hawk followed. The exit door banged closed behind them.

"What did you say to him?" she asked.

"I gave him a couple of hundreds."

"What? That's all it took?"

"He's a volunteer—that's how these cons work. He has probably already been here for a day or two, however long this thing lasts."

"You carry that much cash around?"

"Sure. When I'm trying to travel incognito." He winked.

Incognito. Right. They were trying to stay under the radar.

"Thanks for that. Now that we're here, do we even know she came inside?"

"We're here, so let's look."

Remi took in the room. At the far walls were various booths for crafters and artists. Every age group was represented here, and a good chunk of the people had some form of costume for cosplay events. Lots of Bigfoot costumes, as well as other kinds of mythological creatures, including a variety of aliens.

She pushed through the crowd, Hawk on her heels. A voice Remi recognized spoke over the speakers and all heads turned to the stage. Straining to see, she pushed between a few people until she could. A man—Bigfoot, of course—stood at the microphone. He'd taken off his Bigfoot head and started talking about the upcoming costume competition.

"I know him. That's . . . that's a friend. His name is Hank. He stayed at the lodge with some friends last year. He's really into all this."

"I gathered," Hawk said.

Hanging around long enough to talk to Hank would be

nice, but she didn't have time, and she started back through the crowd, heading for the opposite side. Remi whirled around so fast that Hawk almost ran into her, catching her against him when she lost her footing. She would have tumbled backward and landed on her rear if he hadn't prevented it. And suddenly she was close. So close.

He stared down at her, his face mere inches away. Something electric flashed in his gaze. She looked into his eyes longer than necessary, while he seemed equally unable to disentangle from her. Being here, up close and personal, felt good and right, and she wanted to press into him, trust him with everything, including her heart.

"Remi . . ." Her name came out breathless on his lips.

Even in this noisy place, she heard it. Felt it. No . . . not good. Despite what her heart said, right now she refused to trust anyone that much. Not even Hawk Beckett.

"I—" What had she been going to say?

Then she stepped out of his grip. "She could have seen you with me. That must be why she left the restaurant. I didn't give her forewarning. You're the reason she ran. You have to leave. I'll find her alone."

"What? No," he growled. "You said it yourself. She didn't help much before. Is it worth the danger, the risk to your life, to talk to her?"

"Yes." *I hope so.* "Just pray. Okay? Pray I find her and she helps me."

"Yeah, sure. I'll pray."

His words surprised her. She hadn't even known if he was a believer—in God, that is—but the fact that he agreed to pray gave her hope she hadn't known she wanted when it came to Hawk.

Suddenly, she caught a glimpse of blond hair, a blue jacket, and gray slacks. Remi rushed in the direction the woman had gone. A quick glance over her shoulder told her that Hawk stayed behind at a distance, but she knew he wouldn't let her get too far. She wished she had her phone so she could call the psychologist or text her that Hawk was safe.

Remi weaved her way through a group of rowdy teenagers and spotted Dr. Holcomb entering the restroom. She had to beat a group of women heading that way and dashed past them, heard their shouts of protest as she made it to the door. Then hit it, pushing her way through. And ran into her neuropsychologist.

"I found you!" Remi gasped.

"Shh. Keep your voice down." Dr. Holcomb tugged her into the handicap stall. "Lindie. Please, just call me Lindie," she whispered.

"Why didn't you meet us at the restaurant?"

The doctor was shaking. Her eyes filled with unshed tears. Not the professional woman Remi had seen in the past.

You're scaring me, and I was already scared.

"I'm so sorry," Lindie said.

Oblivious to their conversation, a steady stream of females entered and left the restroom.

"Let's find another place to talk," Lindie whispered.

Remi opened the door and held on to the woman as they fled into the hallway, then Lindie led her toward the exit. Before exiting, Remi pulled her down a side hallway.

"I've remembered a few things, and I need to tell you. You insisted I meet you. That it was important. I'm here now. Please, I need your help."

"You don't understand." Lindie steepled her hands in front of her mouth, then dropped them. "I was paid to keep tabs on you. Threatened. If you remembered anything, I was supposed to contact someone. But please know that I didn't call them. I didn't notify them. I was wrong to insist on seeing you. That was before I knew that they were listening when you left a message. Now they want you dead. And I'm afraid that I'm a target too."

Lindie gulped air between her words, her gaze intense, filled with fear that drilled down into Remi's soul.

"You wh—" *I can't believe this is happening.*

Anger built in her chest until she couldn't breathe. Then the air punched from her. "Then you owe it to me to hear what I know, what I remember, and you can help me with the rest before it's too late."

The doctor shook her head. "Please don't tell me."

"Look, you're already on the run, and you know nothing."

"Exactly."

"I'm not putting you in any more danger than you are already in for agreeing to inform them."

"That's just it, Remi. I never agreed. I didn't inform them, but they had bugged my calls. I'm a liability. Now you need to go deep into hiding until this is all over. One day, it will end."

"I was already in hiding! And now my life is being threatened. I'm not running or hiding anymore. You once told me that I would remember when I was ready. I've started to remember bits and pieces, but nothing makes sense. I thought if we could talk—you know like we used to . . ."

Dr. Holcomb glanced at the door and shook her head, then dragged her gaze back to Remi. "I'm so sorry that I can't help you. I'm taking the ferry across to British Columbia. Someone has been following me, and I hope they don't follow me onto that ferry. I have to go now." Dr. Holcomb pushed past her, down the hall, and through the exit door into the gusty, rain-filled afternoon.

Remi followed her. Lindie kept to the shadows but picked up her pace, heading toward the ferry.

"Who's following you?" Remi ran to catch up. "Who

wants me dead for something I can't remember? If you know what's going on, you have to tell me!"

Lindie paused and turned around. She stood out from under the awning now, her rain-washed face filled with fear and regret.

"They don't want you dead, Remi. Not yet. You have something they want *first*. And then all bets are off." Lindie closed the distance, touched Remi's forehead. "They want what's locked in here."

"Who are *they*?" Remi needed to know who had sent Cole for her.

But Dr. Lindie Holcomb had already turned and rushed toward the ferry ramp. Remi would like to get on that ferry with her, but the woman made it clear she didn't want any part of this, and that was without knowing what Remi knew—that Hawk's *brother* was the assassin after her.

It might be some sort of madness that persuaded her that sticking close to Hawk was a good idea.

22

Growling under his breath, fisting and refisting his hands, he stalked through the crowd after Remi. He'd seen her rush into the ladies' room moments ago. Her friend Hank had finished talking, and now a band was entering the stage. Loud music was about to shift this entire scene, and the crowd would probably grow more raucous. Dancing Bigfoots everywhere. Now, that would be a sight to avoid.

An entire family dressed for the part stood between him and Remi.

"Excuse me. I'm so sorry. Excuse me." He didn't miss the glares from the parental Sasquatches as he tried to cut through. But come on! Maybe they were upset because they hadn't won the contest—*"the best-dressed Bigfoot wins"*—he didn't know.

Didn't care.

He just needed to get to Remi, and he was doing his best to remain patient and act polite.

Frustration fueled his breath as he entered the hallway, then he approached the facilities. A line had formed outside. A couple of women who weren't dressed up exited the ladies' room, and two more pushed in. Had he missed Remi's exit? He didn't feel comfortable going in to check things out, but he needed to know that she was okay.

"Excuse me." Hawk directed his words to a thirtysomething woman in white fur. Was she a Yeti? "I'm looking for someone. Can you ask Remi if she's still inside?" He hoped that anyone coming or going would check.

"Sure." She opened the door but didn't step inside. "Hey, Remi. You in there? Your boyfriend is waiting."

A couple of women in armor exited and gave him a funny look. "What are you supposed to be?" He had no idea why he'd blurted that out. He didn't care.

"Mandalorian. What planet are you on?"

Earth? But he didn't have time to engage and shouldn't have started a conversation. The clueless look on his face must have given him away.

"The Star Wars universe? Hello?" The two women laughed and kept walking.

Good.

Okay. "Remi, you in there?" He opened the door and called into the restroom. Then let the door close.

The woman who'd initially called for Remi shrugged. "Either she isn't in there or she's avoiding you. She might have ditched you for being so possessive that you have to stalk her in the women's bathroom."

He didn't offer a reply. It wasn't like he'd actually gone in, so her claim was completely false. He'd seen Remi go inside. Could he have missed her leaving the restroom? If so, she must have gone out one of the other exits. But where?

Next chance he got—burner phones.

He followed the hallway until he exited the event center and stepped out into the blustery wind. He never should have let her go after the doctor on her own. Once he caught up, she could simply explain he was here to help. Apprehension squeezed his insides. Made his palms sweat. Had this been a trap like he feared, and had someone taken Remi? He couldn't protect a person who didn't cooperate, but he couldn't exactly say that Remi was uncooperative. She had her own ideas about the best next steps.

Hawk stood under the awning as the rain picked up. He took in the full parking lot and, across the way, the ferry station.

A figure rushed toward him from the side of the building. "Hawk."

He grabbed Remi and pulled her with him under the awning and out of the rain. "Are you okay?" He sounded too harsh. "What happened?"

"Can we just go?" Discouragement edged her voice.

They took a cab back to his helicopter, and once inside, he powered the bird up. Turned on the heater to blast away the chill. They hadn't spoken while in the cab, where the driver could overhear.

She shrugged out of her wet rain jacket, donned the headset, then rubbed her arms. "Where to next?"

What had happened? "That depends on what you learned from Dr. Holcomb."

Remi relayed the conversation to him. He took everything in stride. He'd made a list in his head of possible outcomes.

So, they wanted something inside Remi's head. What was Cole up to? Preventing that from happening? She sagged against the seat. He worried that she was exhausted and on the edge of collapse.

"So, you didn't get to talk to Dr. Holcomb. You didn't need her anyway. Remi, talk to *me*. I'm here to listen. You've already remembered a military guy in a helicopter, reaching for you. That's something, and we'll figure this out. Think about the last thing you remember before waking up at the hospital. Where were you?"

"The café across from the cathedral in Novograd. I was there to take pictures for my travel blog."

"What happened to your camera?" he asked.

"I didn't have it on me in the hospital. It wasn't recovered. It was lost."

"Or maybe it *was* recovered. Someone could have it."

She gasped. "The puzzle pieces. I only have two pieces, so I can't be sure, but what if I was the one to take the picture that someone is sending me? What if it's one of my pictures from my trip?"

"If you were to get more pieces—and saw the completed picture—would you remember if you'd taken it?" he asked.

"Or would it even jog my memory?" She huffed.

He hated seeing her frustrated. "It's already coming back to you, Remi. Just relax."

"If only it was that easy."

"What can I do to help?"

"Listening is good. But honestly, I wish I had brought my camera with me. It's beautiful here."

"I wish we didn't have to leave and that we had time to explore. You could get a camera and take pictures as long as you wanted."

She glanced at him. "Where are you taking me now?"

"My former CO that I mentioned. John Marshall. He has to know something." Hawk suspected the reasons why John hadn't been up-front. He was probably monitoring Cole's activities under some classified status. John had been connected to the intelligence community before exiting the military and apparently had remained plugged in. And since Hawk had shown up to stop Cole, his brother might be onto John now and could possibly target him. That fear gnawed at the back of his mind, but John knew how to take care of himself.

"And where is he? Local?"

"Seattle area."

"Can't we just drive from here?"

She really didn't like flying. "I don't want it to take several hours to get there and I'd have to come back to get the bird. Besides, I know just where to land. It'll be a short trip, I promise. I'd say this trip to Port Angeles has been a waste of time, but now we know what lengths someone has gone to. Think about it, Remi. You've been monitored since you arrived at Hidden Bay. Someone has known where you were all along, while you thought you were hiding."

Was there someone at the lodge—a guest, or staff—that was part of watching Remi? His gut tightened.

She didn't respond, and he left her to her thoughts while he finished filing a flight plan and then flipped all the required switches on the dashboard. The rotors started up but needed time to warm up before he took off. In the meantime, he could check the weather again.

"I'm going to take her up now. If you remember anything else, you can share it with me. I'm here to listen and help you figure it out."

"Right. You're the guy to help me get my memories back. And I'm here when you're ready to talk about Cole."

They made a great team. Except he wasn't ready to talk.

This flight would take Hawk's complete focus, but he knew this Agusta was good for it and his skills would get them through. The helicopter lifted and fought the wind. He focused on flying through the inclement weather and thought about next steps. He'd texted his buddy Gordo Bates, a former Weyerhaeuser helicopter mechanic who owned an aircraft salvage business. He had helped Hawk find and put together this bird. Gordo was going to leave

Hawk a vehicle at the warehouse that he could use for a day or two.

After landing at Gordo's salvage yard protected by a fenced and gated-off area, Hawk powered down and allowed the rotors to cool off before shutting down completely. The deep ache of exhaustion coursed through his bones, despite getting a few hours of sleep early this morning. Remi was getting dark circles under her eyes. They needed more rest and sustenance before taking one more step deeper into this quagmire.

Forty-five minutes later, he steered through an industrial section to a gated warehouse turned into a few condos and then drove around the back. They got out, and he led her up the steps to the second floor, where he pressed in the security code and opened the door to let her in, then reset the alarm.

"Where are we?"

"This is just a condo I bought six months ago, after selling my house. It's sparse." He'd been busy trying to track down his brother. Busy with his job. That was before he got fired.

Now he was busy with Remi.

One bedroom. One bath. Anything bigger would have been out of his budget because he spent most of his money on that helicopter. A guy had his priorities. He turned a few lights on in the kitchen and one soft light in the cozy den. Well, it was cozy now that Remi was in it.

"This is . . . nice," she said.

He chuckled. "You don't sound convinced. I haven't put up pictures yet. I'm not much of a decorator."

"But why bring us here? I thought we were going to John Marshall's."

He released a heavy sigh. "We're both exhausted. By the time we get to John's, it'll be late. I thought we could use a reprieve. Eat and rest. Head out tomorrow. Don't worry, nobody's going to find us here."

"Not even your brother?"

He lifted a shoulder. "He doesn't know about this place." *Yet.*

"As far as you know."

"Right." He nodded. "For the last year or so, I've been looking for him so I could face off with him. Try to bring him back from the dark side. I've come close to finding him, but with his training, he's a ghost. I figured he might pay me a visit one day because he doesn't like me in his business. Never did. So, in case of any unwanted intruders—my brother or otherwise—I have security cameras in place." His brother wasn't his only worry. After taking out that terrorist—the incident that got him fired—he'd been threatened by the man's associates in the terrorist cell. This condo had been a good move. But now he'd found Forestview and Hidden Bay. He might settle there instead. *One day at a time, dude.* "I know it's small, but I'm not home that much."

"Do you happen to have extra clothes I could borrow? Do you have a washer and dryer?" She looked down at her attire.

"I have some sweats and T-shirts you could wear if you really want to wash your clothes, but they'll be too big on you."

"That's fine with me."

"And I have these." He pulled a couple of burner phones out of a kitchen drawer and handed one to her.

"Oh, nice. Thanks. You're all kinds of prepared." She smirked at him.

A friendly, teasing smirk.

He showed her the bedroom and the alcove with the stacked washer and dryer, then left her to it. Hawk snagged some clothes out of his closet so he could change too. When she emerged from the bedroom in a T-shirt and sweats hanging off her, he used the bathroom to take a quick shower, then pulled on jeans and a sweatshirt. He headed to the kitchen, where Remi stood at the fridge staring inside the freezer. She peered over her shoulder.

His stomach chose that moment to growl. "Well, what will it be? We have lasagna, lasagna, and lasagna, and—oh, wait—enchiladas. And chicken nuggets. Some frozen broccoli. What's your preference?"

She left him to it and sank onto the sofa. "Whatever you make for you, make it for me too."

He fixed a big plate of chicken nuggets and stuck them in the microwave.

Remi got up and moved around as if searching for a piece of Hawk in this place. She bent over, picked something up, then released a small gasp.

He peered over the counter. "You okay in there?"

"Looks like you dropped something."

He rushed forward to see what she'd found. "That's just . . . it's a picture of me with Cole." He might have set it on one of the bookshelves and forgotten about it. One of them must have knocked it off somehow.

Seeing them together, arms over shoulders, smiling, tore him up inside. Grief engulfed him. He snatched it away.

"Hey." She scowled at him. "Wait a minute."

Remi closed her eyes and sucked in a breath. "I remember . . ."

"What? What do you remember?"

She opened her eyes to look at him long and hard. The way she looked at him, he instinctively knew to brace himself.

"Your brother was there."

"What? Where?" She couldn't mean what he thought she meant.

"The details are fuzzy. He was an important part of a special forces team."

He stumbled forward. "Remi . . ." He couldn't exactly tell her he didn't believe her. It was more that he didn't *want* to believe. "You told me that memories could be wrong. How do you know this is true? You didn't know my brother or remember him before. Maybe it's like you told me, your brain fixed the empty space, filled in the gaps and put Cole there."

Remi's mouth hung open, and he wanted to kick himself. He shouldn't be surprised that Cole was deeply connected to her. He needed to sit down. Think about this.

His head was hurting again. Wow. Had he just said that to her? He lifted his hands, palms up. "I'm sorry."

The microwave dinged. He should have been relieved at the interruption. He wanted to say more, but he had no idea where to go with this. He pulled the nuggets out and put a few on a separate plate for her. Grabbed a couple of bottles of water and then sat with her on the sofa and set the food on the coffee table.

Her actions were robotic, controlled. "I know you don't want it to be him," she said.

"You're right, I don't." What did it matter? Cole was an assassin now. No longer hungry, he stared at the nuggets.

"And I can't say for sure that the memory is correct, but you have to admit it kind of makes sense."

"That your brain would fill in his face, put him on the helicopter?" She'd mentioned it before when he'd described his brother, but he hadn't actually thought it could be him.

"Not what I was going to say, but that makes sense too. I guess we don't know anything more if I can't even trust my memories."

He chewed the chicken nugget but couldn't taste a thing. Then he sat back against the sofa and guzzled the water.

Finally, he said, "Let's hope that you remember it all—I'm talking everything—over the next few hours. Like a floodgate has been opened. And I want you to tell me everything. It could mean the difference between life and death."

"I think you're right—that I'm about to remember it all—and that's what scares me. Dr. Holcomb told me that someone wants what's in my head. She could be lying. Or she could have been lied to."

"Sometimes lies aren't lies but someone's perception. They simply have a different perspective of the events that occurred."

"Or they remember things differently."

He leaned forward and clasped his hands. "Like a soldier who lost a limb. His brain keeps telling him the limb is still there, and he feels the pain of it."

"Or sometimes it's intentional. In the Army, I worked to create a certain image about the military. In other words, my photographs worked to shape the narrative so that it was favorable. Someone could be shaping the narrative for us." She rubbed her forehead. "How do we find out what's real and what's true, Hawk?"

"We stick to the plan. Go see John and find out what he knows."

"Because, like you said, he sent you to Cedar Trails. Tomorrow, Hawk, we could have answers." She leaned back and drank her water.

"Exactly. I'm counting on it."

Remi rubbed her eyes, then rolled her head to look at him. "I want to know more about *you*, Hawk. You and Cole both, and why did you get fired?"

Really? She wanted to know about that right now?

He grabbed his plate and hers and stood. "Do you want more to eat?"

"I'm good for now." She closed her eyes. "You're stalling."

"I have a feeling you're going to fall asleep on me. Let's sleep on it. You get the bed and I'll take the sofa."

But it was too late. Remi had conked out. Great. He didn't want to be a jerk and leave her to sleep on the sofa while he had the bed.

He stood, then urged her to stand too. If he picked her up like some damsel in distress, she might actually slap him. Her eyes grew wide. "What—"

He took her hand to lead her. "I'm tucking you in. I'll be on the sofa if you need me. You're safe." But he wouldn't promise because no place was a hundred percent impenetrable.

Hawk was surprised that Remi let him tuck her in, and she smiled as she sank into the bed and onto the pillow, closing her eyes. "Night, Hawk."

"Good night." He covered her up, fighting the urge to lean down and press a kiss on her cheek.

Well, he lost that battle. He leaned in and kissed her forehead.

She was asleep and hadn't felt a thing. Just as well.

23

*S*omething feels wrong.

It gnawed at the back of her neck.

Her agitation growing, Remi tossed and turned, then finally opened her eyes. The room was dark, but light filtered in from beneath the door.

Heart pounding, she sat up and gasped.

Where am I?

Oh . . . yeah. Hawk's place.

Listening to the muted sounds of rain dancing on the concrete outside, she released her pent-up breath and eased back onto the pillow. The storm wasn't as violent here on the other side of the Olympic Mountains. Was that the reason she felt unsettled? She'd grown accustomed to the crashing waves and now her mind, her heart, missed those sounds. The absence of those comforting noises made her feel displaced.

The sounds. Remi sat up again. She had thought that Hawk reaching for her, his hand, had triggered the memory. But that wasn't it at all. Hanging from the rope over certain death had been what triggered her memories. It was the rope, not Hawk. She wasn't exactly sure how or why, but she just knew that's what it was.

The crashing waves and the rope were sensory details.

She struggled to breathe as the past came roaring back. She dreaded and welcomed it at the same time. Squeezing her eyes shut, she let images overwhelm her mind as violent sensations rushed through her.

Remi was there now, in the past, living it all over again.

They had to hurry and get out. She had to escape. Cole reached out of the helicopter for her and pulled her inside. The next few moments were a blur. Then suddenly the helicopter hovered over water. Remi was falling into the blackness. The darkness. The Baltic Sea?

Another image slammed into her. An explosion in the air. Debris falling to the water.

She gasped. Couldn't breathe.

Anguish filled her, and she pressed her face into the pillow and sobbed. Everyone had probably died. Remi lifted her face and swiped away the tears. Cole Mercer wasn't dead. And Remi had survived. Had Cole jumped? Her thoughts remained fuzzy about much of what had happened and why she had even been on that helicopter. Remi wasn't sure she wanted to know what happened. Sitting up in the bed now, she continued to wipe at the tears that wouldn't stop coming.

She thought about the Nebraska farm and her childhood. She'd just been a normal kid growing up in a rural community, and then living on the outskirts of Omaha had felt like living in the city. She and Mom had done okay for themselves.

God, I miss that. I wish I was back there and Mom was still alive. Why'd she have to die so soon? If only she was still alive.

Remi would be there with her now. Maybe they would have expanded the house. Added rooms. Created some kind of new recipes they could sell at the local mom-and-pop shops, which would have been a lofty goal for the two of them. Running a bed-and-breakfast had been a big step. But they'd been happy.

And Remi had just been too devastated when Mom had died of a heart attack at forty-eight. She thought about that cold, rainy day when she signed the papers after selling the bed-and-breakfast, then walked into the Army recruiter's office there on the corner of Main and Chestnut. Maybe she regretted that decision—just a little. She'd grown as a person. Learned so much. But if she hadn't sold the bed-and-breakfast, she wouldn't be here now, running from an assassin.

Lord, I know we're not supposed to think back to the past and wish we'd made different decisions. It doesn't do any good. But please help me find my way now.

She had no idea what time it was and didn't want to know. Remi would have preferred to go back to sleep, but her mind was awake now. She hoped to remember everything, but until then, could she piece together what she knew? What did it all mean? At least it was coming back to her, though slowly. And if she figured it out, what would she do with that information?

She had to reach out to someone who could help her, but at the moment, she had no idea who to trust. And she'd really like to know much more about Hawk before she told him *everything*. Just like Dr. Holcomb had been used as a spy to help her remember, or at least inform them if she did, Hawk could also be a plant.

She hated to consider it, but he'd shown up at a weird time. Could everything that had happened been to gain her trust? How could she truly know? She got out of bed and searched the dresser drawers.

She found nothing interesting in the drawers. Slipping out of the bedroom, she crept down the short hallway to find Hawk sleeping on the sofa, his gun in his hand and resting on his stomach. Well, that was comforting. Not. A digital clock on the kitchen counter told her it was two in the morning. She tiptoed over to the bookshelf and found only a few books. No pictures. Tugging out one of the books on the shelf, she looked at the title. *Fatal Traps.* She flipped through the pages, forgetting that she intended to remain quiet, and saw that it was about helicopters. No surprise there.

"Why aren't you in bed, asleep?" He half mumbled the question.

She snapped the book shut. *I was snooping.* "Couldn't sleep."

"Interesting reading, don't you think?"

After returning *Fatal Traps* to the shelf, she moved around to the sofa. He was still lying down, an arm across his eyes. He looked relaxed and yet on high alert, all at the same time. How did he do that? She wanted to know more about him for all kinds of reasons, but she couldn't deny that she wanted to know Hawk the man. What would it feel like to have his arms around her, not to protect her but to hold and cherish her? To kiss her?

And with the unbidden thoughts, her cheeks flared. She was glad his arm covered his eyes so he couldn't see.

She had a vague memory of him walking her to bed. Had he kissed her on the forehead? Nope. She must have dreamed it.

"I'm going back to bed now."

"Try to sleep. We have no idea what happens next."

She rushed back down the hallway into the bedroom and

closed the door behind her. Once back in bed, she struggled to shut down her thoughts about Hawk. For what seemed like several more hours, she tossed and turned, growing more anxious and agitated. Then finally . . . sleep, sweet sleep.

Until she sensed someone in the room with her.

24

Hawk flipped on the bedroom light. "We need to leave."

"What? Why? You wanted me to go back to sleep and I finally did." Remi sat up and rubbed her eyes.

"I got an alert. Someone entered through the gate. I've been watching them drive around and case out the place. They'll figure out where we are soon enough."

"You're sure they are looking for us? Who are they?"

"It's Cole."

"Why leave? If we stay, you can face off with him like you wanted. We can find out what's going on and get answers. Why would you want to run from him?"

"I'll face him when the time is right. When it's just me and him." He couldn't risk Remi getting hurt. Keeping her as far away from Cole as possible was for the best.

"But don't you see? We could find out what he wants." In sweats and a T-shirt, Remi climbed from the bed and finger-combed her hair.

His too-big items hung off her form and he couldn't help but grin—inside. He wouldn't let her see. Her tousled hair and sleepy eyes made him want to pull her into his arms and cocoon her. Protect her. Let her rest as long as she needed. He reined in his thoughts before he stepped closer.

Once he was close, he dragged in a hard breath. "Remi, trust me. Now is not the time."

Her lips shifted into a flat line. Then her eyes widened. Those beautiful big eyes. And utter determination to win, to beat the odds.

Remi glanced down. "I can't wear this."

Her words surprised him, and he almost laughed. He gestured to the dresser. She spotted her folded clothes.

"You were asleep, and the dryer dinged. Now you have something to wear."

Her smile was adorable. "Thank you. Give me a sec."

She slipped into the bathroom and shut the door. Using his burner phone, he logged into an app and viewed the cameras he'd set up outside. Cole was nowhere to be seen. But the car he'd arrived in was parked at the far corner of the building. Hawk was surprised Cole had driven and parked. He had to know that Hawk would have cameras. But maybe he was getting desperate and running out of time. And his brother was probably already trying to make his way in. If he was working with a hacker, he could have already hacked into Hawk's camera system and manipulated what he was seeing now. His special forces brother was highly skilled in a thousand ways.

"Remi," he whispered.

The bathroom door cracked open, and she slipped out. "I'm ready."

"Grab our coats. They're on the bed." He'd brought them when he'd come to wake her up.

He yanked the curtain wide and opened the sliding glass door. They slipped out onto the small balcony in the still-dark early morning. He sucked in a breath of the brisk air.

"Uh, what now? How do we get down?" She whispered the question.

"We shimmy down the tree." He reached out and touched the needles of a lofty evergreen.

Her eyes grew wide. "You're kidding."

He smiled, then positioned a fire escape ladder over the rail.

She arched a brow.

"We need to hurry. I'll go first."

He climbed over the rail and then down a few rungs before dropping to the ground with a *thunk*, then quickly glanced around. Seeing nothing, he watched Remi slowly crawl down the ladder.

On the ground, he took her hand and led her around the warehouse and over to the office complex next door, then down a stairwell that led into its underground parking garage. "Is this all part of your escape plan? I mean, if you ever needed one?"

He'd thought through it a number of times, and this wasn't exactly ideal, but it worked. "I guess you could say that. This garage is not connected to the condo warehouse, and it could take Cole time to figure out our escape."

"He's your brother. He thinks like you. It won't take him long."

Unfortunately, she was probably right. He used the fob to lift the hatchback, reminding him where he'd parked the Chevy Blazer. When you had an assassin for a brother who might decide to come for you and you'd killed a terrorist and people threatened you, it made sense to have a trick or two up your sleeve. Park a car in a random garage. Honestly, he was surprised he had to use the Blazer and even more surprised that the battery hadn't died and it was still there and waiting. He'd figure out how to return Gordo's vehicle later. Hawk was all about old vehicles, old helicopters, and apparently, condos in old warehouses.

Once inside, he started the Blazer and let it warm up. He pressed a button on his cell that was effectively a kill switch for the computer in the condo.

"I feel like I'm in a spy movie, Hawk. And I don't like it. I'm just a farm girl turned Army photographer turned girl with amnesia on the run. Get me out of this nightmare. What is going on?"

"You know as much as I do. You might even know more. Did you remember anything else?" The tires squealed as he peeled out of the parking lot a little faster than he intended, and he took a side street.

"I'm going to need coffee before I talk. And I need you to talk about Cole if I tell you. Tell me about him."

"You and your hard bargains. Okay, I'll drive through a coffee kiosk. Grab food and a couple of Americano grandes to go. But I need to put some distance between us and the condo." And Cole.

"Triple shot."

"Triple shot it is. And then we're heading to John's." Though Hawk had no idea if the man was at home or traveling. It was a start. He preferred seeing the man's face and asking the questions in person. Not that he thought for a minute that John would lie to him but that he might have to keep secrets, and Hawk wanted answers. John had opened this proverbial can of worms when he sent Hawk to Cedar Trails, so he owed him an explanation. More than one.

At 4:30 a.m., after ordering breakfast and coffee at a drive-through coffee kiosk, he steered onto the freeway. "It'll be a couple of hours before we make it there, which is fine. It'll still be early morning. So, tell me what you remembered."

"That Cole was there, which I told you. I also remembered

that I wasn't in the crash. I fell out of the helicopter, I remember falling. I remember an explosion and crashing. I don't know who lived and who died. If the whole team made it out. Something had gone wrong. And Cole was the one to reach for me."

That disturbed Hawk as much as anything. "And if Cole was on the bird, that mission, then he survived and not everyone is dead."

"It was a special forces mission," she said. "I don't know what I was doing there."

"You were taking pictures. What else?"

"Not while I was on the helicopter. I wouldn't have been on a special forces mission. I wasn't in the Army anymore. So my presence there makes no sense."

"Well, at least it's coming back to you," he said. "This thing is coming to a head, and probably faster than we're ready for."

"What do you mean?"

"Just that we need to be ready for anything."

"And I can do that once *you've* told me everything."

He groaned to himself. Yep. He'd agreed to that. He took a long swig of the too-hot coffee. Took a bite of his breakfast sandwich. Swerved into the middle lane and watched the mirror for any tails. Early morning traffic would pick up and get heavy within the hour. It didn't appear anyone was onto him yet, and his Blazer couldn't be tracked. Remi was right. This was like a spy thriller in too many ways, and he wanted to get them both out of this plotline before it was too late.

"I was a deputy pilot for the sheriff's air support unit."

"Wait, I want to know, I really do, but I think I need to hear about Cole first. Tell me about your brother. He's the reason this is happening."

"He's one part of it, yes." Hawk's stomach churned. He really didn't want to hash through this again. It was still

200

too fresh. Too raw. "It's all related, so let me tell it my way, okay?"

"Oh, yeah. Sure. I'll shut up now."

She was cute. More than cute.

Time to focus on the road now and, unfortunately, the recent past. Might as well get this over with. "I was in a high-speed aerial pursuit to capture a dangerous terrorist and wanted fugitive. Red Notice kind of thing."

"Red Notice kind of thing?"

"Interpol stuff. Someone wanted by other countries who has been put on a watch list called a Red Notice. His name was Andre Aslam, part of a terrorist cell called Blackfire. On the side, outside of my duties, I'd been searching for any information that could lead me to Cole. He'd gone missing two years ago. Same time as your incident."

"So, see, it makes sense. He could have been there."

"Yeah, he could have. I'd heard that Cole had gone rogue and was a very specialized hired gun."

"Where did you hear this? Let me guess, your former CO."

"Yes. He couldn't tell me much, just that through intelligence channels, he'd learned that Cole was working with an international criminal organization."

He paused and let that sink in all over again. Like he'd just heard the news yesterday.

"You must have been devastated."

"That's an understatement."

"I don't mean to interrupt the flow of this, but could you have ever suspected it? What could have caused such a big shift in your brother?"

What indeed? Hawk had struggled to come to terms with it. He and Cole loved each other growing up, but they'd always been competitive, and at times, that had taken them to dark places. But they'd always had each other's backs.

"And what about your parents? Are they still alive?"

Remi was good at asking the questions. He pursed his lips.

"Oh. I'll stop and let you tell me."

"They're gone. I'm glad, honestly, because Cole's behavior would kill them now."

"I'm so sorry."

Before she could ask, because he knew she would, he told her. "Car accident. Five years ago." Dealing with the aftermath was the reason he'd left the Night Stalkers. "The thing is, Cole and Dad never got along, and I get it. I understand. Dad always favored me. I wish he hadn't, but he put pressure on Cole to measure up, and it was wrong. Just wrong."

"Could that be the reason Cole has gone to the dark side?"

"I don't know. I can't fathom it. Despite all that, Cole was a great guy. Everyone loved him. Dad was hard on him because—in Dad's mind anyway—he was simply trying to push Cole to be the best man he could be. Even if that had been the reason, there had to be a catalyst. Something to send him in this direction, and it sounds like it happened about two years ago."

"Because that's when he disappeared? Did his unit inform you that he was MIA?"

"No. He disappeared in that I couldn't contact him or find him. He didn't respond. I thought he was just on another mission, and sometimes he was deep in the bush somewhere in the world and would get back to me when he could, but it had been going on too long. So I was worried that something had happened to him and was telling John about it, and that's when he told me. He hadn't wanted to tell me that he'd learned that Cole was working as a mercenary. A hired killer. That he hadn't reenlisted. His unit had been killed but he survived." And Remi's story, her timeline, fit. "I'm hoping that John will shed some light on things."

"I'm sorry about all of it," she said. "Really sorry."

"Me too. I'm sorry that he's after you." He could barely comprehend it.

They sat in silence for a while. Then Remi asked, "What about this Andre guy? You were telling me about him and how it's all connected to Cole."

"I'd cornered him. It was a multiagency effort, and I had him. And he mentioned Cole to me. Said that he knew my brother and had information. He shocked me with that." Hawk hated this part. He really hated it, and it was all on him. "He slipped through my fingers."

"What? How?"

"The details aren't important." No need to talk about his failures. "Then he escaped in a helicopter, and we were called in on an aerial pursuit in Snohomish County. I decided this time I wasn't going to let him get away. These helicopters are equipped with so much technology. More than you could imagine. Infrared, zoom cameras, GPS mapping, what we call 'night sun,' which is a powerful spotlight." Man, he missed flying for the sheriff's department, but not the rules and not the politics. "The county works with multiple agencies. It's something, and after what I pulled, I'm not sure I can work in law enforcement again. But I was so close, why would I let him go?"

"So, what happened?"

"The sheriff tried to reel me in. Gave me some excuse to stand down. But I wasn't having it. If I lost the guy this time, I might lose Cole for good. But Aslam was more daring than I am, let's say, and he came around behind me in his bird so that he was pursuing me. Jake was an aviation deputy riding shotgun. The helicopter didn't need a copilot. But he wanted to take this guy down too. If we didn't catch him, he could follow through with his plans. Jake's dad had died on one of the planes that crashed into the World Trade Center towers on 9/11."

Hawk's heart pounded at the memories. Maybe he shouldn't tell her while he was driving because his foot was pressing hard on the accelerator. He took a few long breaths and then slowed. Checked the rearview mirror. His exit wasn't for another thirty-plus miles. He'd finish the story by then.

"Let's just say that two helicopters went down that day. We collided. Mine went down in Lake Stevens. Aslam was killed, and so was Jake. He drowned." The memories were excruciating.

"It was a moral dilemma, Hawk. You made a judgment call."

"If I had followed orders to stand down, Jake would still be alive. I can't know if Aslam would have been caught, but I can know that Jake would still be alive. And a less important issue, but I would still be working for King County."

"Do you feel guilty that you survived?"

"I survived with barely a scrape. I don't know how, and it seems all wrong. Everything has felt wrong since that day."

"How is that possible?"

He shrugged. "It's like when someone is pulled out of a car that's crumpled and destroyed. I don't know. I just know that we should have caught the guy. But he chose the way of death and tried to take me and Jake out too. I couldn't have known he would do it." Maybe his boss had. "I just knew that Aslam had to be taken out."

"But you still blame yourself, don't you?"

"I'm responsible. Sure I am. I disobeyed an order. Jake and I both did, and not in any way is this a comparison to the lives lost, but I cost the county a lot of money on that helicopter. If I had followed my orders, we'd have the helicopter, but again, more importantly, Jake would still be alive."

"And Aslam would have gotten away and possibly followed through with a terror attack. So, ask yourself, was it worth it, then? The risk?"

"Knowing what I know now, of course not. We could have lived to fight another day, as the saying goes."

"I'm sorry that happened, Hawk," she said. "That's a huge burden to carry. Like this burden you carry for Cole. He's turned to the dark side and you're chasing after him to save him."

"Yeah. He's my brother."

"Anything more you can tell me about this man who wants me dead?"

"Or alive. We can't be sure what he wants, but obviously it has something to do with a lost mission."

"Is that what we're calling it now because of my lost memories?"

"That, and it sounds like it was lost all around. A downed helicopter. People are dead. Whatever the mission was, it didn't get accomplished. Since you were on board, I'm kind of thinking some kind of rescue mission or an extraction."

"But that would mean I was running from something. Trying to escape. I was just a tourist with a camera."

Exactly. Hawk's throat tightened and he wasn't sure he could keep talking. What more was there to say? Remi pressed her hand over his and squeezed. He soaked up the reassurance from her soft, warm skin.

"We'll figure this out together, Hawk. I know you want to find him and talk to him. So I understand why you want to face him on your own terms. Maybe whatever happened on that helicopter is the reason for his descent into a dark world. I don't know."

Yeah. Lots of possibilities. That's what worried him the most as he steered out toward the Fletcher Bay Marina.

"Where are we going now?" Remi asked. "Are we almost to John's house?"

"Almost. We have to take a boat."

"What?"

"You can only get to his house on a boat."

Remi sighed. "He lives on an island, then."

"Yes, an island that's only connected to the rest of the world via boats."

"What about helicopters?"

"He doesn't have a pad. If he did, we would have been there last night."

"This seems like a complicated way to live."

"Coming from a woman who lives in Hidden Bay with no cell or internet service, and satellite is iffy. GPS can't even find you."

"It's only a complicated way to live if you want to be in contact with the outside world."

25

Remi appreciated that the enclosed and heated pilot-house on the boat Hawk had rented protected her from the cold and rain. Sitting behind Hawk as he steered the boat, she studied him. He was focused on navigating across the rough water in Puget Sound. Now that she knew Cole was his brother, she could more easily see Hawk's resemblance to the image of the man in her mind reaching for her from the helicopter. She'd never actually seen her attacker's face. When she'd fought him in the woods, it had been dark and raining, and he was well layered just like when he'd fought Hawk near the cabins.

If Hawk hadn't run into him again later that night, they still wouldn't know who was behind this. Except, Cole was probably not actually behind it. He had to be working for someone.

Despite his multiple attacks. Despite the fact that he'd abducted Jo, calling him a "hired assassin" wasn't adding up. If he was a cold-blooded assassin now, Jo would have been thrown into the furious ocean. Her body wouldn't have been found for days, weeks, if ever. Instead, Cole had kept her hidden but alive, maybe to release her at a future date after he completed his mission.

But what was his mission exactly? It seemed like he wanted to kill Remi. He'd approached her with that knife, after all. Then again, he'd come after Hawk and Remi in the forest in the dark. If he used all the skills he'd gained in the military, he could take her out in an instant, no trouble at all. If he simply wanted to find out what was in her head, like Dr. Holcomb had insisted, Cole could have taken Remi, abducted her, and tried to torture it out of her. But Cole might know that wouldn't work.

She shook her head. Something more was going on here. Regardless, she hoped Hawk would find Cole and then Cole would confess his wrongdoings and turn himself in. But nothing was ever that easy. Happy endings weren't the reality, and she was only fooling herself. As much as Hawk and his brother were similar, they were very different.

"We're almost there," he called over his shoulder.

She took in the beautiful greenery and a few small hills that sprung out of the water. "It's a *small* island."

"Yeah. Only a few residents, so no ferries or bridges. Boat access only."

Hawk circled around to dock at a private pier. He jumped down and secured their boat. She joined him on the dock. They hiked forward, and Hawk glanced around, maintaining situational awareness like the Army-trained pilot deputy he was. After his brother had found them at the safe house that supposedly he wouldn't be able to find, Hawk's hyper-awareness was appropriate. Remi's handgun was tucked in the small holster at her side, reassuring her.

"Tell me about this man we're going to see."

"What more is there to tell?" he asked.

"Was he there during that mission that went south?"

"Which one?"

"The one you just told me about, with King County, where you were fired."

"No. Why would he be?"

"For support. You made it sound like you were close." This was like pulling teeth.

He didn't respond and continued his pace.

The house came into view behind the trees—a spacious multistory bungalow. *Nice.*

Hawk hiked up the porch steps. This guy had a great job or he had family money to afford a place like this on an island in Puget Sound. She suspected Hawk's family had money too. A helicopter, she didn't care how old. *Cha ching.* Home in Seattle. *Cha ching.* Then a condo and a Chevy Blazer in addition to the Ford truck. *Cha ching, cha ching.* But she hadn't asked. None of her business.

Hawk rang the doorbell. The guy must have had cameras all over the place like Hawk did, for the same reasons—or possibly even more reasons, depending on his job. If he'd directed Hawk to Cedar Trails Lodge, then he had his finger on the pulse of a covert operation or two. But maybe Remi shouldn't make so many assumptions.

He shifted to look at the water behind him, then pressed the doorbell again. Nothing. Nada.

"Come on, John. I know you're inside." He looked at the doorbell camera when he spoke.

"Unless he has another boat. He might not be home." Remi kind of mumbled so maybe only Hawk could hear. Or maybe he couldn't.

But he angled to look at her and arched a brow. Yeah, he'd heard. She shrugged.

He shoved both hands through his hair. "We ran into Cole just like you thought we would. We, as in Remi Grant, in case you were wondering who the woman with me is. We need answers. Come on, man."

Hawk knocked this time instead of using the doorbell. At his touch, the door opened slightly.

Remi sucked in a breath. The door wasn't latched shut. Maybe John just hadn't shut it hard enough. That happened to Remi sometimes. But a former military guy who worked in intelligence and had cameras everywhere—she could see some, and probably a lot she couldn't see—leaving his door open?

"Tell me we're not going inside," she said.

Hawk sent her a look.

Keep quiet.

He wasn't about to leave without checking on his long-time friend. He readied his handgun and toed the door open, then stepped inside, his back against the wall. She took his lead, drew her weapon, and followed him inside.

God, please let John be all right. Even as she said the prayer, she suspected he was probably not okay and they were walking into danger. She followed Hawk through every gorgeous room in the house—who was this guy's decorator? His wife? Remi hadn't heard Hawk mention a wife. Maybe she should have asked.

The last room was down the hall. The door was cracked enough for her to see the bookshelves in deep mahogany. His office? Tension rolled off Hawk as he glanced back at her, cautioning her with one look.

They might find John and it might not be good. He crept forward, leading with his gun, cleared the room quickly, then rushed forward and dropped to one knee.

A man lay on the floor.

Hawk pressed his finger against his carotid, and then the man's hand flew up and gripped Hawk's arm. "You made it."

"What happened?" Hawk asked him.

Remi couldn't believe her eyes. Her pulse skyrocketed. She gulped for air and pressed forward. "I . . . I know you."

The man held his hand up as if to speak but coughed up blood instead.

"Now isn't the time, Remi," Hawk said.

He could die. There might not *be* another time.

"You . . . you asked me questions while I was in the hospital. Then you followed me from the hospital in Germany. I saw you in Nebraska."

Hawk was right. Surprising him was a good idea. But someone else had beaten them to it.

26

C ome on, John, hang in there." The man had survived so many missions overseas, he couldn't die now. Hawk refused to let him and pressed his hand against the gunshot wound. At the same time he tried to save John's life, he struggled to believe his ears. To comprehend Remi's claims. She glanced between him and John with wide, accusing eyes. He could deal with that later.

John was going to die if he didn't get medical attention. That was Hawk's priority. "We need to call 911!"

Remi held her phone up. She had already tried. "The signal isn't going through."

"Couldn't . . . call . . ." John struggled. "He . . . disabled . . ."

Someone had disabled cell signals and electronics? "Remi, can you help me?"

Without hesitation, she dropped to her knees by his side and pressed her hands against the wound.

"I'll run out to the boat and use the radio to call for help," he said. "I'll see if I can find a medical kit with something we can use to stop the bleeding."

He hated leaving his mentor, his friend, in what could

be the man's last moments, but John needed help, which included Life Flight off this island. It wasn't ideal for a helicopter to land, but they could hoist him up.

He started to get up, but John grabbed his wrist, proving he still retained much of his strength, which surprised Hawk.

"Careful. He . . . Cole . . ."

This had to have happened moments before they arrived or else John would already be dead.

"Is he still here?"

John said nothing but closed his eyes. He was fading fast. "Remi, stay sharp. Keep your gun ready. John is one of the good guys. There's an explanation for everything. We need him alive so we can learn more."

He cringed at his attempt to persuade her, as though she would deliberately facilitate his death, but Remi was only human and could have doubts about saving a man who she believed might intend her harm. Still, she appeared to be completely focused on helping John, and Hawk shouldn't doubt her.

"I've got this." She nodded to Hawk.

He left John in Remi's hands and rushed through the house, gun ready in case he faced the enemy. His brother. How had Cole beat them here? Or had Hawk misread the situation at his condo? Regardless, he hadn't wanted to leave John or Remi in case Cole made an appearance. Hawk's options were limited.

Carefully, he stepped out the door and then eyed the surrounding grass—no bushes for someone to hide in, but beyond the small yard, trees filled his view. He bounded down the porch steps, watched his six as he covered ground, especially moving through the trees. Once out of the trees where someone could have hidden and ambushed him, he was exposed. Every egress had vulnerabilities.

Protect me, Lord!

Hawk raced to the boat and hopped on. He got on the radio and called for emergency assistance. Then he searched the boat for a medical kit. Found one, but it didn't include gunshot wound powder. He exited the boat and headed back to the house while taking in his surroundings. Gray skies. Rain. Wind. No other boats were about. And no Cole.

Then again, Hawk would only see Cole if and when he wanted to be seen. Myriad emotions—anger, agitation, apprehension, and a familiar fear that all would go south—twisted in his gut as he ran back to the house. Once he entered, he prepared to face anyone and anything as he made his way back to Remi and his former commanding officer.

Voices echoed down the hall. Raspy mumbling, along with Remi's upset tone. When Hawk finally entered the office, Remi was no longer pressing her hands against the wound.

"I found the Celox and gauze. He told me where to find his medical supplies." Her big blue eyes held his gaze. "It was a risk, but I didn't think he would survive otherwise."

He still might not make it.

"What did he say to you?"

She frowned, unshed tears in her eyes. "Later, okay? So, what now?"

He understood, but there could be more questions to ask.

"You can go wash your hands." *And wipe your eyes.* He knew she wanted to swipe the tears away but would only get blood on her face.

"Okay, but then what are we doing?"

"We're waiting for the police and emergency services. The bathroom's just across the hall. Get cleaned up."

He went with her just in case Cole had decided to make an appearance and ambush them.

She stood just inside the bathroom door and made to close it. "I'm good, Hawk. Go talk to him."

He had a line of sight to the restroom and so returned to John's side. He was pale, but they'd slowed the bleeding for now. Nothing here to start an IV or fluids, so they'd just have to wait.

Hawk couldn't lose this man. He'd been a pillar in his life.

Lord, please save him. Hawk found himself crying out to God more than he had in far too long, and maybe that's what despair did. It brought a man to his knees before God.

John coughed, and Hawk gripped his hand. "You with me, John? Stay with me."

The man twisted his head around and looked at Hawk. His eyes weren't glazed over but clear. His grip strong. That's why John had been his CO, his friend, and mentor. His guide. He was as strong as they came. Still, seeing him like this gutted Hawk.

Hawk didn't want to press him too much, stress him out, but if possible and John was willing, Hawk needed answers in case this was his only chance to get them. "You sent me to Cedar Trails Lodge."

John nodded. Coughed again. At least now he wasn't hacking up blood. He shouldn't talk, he should just rest, but so much was on the line and Hawk suspected that John knew that better than Hawk.

"I told you that I still had connections in the intelligence community," John said. "But I didn't tell you everything. The company I work for—Conclave Assets—is an import and export business, but it's just a front for an intelligence firm."

So, John was more than just connected to that community. He was in it. But how deep? "A private firm? Or government agency?"

"Private."

"What *kind* of private intelligence?"

"Contract with government agencies. Cover everything including international and counterintelligence."

The government didn't have enough spies, so it had to contract out for them? Hawk nodded, absorbing John's words. And he wanted to know much more. When would emergency services arrive? This man had to survive.

"I was tasked to find out if she remembered anything in the hospital, and then when she didn't, I followed her. I've known she was at Cedar Trails Lodge from the beginning. I arranged for Dr. Holcomb to send her there and to inform me, but someone else was listening. When Cole came up on the radar . . ." John paused to catch his breath. He closed his eyes and Hawk feared the man had said his last words, at least for the time being.

Remi returned to the room but kept her distance, giving Hawk and John a moment.

"I suspected he was a threat to Remi, and you'd been searching for him."

"You orchestrated her being at the lodge to keep her safe and sent me to interrupt Cole's plans. Why not tell me what I was walking into?"

"Security clearance."

Remi had somehow ended up involved in a special operation that was classified. What had she forgotten? "What's so important for her to remember?"

"Tied to Charles Whitman."

"Who is he?"

"He's dangerous. An arms dealer and a threat to national security."

Hawk didn't understand any of this.

"Then why aren't the feds involved? Why didn't you tell me so I could be prepared?"

John closed his eyes.

The man was probably done talking, and he shouldn't have been sharing information with Hawk, but given the circumstances and the fact that he might be dying, John was ready to give up at least some of the intel.

John grimaced in pain. "Operation Blackout."

The operation had a name. "What is it? What can I do to help?" Where was that helicopter? Emergency services? Where were the harbor police? How long did it take to get to one stinking, small island?

John opened his eyes again. "Classified intel. You need to be gone before the police get here."

"You can't have us talking. You shouldn't have told us." Hawk shook his head.

"Doesn't matter if I told you or not."

"I'm not leaving you," he said. "Your Conclave Assets can just clean up the mess." And leaving the scene of a crime would make Remi and Hawk look bad.

When John didn't respond, Hawk felt his pulse and found it thready. He'd been hoping that it would remain strong.

"Come on, John, don't die on me!"

"I'm afraid that is a foregone conclusion," another voice spoke up.

Hawk pivoted, but Cole had made his move while Remi and Hawk were distracted by John's words.

Cole stood with his weapon thrust into Remi's side. "She's coming with me. You shouldn't have gotten involved, Hawk."

Fear for Remi strangled Hawk. Her gaze held his. He wanted to tell her how sorry he was a thousand times over. No one else was going to die on his watch.

"Cole," he said. "Please stop this. Whatever you've gotten into, we can fix this!"

If he was taking her now instead of killing her, then Cole needed her alive, and he needed her memories. If Hawk made a move for her now, would Cole shoot Remi? Or his own brother? He wanted to signal her to make a move and he would take Cole out, but Remi subtly shook her head. She knew, like Hawk knew, that he simply couldn't take that risk.

Hawk didn't recognize the man before him. Those angry, dark eyes didn't belong to the brother he'd grown up with. Cole aimed his gun at Hawk and fired.

27

Gunfire echoed in her ears. Her heart jumped to her throat.

"Hawk!"

He dropped behind the desk, and she couldn't see him. "Hawk!" Her screams went unanswered. Had he been shot? Was he okay? She tried to break away from Cole and disarm him, but all muscle and ultra-skilled, he easily out-maneuvered her and pulled her closer to him to haul her out of the office. How could she have been so focused on John's words that Cole had slipped into the room and grabbed her?

My mistake could cost everything! It could have already cost John and Hawk their lives. Anguish engulfed her. "Let me go! Did you just shoot your brother? Are you crazy?"

She wasn't going to let him get away with it. Get away with her. She'd fought this guy before. He dragged her down the hallway, because no, she was not going willingly. Her chest tightened with grief that threatened to paralyze her. Strength tried to drain from her limbs.

Cole was winning this fight, but she wouldn't give up. Remi tried to twist her arm out of his ironclad grip as he marched her out the door and into the tumultuous weather. She angled her face to look at him. Take in his features. He'd dropped the whole mask thing because maybe at this point, it was worthless to hide his identity.

"Did you kill him? Your own brother? How could you?" She seethed the words.

Her whole body shook. Tears choked in her throat. She couldn't afford to be weak.

Hawk could still be alive. I can save him if I can get free.

"Let me go. I don't remember anything, so all of this is for nothing. You hear me? I don't know what happened to you, but you broke Hawk's heart." She refused to let the sob caught in her throat break free.

Cole continued to urge her along the pier, and she couldn't forget that he also aimed a handgun at her. He was a skilled assassin, and Remi couldn't fight him and win at this moment. But like Hawk had said, she would live to fight another day, or maybe later this same day. She'd just have to watch for her chance.

"Tie your ankles," he said.

"What?"

"Put the plastic ties around your ankles."

He rested his handgun against his chest. Now wasn't the moment for her to make an escape, but plastic ties now would mean a tougher escape later. He then tied her wrists, never once looking her in the eyes. Then lifted her over his shoulder. He climbed onto the boat with ease as if Remi was a ten-pound bag of russets. Then he set her in a chair inside the pilothouse.

He stared down at her. "Are you going to give me any trouble? Because I don't need you awake for this ride."

What did that mean? "No trouble." At least not yet.

He untied the boat and then hopped on, started the engine, and steered away from the pier. She refused to let tears surge, so instead gave him her best deadly look, which he couldn't see with his back to her—as if he would be intimidated by her if he *could* see.

"Why are you doing this?"

But Cole was focused on getting away from the island and apparently the police. In the distance, she spotted the harbor police finally responding to the calls for help and closing in on the island.

Too little. Too late.

She glanced behind her. *Please, please, see this boat. Come after this boat.* But no one was following yet.

Rain and wind picked up.

Closing her eyes, she prayed.

Lord, help me! Save Hawk and John. Please make this situation right. Too much is going wrong.

Remi realized she had felt abandoned for a good long while. She tried to ignore it, but deep in her heart she was alone. No, that wasn't true. God was with her. He would never leave her. But right now, he felt far away in all of this.

How has it all come to this?

How had the bad guy gotten her? Okay, so maybe those tears would come now. But they were angry tears. She closed her eyes and thought of her favorite Scripture passage, the one she had on the wall in her office. She had no doubt that God had sent her to Cedar Trails Lodge because, while there, she'd gotten closer to him. She'd taken the amazing photographs and come to love the ocean. But at the same time, fear had blocked her memories. Even though she was drawn to the ocean, something dark lurked there, waiting for her.

Maybe . . . maybe that's why, when Hawk had pulled her up from falling, she'd had the sudden image in her head of a desert. Her memory had been wrong. That had to be it. Her mind could not go to the ocean, so instead it produced a desert, but a hand reaching for her as she climbed a ladder had been correct if she could believe anything.

Cole accelerated and she held on for dear life. Sea spray slapped her in the face, adding to the chill factor. Remi focused again on the Scripture.

"The waves roar, O Lord, the waves roar, the waves roar and crash. Above the sound of the surging water, and the mighty waves of the sea, the Lord sits enthroned in majesty." Psalm 93:3–4.

God, you are still on your throne. Please help me.

Cole sped across the choppy water that jolted and bounced the vessel. The boat slammed into a bigger wave, and Remi was thrown from the seat.

She grimaced in pain but didn't yelp.

Surprisingly, Cole turned and glanced at her. "Are you all right?"

A strange question coming from him. She was too stunned to think of the right response. *No. I'm not okay, you jerk! I'm tied up. You abducted me. It's cold. I don't have a coat. Let me go, you murderer.*

She said nothing at all, to give him a taste of his own medicine.

He glanced back again, his expression one of concern. "You're cold. We're almost there and I can't stop."

Where was he taking her?

Then another glance. "You have to remember before it's too late."

Wasn't it already too late? She couldn't make her brain comply.

Having fallen out of the chair, she was still on the deck. He hadn't left the helm to put her back and instead remained focused on escape. With her arms and legs tied, where was she going to go?

Maybe he wouldn't notice if she inched away. Remi half

slid, half crawled away. The rain and wind lashed her once she was out from under the protection of the partially enclosed pilothouse. Then she crawled up onto a bench next to the rail. With the bouncing vessel, she feared at any moment she might be thrown into Puget Sound. Cautiously, she peered over the rail, hoping to see another boat that she could somehow signal for rescue.

She tried the trick she'd read about to free herself, but she couldn't pop the plastic ties off. She should crawl back into the wheelhouse before she froze to death or Cole caught her out here. Cole glanced over his shoulder. He'd caught her, but he didn't leave the helm to move her back closer to him. He was trusting those plastic ties to keep her close. She took the opportunity to glare at him. He returned his focus to the rough waters and continued speeding north. Where was he taking her?

To Charles Whitman? The name wasn't jogging anything in her memory. What was it going to take for her mind to free the information? Maybe she had no memories that pertained to this situation, none that were important anyway.

Remi shifted to peer over the rail again.

Another boat chased them.

Hawk! Hawk was alive, he'd survived. The gunshot had merely been meant to send him into hiding. Cole couldn't lose the guy. Hawk wouldn't give up. His determination infused her with hope.

And neither would Remi. She might have been haunted by her past, attacked and abducted, but now she was more determined than ever. She doubted Cole realized that his relentless pursuit, his psychological games, only made her stronger.

Remi carefully balanced and stood on the deck, hoping that Hawk would see her. She was counting on him to watch her make a risky move.

The boat hit a wave and flew up into the air, tossing her up as well, then suddenly swerved, cutting to the left so that she landed in the water. The shock of cold rolled through her. Heart pounding, she sucked in a breath before her body sank. While jumping out of the boat had been her plan, she'd wanted to make the choice of when and how. She kicked her bound legs, but it wasn't enough to keep her above the rippling waves that pounded her down and under.

28

Heart jackhammering, he laser-focused on the spot where Remi had disappeared beneath the chop.

She'd been standing when they hit the wave head-on, and then Cole had turned hard to port.

"Remi!" he shouted to the wind and rain, then slowed his boat as he approached. No time to drop anchor, he killed the engine. He risked the waves pushing the boat away from the spot where she'd gone in, but he couldn't risk hurting her with the boat or motor.

His shoulders tensed as he searched the water on both sides of the boat.

She hadn't come back up. He kept watch on Cole's vessel. His brother could turn around and come back as soon as he realized Remi was no longer with him. Or Cole could keep going because the harbor police were out searching the waters now.

Hawk was going in after her. He grabbed the flotation device and jumped in. To dive, he'd have to leave the device and hope it was near when he came up with Remi. Because he would come up with her. He wouldn't accept defeat.

He dove into the dark, cold waters and swam until he

reached the calm below the chop. He could barely see in the murky dimness. He spotted her struggling to reach the surface. Struggling and failing. Bubbles rippling from her mouth. He had to reach her before it was too late. Kicking hard, he grabbed her arms and dragged her up, shoving her above the water. She gasped and coughed.

"What took you so long?" She didn't smile with her question.

He was just happy he got to her. He'd wanted to find his brother and somehow fix him, and now, all he wanted to do was strangle him. But he let the anger go. They had to get to safety.

"Where's the boat?" she asked.

Where was the life preserver? Both were washed well out of reach in the brutally rough waves. They couldn't tread this for long. Except . . . wait . . . a Seattle Harbor Patrol boat sped toward them.

And slowed. Relieved, Hawk swam to the boat, pulling Remi with him since she was helpless with her wrists and ankles tied. A marine police officer assisted them aboard, cut off her plastic ties, then escorted them below deck, where it was warm. He offered them each blankets.

"Thanks." Hawk used it to wipe his face off and wrapped it around his body.

Remi did the same and then she sat in a booth.

"Glad to be of assistance. I'm Sergeant Medford."

"Hawk Beckett and Remi Grant. What's happening?" Hawk asked. "You're not letting him get away, are you?"

"Not letting who get away?"

"The man who shot John Marshall, and who abducted her." Hawk's voice hitched up with his anger.

"Why don't you tell me your version?"

"I will, but I want to know you're not letting him get away."

"The Harbor Patrol officers are handling this. Now, your version. Your statement." The man studied Hawk. "You're that pilot with King County Aerial Unit, aren't you?"

"I was, yes."

"You can't stay out of the news, can you?" He arched a brow.

Hawk shared a glance with Remi. "I guess not."

"John. How is he?" Remi asked.

"Last I heard he was being airlifted to UW Medical Center. Still alive."

"Where are you taking us?" she asked.

"We're heading back to the marina and dropping you off. I need to get your statements, please."

They each shared the events as they'd unfolded, but Hawk never mentioned that Cole was his brother, and the sergeant didn't ask questions that would require him to reveal he even knew who Cole was. That made him curious about what John had said, if he'd said anything at all to them. Hawk had taken off after Cole and Remi as soon as he could. Cole was a ghost, and if he took Remi, she'd be lost for good. Hawk didn't feel right about leaving John, but at the same time, he had to save Remi. Though that decision had been excruciating, it really wasn't that hard to make. Remi needed him. His friend had remained strong, though in pain, and Hawk had done all he could do for him. John had also urged Hawk after Remi, even as he was already halfway out the door.

Hawk had exited the house in time to watch Cole speeding away in what Hawk had previously assumed was John's boat.

"Why were you there to see Mr. Marshall?"

"He's my old CO. A friend." And that's all Hawk would say. He wasn't obligated to share more. Hawk half feared that he and Remi would be detained for more questioning.

Medford might have read his mind. "Marshall told us his version of what happened, and it jibes with yours."

Hawk would share the facts as he knew them, but he wouldn't answer questions that hadn't been asked or volunteer information. The Harbor Patrol dropped Hawk and Remi off at the marina where Hawk had left his vehicle. The police were out in full force to capture Cole Mercer.

Hawk's brother.

He'd seen Cole in action. Seen it with his own eyes. For John to tell them he'd been shot was one thing, but for Hawk to see it was another. Cole had fired at him as well, but he'd merely been throwing down cover so he could exit and escape with Remi. Hawk should take some comfort in the fact Cole hadn't killed her and so he wanted her alive for the moment. But for how long?

Inside the vehicle, Hawk cranked up the heat and let it idle.

Shame flooded him. Shame and grief. *God, I don't even know what to think or do.* His goal had always been to find his brother so he could somehow pull him back from the edge and save him. Then his mission had shifted to add keeping Remi safe as they searched for answers.

Hanging his head, he released a heavy exhale.

He felt hollowed out.

Maybe Hawk wasn't the person to save Cole, and he wasn't sure anyone besides God could.

God, are you listening? This isn't who Cole is. Please, save him!

Because I don't know what I'm going to do if he stays on this path or gets killed and is lost forever.

Remi had been quiet the entire time. She was likely in shock, and his concern for her kicked up. If only he could just take her back to the lodge and she could return to her life. The life she lived there in an effort to hide from all this.

Admit it. You have no idea what you're doing. Hawk squeezed the bridge of his nose. Then he reached over and lifted her chin. Turned her face toward him so he could see her eyes. A bold move on his part. "Are you okay?"

But he knew she wasn't. How could she be? He dropped his hand, but she kept her face turned toward him, her eyes locked with his. Her breaths quickened and his fear ratcheted up.

"What is it?" he asked. "What's the matter?"

"We're in a lot of trouble," she said. "More danger than we thought."

As if the news of Operation Blackout weren't enough. "Why do you say that?"

"Because . . . it's all coming back to me."

29

Memories bombarded her, rushed at her, igniting emotions, and filling her with dread. A hammer beat her head and she pressed her fingertips against her temples as if the action could stop the pain. Her chest constricted as she tried to breathe, but fear and terror paralyzed her.

Hawk gently grabbed her arms. "Take a deep breath. Just calm down."

The images . . . everything that had happened hit her all at once as if a curtain had suddenly lifted to reveal what had been hidden in her mind this whole time. Those memories had always been there, just beyond the veil, but she hadn't been able to access them.

"Remi, look at me. It's going to be okay."

How could he say that? He had no idea. Too much information hit her at once and none of it good.

"Breathe, Remi, breathe." He grabbed her hands. "Look at me."

She blinked a few times, then stared at him, his face filled with concern. Compassion. The cab filled with the sound of rain pummeling the truck and pavement. *Focus on Hawk.*

She drew in a breath, then released it. Then another. And another. In and out.

"Good, you're doing great. Keep it up."

Leaning back against the truck seat, she pulled her hands free from his and closed her eyes.

"Take your time," he said.

But tell him everything.

She opened her eyes again to peer at Hawk.

"Look," he said. "John already told me the operation name. He already gave me information, if you're concerned that Operation Blackout was classified. He was basically reading me in."

"Who *is* he to read you in? For that matter, who is he to read *me* in? I'm not *on* this mission, and I was never supposed to be part of it. I was just in the wrong place at the wrong time." She shook her head. "Classified or not, you need to know if you're going to finish this with me, and we'll deal with the fallout."

"I'm good with that."

She could do it. She had to tell someone. Hawk was it.

"I was at this café in the capital, Novograd. Sitting outdoors, taking in the sights. I planned to visit a castle that day."

"For the travel blog," he said.

"Yes. I hadn't gotten up the nerve to start it. Maybe if I had, then we'd have that record. But I kept seeing this guy, you know? Thirties. Glasses."

"You mean he was following you?"

"No. He kept coming to that same café. I was there for three days. I was taking shots of a gorgeous cathedral, you know, with the domes like you see in Russia. I decided to capture him in the photos. That's when I realized that someone was following *him*. I noticed the follower was packing too. I wasn't sure what to do. Warn him? And put myself in danger? Or mind my own business and leave him to his own troubles? Then the strangest thing happened. He approached and asked if he could sit at my table and then he sat down before I could respond."

"What would you have said?"

"I would have said yes. It would give me a chance to warn him. He smiled and spoke very good English, but with an accent. Turned out he wasn't happy that I had taken his picture. I showed him the pictures, and that's when I told him he was being followed.

"A bullet grazed the chair he was in. We both ducked. People screamed. I'm not sure if he grabbed me or I grabbed him, but the next thing you know, we're running down alleyways, and I was lost. But now and then, whoever was after him would catch up and bullets would fly again. Hitting much too close for comfort. I did what I could to protect this stranger, pushing him into doorways, yanking him down other alleys, whatever it took to cover and protect him so the bullets wouldn't hit either of us. I guess my former military training just kicked in or maybe it was the will to survive."

Remi shook her head. "We ducked into a church and hid in the confessional. Not sure how long we were there, but it had to be hours. He said he was trying to escape the country and asked if I could help him get to his extraction point."

"Why would he want you to do that?"

"I think he was scared, for one thing. Plus, he knew that I was an American and had been in the Army." She shrugged. "When you're hiding in a confessional, you say a lot of things. Like, I learned his name was Sergei Petrov. I had helped him stay alive so far, and so he seemed desperate for me to stick with him until, and I quote, 'the Americans get him out.' At first, he even believed that I was part of the extraction team, sent there to watch over him and assist him to the meeting place. To be honest, at that point, I felt I needed an extraction too. I had no idea what I'd gotten myself into."

His expression remained grim. Serious. "Where were the Zarovian police?"

"Oh, they showed up, searching the city. We slipped out of the church late at night and headed into the countryside. Sergei warned me against talking to them. He was a wanted man, and I had just helped him. I decided I'd be better off letting the Americans who were extracting him figure this out, so I agreed to help him get to the extraction point. We found our way to a small village at the base of the Carpathian Mountains, then we were extracted."

"Give me the details."

"Soldiers—American soldiers—showed up. We didn't even know they were there. Two of them. They took us to wait for a helicopter. There was an argument at first over taking me too, but Sergei refused to go without me. He was bluffing, of course, but if I stayed behind, then I was going to be running anyway. The helicopter started lifting off, and I climbed up the ladder. Another soldier was behind me, but Cole reached for me. I wasn't over water or in the desert like I initially thought."

"So, Cole was there to help initially." Hope rose in his eyes.

I haven't finished the story!

"Sergei must be some kind of high-payoff target," he added. "What else do you know?"

"Well, I know a lot. More than I'm supposed to. With all those hours together, he told me more than he should have, but he was nervous. I think he just needed to talk. He was afraid. He's a scientist, a physicist, who developed technology and weapons for the Zarovian military. Well, he *was* anyway. He's dead now. He'd been working on a new project but learned that someone within the government agency in which he worked was selling the project to an arms dealer—Charles Whitman. I didn't recognize his name when John brought him up, but Sergei told me about him."

"Now we know where Whitman fits in."

"Sergei didn't feel comfortable with what he knew would happen to his project. He spoke to his supervisor about his concerns, and a week later, that man died—radiation poisoning."

"Murder?"

"Yes. The effect was instant. Sergei feared for his own life. He couldn't tell another soul. When Sergei was speaking at a conference in Europe, someone within our government approached him."

"A CIA operative?"

"Maybe. He didn't say. And arrangements were made. If he delivered the project to the US instead, so that it wouldn't land in the hands of a notorious arms dealer who had arranged to sell it to a terrorist group targeting US soil, then he could be extracted. He couldn't just get on a plane to the United States. Zarovia is a post-Soviet democracy."

"So, still struggled with political instability. I get it," Hawk said.

"He was too valuable for his government and, unfortunately, to the unscrupulous government official who planned to sell to the arms dealer."

"And the tale grows darker still," Hawk said. "Sounds like US intelligence was hard at work thwarting a plot against Americans. What else do you know?"

"Sergei was able to have the device sent somewhere."

"It's crazy to think he got away with that when it sounds

like he was being watched closely." Hawk rubbed his forehead, looking more haggard than she'd seen him in the almost three days she'd known him.

This was bad. Really bad. Dangerous bad.

"What about this device you mentioned?" he asked.

Remi had a sudden thought, and she could hardly breathe. "You're not a spy, are you? Sent to get close to me and find out what I know?"

"While that's within the realm of possibility, no, I'm not a spy." His smile was filled with sadness and compassion. "Remi, you're in so deep."

"Well, since you're not a spy, are you sure you want to know? Because telling you could put you in danger."

He scoffed a laugh. "I'm in this with you now."

They remained sitting in his vehicle in the parking lot, the rain coming down in sheets. He was probably waiting for her to get to the part about his brother. Maybe he couldn't drive and focus on the conversation. She didn't blame him.

"What's this about?" he asked. "What's the device that Sergei sent?"

"I'll get there, Hawk. But I think you want to hear this next part."

"Cole."

She nodded. Tears spilled, and she didn't care. "On the helicopter extraction that night, I was strapped in next to Sergei. He should have felt relieved, but he was so nervous. I remember he looked at me when I tried to reassure him and said, 'You don't understand. They don't let you go. Ever. I'll never be safe. I'll never be free, and neither will you.'

"Then chaos erupted. Alarms sounded. The helicopter started spinning. There was lots of shouting and cursing. I think the pilots were trying to land before we crashed." Remi squeezed her eyes shut, but she couldn't stop the flood. She'd been a soldier. She should have been able to tell this story without tears, but her emotions were running high as she relived it.

"It's okay, Remi. I'm sure it was terrifying."

She opened her eyes. "I know you understand. You've been through it. I'm glad you're here, Hawk. I'm glad you're the one in this with me." And she was. She truly was. She squeezed his hand.

"I need to know what you were going to say about Cole."

Right. She released his hand and wiped her cheeks. "I don't know what I saw, really. There was fighting in the group. Sergei told me the extraction had been compromised and we needed to jump. He said we were over water. I think he pushed me out. It all happened fast, and I'm having trouble with details. I remember seeing an explosion."

"What happened next?"

"I woke up in the hospital."

Hawk shifted in his seat. "And this device, the reason they wanted Sergei?"

"Some leading-edge electromagnetic-pulse device. He called it the Tempest device."

"An EMP device. The name Operation Blackout makes sense now. An EMP knocks out all electronics. But that's nothing new." Hawk sounded almost incredulous. Definitely suspicious.

"No, but . . ." She squeezed the bridge of her nose. *Focus. Remember.* "The military is always looking for cutting-edge technology. I don't think Sergei wanted to be in weapons, but he was forced there. He explained the big race between countries. Everyone wants high-powered electromagnetic weapons for both offense and defense. It could mean the difference in gaining the upper hand and winning in a conflict."

"Yeah, but what did *Sergei's* device bring to the table?"

"He developed an extremely portable and compact weapon with focus targeting. I mean, it could even be used from a drone."

Hawk nodded. "In other words, in enemy hands, a critical infrastructure or military equipment could be taken out while our enemies wouldn't be affected by that same pulse. So, the terrorist organization that wanted to use it against us could be planning for something catastrophic. Take out Air Force One or other planes. I can think of so many terrible possibilities. Maybe they planned to target a nuclear reactor. I don't know."

"I do."

"What do you mean you do?"

Nausea roiled inside. "Sergei hacked into the traitorous official's email and learned of the plans. First, I asked Sergei the same thing—I mean, about the nuclear reactor. He said with all the multiple fail-safe systems in place, an EMP couldn't do much. Especially since those shutdown systems are analog, they wouldn't be affected."

"But what more? If not that, then what are they planning to target? The power grid?"

"One of our most vulnerable critical infrastructures—the water supply. They're planning to target the water supply and distribution networks of multiple large populations, introducing a radiologic threat agent—"

"Wait. You mean, radioactive material?"

Remi had to slow her racing heartbeat. "With the Tempest device, they can specifically target and disrupt the contamination detection systems, and communications as well, so that after they contaminate the water, millions of people could be affected before anyone even knew what was happening—because, again, it's very specifically targeted and affects nothing around the target. When someone makes the discovery, their ability to stop the flow of water—

anything at all—would be taken out long enough . . ." She hung her head. "Why do people come up with such horrible ways to hurt other humans?"

"I don't know, Remi. I just don't know."

She stared out the window at the rain, pure, unadulterated water falling from the sky, washing the air and the earth. "I'm not a scientist and I think Sergei did a great job explaining it, but I wish he hadn't. Why didn't I ask him to stop? Now I know something I shouldn't know." Something too horrible to imagine.

"I'm done sitting here. We need to get moving." He turned on the wipers, then exited the parking lot, steered through the side streets, then sped onto the freeway.

Fear had edged his voice, and it added to the terror already coursing through her. Rain whipped the windshield, and the wipers moved fast, the rhythm beating with that of her heart.

Hawk glanced at her and back to the road. Back and forth.

Remi. The road. Remi.

"And Cole knows this, or suspects you know it, so he wanted you dead. But . . . now he wants you alive. What haven't you told me?"

"You want to know why he suddenly needs me. What could I remember that's so important? Someone wants the information before they kill me." Remi knew. Now she got it. *Oh, Lord in heaven, please help me!* "I know where it's hidden. The science. The documents explaining the build. And the prototype device."

"Why did he tell you that?"

"In case he didn't make it. In a way, he was in the wrong place at the wrong time just like I was. In that way, we're the same. Who knew a camera could get me into so much trouble?" She shook her head. "I wonder if it's already too late."

"This was never supposed to be your battle, your fight."
Remember before it's too late.

She sucked in a breath and looked at Hawk. "Is there some sort of countdown, a timeline for when the weapon will be used?"

"Someone has to find it first." He gave her a hard look.

And Remi might be the only living person who knew where the device was.

30

And that's why they needed to hand this off to someone else as soon as possible. Hawk had been pulled into this quagmire from two directions that had intersected.

Remi and Cole.

"I hope that John is recovering, because he knows about this," Hawk said. "He needs to know what you just told me."

John could be off the project now, but he was their best chance at containment.

"So, you want me to tell your former CO, John, what I've remembered." She almost sounded incredulous.

That confused him. "Why wouldn't I?"

"He questioned me. He followed me."

"And there's a good reason for that. Did he explain that to you? I heard you talking."

She shrugged and shook her head. "He said he was protecting me."

"You sound like you don't believe him."

"I don't know what to believe."

"Well, what we do know is that John is connected to this through his intelligence contacts. It seems to me he protected you." If John had sent Hawk there for that purpose, he could have informed him. That didn't sit right with him, but there were too many moving parts right now. He knew for sure that Cole was a big part of the chaos.

"But can you trust John, Hawk? We need to be absolutely sure."

"I'm as positive we can trust John Marshall as I can ever be about anything. And handing this off is the best thing we can do. You can get back to your life." He hoped. Remi had been put in a precarious situation by this Sergei Petrov. What had the guy been thinking? What an idiot. Scientists could be idiots, couldn't they? He clearly was unaccustomed to clandestine operations and had dumped all the secretive intel on Remi, a civilian, because of proximity, fear, and pressure.

Once Remi was out of danger, then Hawk could focus solely on Cole. For what purpose, he was no longer sure. When John had given him the intel that Cole had gone to the dark side, Hawk had held on to hope that the information was inaccurate. But Remi's story confirmed that Cole had been involved with this Sergei business from the start. He wasn't simply a hired assassin. He could even be working with Whitman. Maybe it had been the plan to take the helicopter down before Petrov was in American hands. But they were missing a lot of information to know the reasons the extraction had been sabotaged.

"Can I really get my life back?" she asked. "How do you suggest I do that? Because from where I'm sitting, I don't see it."

"If we can hand this off and somehow transfer the information that makes you the target, then you can go back to your lodge and still be there at the height of storm-watching season."

Yeah. He was dreaming. When did things ever go that right? But a person had to dream sometimes to make it through.

"I'll think about it," she said. "But before I talk to him, I want to know more about it. I want to do some research of my own. What if there's something more? Something else I need to do? Some agency I need to provide with this vital information?"

"I agree," he said.

"You do?" She arched a brow as if agreement from him was foreign to her.

"Yes. That's why . . ." He steered through the gated community of his condo.

"We're back at your place?" she huffed. "Why? This place is already compromised."

"Cole is on the run. I know my brother. He isn't going to come back here."

Could Hawk be absolutely positive about that? He hadn't thought Cole would find it to begin with. And he didn't miss Remi averting her gaze right after the slight roll of her eyes.

"How safe could it be if he found you and was able to break in?"

"While that's a good point, it's the safest place at the moment. And we're here. You think because Cole has changed and he's so different now that I don't know him?"

Now that he said the words out loud, he doubted them. He didn't truly know Cole. He didn't understand what was going on. Regardless, he had already reviewed footage from the cameras around the area on his burner smartphone. Nothing. He did it again in case something had changed since he'd last checked. Usually he got an alert, but that didn't always work. They should be safe here for the time being. His brother wasn't here. According to his cameras, Cole hadn't approached the condo. The suspicious vehicle that had set Hawk on edge had finally left. No one besides the few usual tenants who'd snatched up a condo deal in the old renovated warehouse had entered the parking lot.

They got out of the vehicle, climbed the stairs, and entered the condo.

Remi had to be reeling from the sudden burst of total recall, because *he* was reeling from the story she'd shared.

"I need to catch my breath," he said. "I'm sure you do too. I'll cook a frozen casserole for a late lunch. You can clean up, shower if you want. You got dunked in salt water after all."

"Yeah, I need to get out of these clothes. I can wear your too-large sweats and T-shirt and wash these again."

Hawk decided to cook the frozen lasagna in the oven rather than the microwave, that way it would taste only a little bit more like a home-cooked meal. He hadn't had a home-cooked meal in far too long. Remi emerged with wet hair and wearing a Seahawks T-shirt and navy-blue sweatpants that hung off her, even though she'd tied the pants at the waist. She hiked them back up and scrunched her face. She was too cute.

She eased onto the couch and rested her head. Closed her eyes. "If we keep this up, we should stop by a store so I can grab some more clothes, you know, just to switch things up."

He hoped this would end sooner rather than later, but she was right. "Good idea. My turn to clean up. The lasagna won't be ready for another forty-five minutes or so."

After a quick hot shower, Hawk felt three thousand times better. When he came out, Remi had set the small table with dishes. He only kept four plates, which was more than enough.

"You know what's weird?" she asked.

"No. What?"

"You don't have nearly enough windows in this place, and the view isn't that great either. I'm feeling claustrophobic."

"I figured you'd say as much. After all, you lived on the coast and got to watch the ocean every day."

"Yeah, I really miss my lodge. I got accustomed to the panoramic view." Her hand covered her heart. "Did I just call it mine?"

He nodded. "You did."

"It's not mine, not by a long stretch. But I miss it. When I first stayed there, it was to have time to get my memories back. Dr. Holcomb said to just focus on nature and enjoy the peace and quiet, far away from distractions. I started taking pictures of the ocean. Of the forest. It was magical."

He smiled. "The waves crashing against the rocks enraptured me too."

"Enraptured, huh?"

"What? Can't I use big words?" He moved to the kitchen to get them water.

"Of course you can. But it sounded unnatural coming from you."

"It's just that I can't think of any other word to describe it. And it's how I felt when I saw your photos, so I get it."

"My photos made you feel things?"

"Enraptured." She was right. That did sound funny, but it was still a good word.

He slowly approached. She'd been through so much. When he'd pulled this woman from certain death, he couldn't have known that her beautiful eyes would snag him, draw him in. Nor could he have known their lives were already entangled.

She stared at him now, her gaze shimmering with expectation. "Really?"

The question was almost breathless, and he couldn't help himself. He stepped closer and looked down at her. *Believe me . . .* "Really."

He felt the draw, the pull, and the crazy desire again to kiss her. Yeah, it was crazy. She was in danger. Vulnerable. He'd be a jerk if he followed through, but he could at least try to ignore the fact that he wanted to. He took a step back to give them both room to breathe. Clear their heads.

And then, of all things, disappointment flooded her beautiful gaze. Hawk couldn't win, but he was doing the right thing. And the sooner he got her back to the lodge, the better for them both, at least on a more personal level.

The oven timer dinged. "Lasagna's up."

"I'll get it," she said.

"No, you set the table. I'll get it." He rushed to the kitchen, grabbed oven mitts, and pulled the steaming casserole out.

"Normally it needs to rest for a few minutes." Remi had come up beside him after setting the table. "Or else it'll just fall apart. It needs to set."

"Okay." And there she was in his space again, but he could tell that her thoughts had moved away from whatever the oven timer had interrupted between them.

"I didn't plan to stay so long at Cedar Trails. I mean, why would I want to stay there when I had planned to travel the world and write a travel blog? But I didn't have unlimited funds, so I'd need to do it on the cheap," she said. "Obviously I got caught up in my life at the lodge. I pretended it was my *real* life."

"It was your real life. It is your life. The here and now. This present moment is your life. Not the past or some future dream that may or may not come true. It doesn't matter that circumstances seemed to bring you here, that's part of it. Haven't you heard the old saying that life is what happens when you're busy making plans?"

Looking at him, she ducked her chin. "Wise words from someone so young."

She made him laugh with that one. He hadn't laughed in a long time. "I don't know whether to be hurt because you didn't think I could say the word *enraptured*, and now you act like I don't ever say anything that comes across as wisdom."

"It was meant to be a compliment." She sent him a soft smile.

He didn't let his gaze linger on her lips but started cutting up the lasagna. "I'm hungry, and I'm not waiting any longer."

She left his side and rushed back to grab the plates from the table. "We can just plate it here. It's easier."

Using two spatulas, he tried to get a square piece onto each plate, but the layers didn't remain completely intact. "Doesn't matter. It tastes the same."

"Thanks for making it."

They took their plates back to the table and dug in and ate in silence for a few moments.

"You said you missed the lodge," he said. "You can't wait to get back, can you?"

"I miss the breeze."

"You mean the wind. There's rarely anything breezy on the Pacific Northwest coast."

She smiled. "Okay, I miss the wind. And I love the storms, as long as I don't have to be standing out in them or hiding

246

from a villain, but I fell in love. I guess I sort of lost myself there."

"Or . . . maybe you found yourself."

After she finished a bite, she angled her head as if thinking. "Maybe."

Yeah, Hawk had a feeling that Cedar Trails Lodge might be her permanent home. She'd fit in and, before everything had hit, was in a good place.

"But then again, I was pretending that I didn't have this dark secret chasing me, closing in on me." Her shoulders dropped. "Honestly, I hoped it would go away silently. I should have done more to find answers before things got out of hand."

"You were doing what your doctor advised. Don't beat yourself up." He could go down that dark and lonely road too, and he did often, wondering what he could have done differently to prevent his brother from traveling this path that led nowhere good. But he had to accept that he had no control over his brother, over others. No control over their decisions.

"Listen to me, whining about my life. Hawk . . ." She slid her hand across the table as if she would press it over his, but she just left it there. Just reaching out from her heart? "Your brother. I'm so sorry this is happening."

"After everything Cole has put you through, you can say this?"

"Yes. You didn't make the decision for him. He isn't . . . you. And I can't imagine how hard it must be."

I believe you. He saw so much compassion in her expression, his heart melted, but with the thaw he felt so much more anguish over his brother. He cared deeply, grieved so long, that he had to build up a wall to protect himself. Anyone would. If he was going to make it through, he needed to keep that wall up, so he pressed his hand over hers, felt the warmth there, the softness of her skin. He ignored the sudden longing that coursed through him. The need to be close to someone and build a life. He pulled his hand away and then stood, grabbed their plates, and moved to wash them in the sink. He had to focus on what to do next.

He finished washing the dishes while Remi sauntered around in the living room. He didn't want to look at her and see disappointment again or that he'd hurt her. It seemed unreasonable that he was even thinking along these lines, under the circumstances.

He dried the two dishes and the utensils and put them away. Wiped down the counter. Frowned at the leftover lasagna. Would they stay here long enough to finish it off? He covered it and stuck it in the fridge. Then headed to face Remi in the living room.

She'd taken a corner of the sofa, her legs propped up and her chin on her arm.

"Look, we'll wrap this up as quickly as possible. Talk to John in the hospital. And if all goes well, you can go back to the lodge and be free of the past."

"I'd love that. I really would. But I can't shake the feeling it won't be that easy."

His fears exactly. But he couldn't let that distract him. At the opposite end of the sofa, Hawk sat on the edge. "It's time to figure things out."

"Like who all the players are besides Cole."

A traitor to his country. Hawk couldn't even think about his brother now without seething inside.

"I'm not sure we need to know any of that. We're not taking this on. We just need to make sure that we deliver the information to the right person at the right agency. You've been targeted, and that's before anyone knew with certainty that you held on to high-value information."

"So, you think John will know how to help. But what if he doesn't? Who do we talk to? The FBI, CIA, DOD? And I could keep going with all the many government agency acronyms."

"Probably the Department of Defense. Operation Blackout has to be some kind of SOCOM—Special Operations Command—mission."

"Do you know the guy at the top so you can call him and get me an appointment? Because if you don't, how do I find the right person to talk to? How can I get someone to take me seriously when I say I have information that involves national security? The feds must get all kinds of kooks. And I can't afford to tell just *anyone* my story, really. It's too risky. As for John, have you heard anything? Is he even still alive?"

He shook his head. "John's wife died three years ago, so it's not like I can reach out to family. I don't know his kids. Since I'm not family, I can't call the hospital to ask about his status."

"No, but you could call. He's a patient. Maybe they'll put you through to his room. If he doesn't have a room, then we know he's either in surgery or recovery, or if nothing else, then maybe we'll learn that he didn't make it."

"You have a point. I'm holding on to hope that he'll reach out to me when he's able, and that he'll recover from the bullet wound." Inflicted on him by Cole. Law enforcement alerts had to be out on his brother by now.

Hawk seethed inside. He grieved. Two conflicting emotions battled for attention.

He checked the communication app where John would reach out to him, but there was no activity. Surely the man would reach out as soon as he was able. He understood how important it was. Under normal circumstances, Hawk would be at the hospital in the waiting room, eager to know what was going on, but with Remi being targeted, he'd wait until he knew John was ready to talk to them.

"Whatever we do next," Hawk said, "I want to make sure we're not digging ourselves even deeper into the wrong side. Let's find out what we can in case John is unable to help."

Remi paced and pressed her fingers against her lips. He wasn't entirely sure she'd heard him.

"Let's say Charles Whitman is still actively after the device," she said. "He could have been the one to hire Cole."

"To kill you?"

"But that's just it. Cole didn't when he had the chance. And I have no idea who could have sent me the message to remember."

"Do you know what the puzzle pieces were about now?"

"I only had two pieces before we left the lodge. It's hard to tell, but it could have been the church next to the café. But now that I've remembered everything, I don't think the image that the puzzle pieces would create—if I ever get them all—matters."

Her eyes grew wide. "Wait. How does someone *know* that I'd forgotten something important? I'm the only one alive who can know that. If Sergei was alive, he would know what he told me. No one was with us in the confessional or on the journey through the countryside to the village."

"See, here's the thing. You were *seen* with Sergei. He approached you right before someone tried to take him out, and the hero in you instinctively took over."

"The hero in me? How about the survivor in me. Someone was shooting. Everyone ran."

"Yeah, but *you* ran with Sergei. Sergei approached you, sat at your table, then you left together. On the surface, that could be taken to mean you planned everything and that you know his secrets. And maybe someone wants you to remember before Cole comes for you. It could be as simple as that. Whoever is behind targeting you, whoever is behind wanting to know your story, they *suspect* that Sergei could have told you vital information. And guess what—he *did* tell you vital information."

"And I wish he hadn't."

"That means you know more than anyone else. Even Charles Whitman."

"I'm being hunted by an assassin and an arms dealer."

God, help me protect her!

31

anger was closing in.

Remi feared her days were short. "I ran from John, but now I see that he was just trying to protect me . . . at least from a distance." She shared a look with Hawk. "And he almost paid with his life."

"In general, I trust no one, but if I'm going to trust someone, John's the man. He saved my life, Remi. Back on a mission. Risked his own to save me. So it's all going to work out. He knows about the operation. He'll know who you need to talk to. And he can make that happen."

It was their best next step, unless they wanted to retrieve the device themselves, but she wouldn't touch that with the proverbial ten-foot pole. That would be foolish and dangerous. Knowing the location was already too much. She appreciated that Hawk had never pressured her about *where* the device had been hidden.

Over the next hour, she finished up her laundry but stayed in the sweats. She found Hawk at the table on his laptop, his expression dark as he worked.

"Anything from John?" she asked.

He looked up from the laptop and shook his head.

"If it's all the same to you, I'm going to take a nap."

"I think that's a good idea. Honestly, I don't think we'll hear anything from John or find anything out today. It's too soon. We'll plan on staying here for the night. Get some rest. Eat leftover lasagna for dinner." He grinned.

And she smiled in return, then headed for bed, hoping she could put the events of the day, and her memories, out of her mind and get some rest.

Lord, please let this be over soon.

She was beyond done with this metaphorical storm and ready to get to the lodge she called home. At Cedar Trails, her only concern was for her guests, and she found hope and inspiration in the beauty of God's creation and the power of the waves during the storms. She longed for the calm that came after.

Because right now, her mind was spinning with catastrophic images and morbid memories.

A helicopter crash.

Sergei Petrov dead.

The special forces team dead.

Murdered?

All Remi could think about was ridding herself of this burden. In her job in the Army, she worked to take pictures and present a positive image of the good guys doing their jobs.

Why had Sergei shared so much? Why had she let him? Now in her head she carried around military secrets that dangerous men wanted and that could pose a national threat. Inside, she was screaming. She should have known better than to get involved with a stranger on the run from gunmen, but she had. There was no returning from that decision. And she'd needed to know what kind of trouble she was in by helping a stranger. The gunmen could have been sent to make sure that Sergei didn't defect with his country's most important military secrets. From his government's point of view, Sergei was a bad guy. A traitor. She wasn't sure if they had been informed of his death.

She hadn't realized the knowledge would end up putting her in so much danger even two years later. Then again, the information in the right hands could save people. She had a responsibility to deliver it.

After an entire hour of trying to fall asleep—because her body said she needed it, but her mind refused—she crawled out of bed. Remi found Hawk still sitting at the table.

He looked up from his laptop. "Did you get some rest?"

"No." Remi sank into the comfy sofa. No wonder Hawk wanted her to sleep on the bed. The sofa was better.

And the next thing Remi knew, she woke up . . . on the sofa. She laid her arm over her eyes. She got the distinct impression she'd taken a very long nap, when she hadn't meant to fall asleep at all. She peeked out from under her arm when she sensed that Hawk stood over her.

"What . . . is dinner ready?"

"You missed it. We're eating leftover lasagna for breakfast. That okay?"

"What?" She sat up. "I slept through the night?"

"Yes."

"Why didn't you wake me up?"

"I tried."

"You didn't try hard enough."

"Well, full disclosure, I didn't try at all. I let you sleep. You needed it."

"Did you take the bed, then?"

"You had the sofa, what else was I going to do?"

She rubbed her eyes. "Any news from John?"

A ding suddenly came through on Hawk's burner cell. "I

was going to say no, but let me read this. It's from John. I sent this number to him via an app we use to communicate. It's easier."

"What does it say?"

"He asked us to come to the hospital. He'll have a security detail in place so we can talk there."

Remi wasn't so sure this was a good idea. "You don't think Cole will try something there?"

"Security is everywhere. And we *need* to talk to him. You can tell him what you remember." Hawk frowned. Was he second-guessing this decision because she was?

"Let's go, then. Honestly, I can't eat lasagna for breakfast. Let's just grab coffee and food on the go."

A half hour later, she'd showered and changed into her clean clothes, and Hawk drove through a coffee kiosk in Gordo's vehicle because Hawk intended to return it today, if possible. After coffee and croissants were acquired, Hawk steered them back onto the freeway.

"Oh, Hawk, I put your clothes I wore last night in the wash. Don't forget to put them in the dryer or they'll mildew." Wow. Had she really just said that?

He laughed. "I'm sure you're ready to get into your own closet in your own place."

Yeah. Her own place.

"While that sounds nice, you know as well as I do that until the device and information are retrieved, I could still be in danger. Even then I could be looking over my shoulder for a long time."

He pressed his hand on the console near hers. She sensed he might reach for her hand. Touch her arm. Something. Maybe she would be the one to do it because she needed his touch and reassurance. She hadn't realized just how much.

"I'm in this with you for as long as it takes," he said.

"I appreciate that." But she wasn't sure that it was necessary. At some point, he'd have to go back to his life, and she'd go back to hers, whatever the future held for her.

Hawk was a good man, and she'd known a lot of good men. That's why she couldn't fathom that his brother would be his polar opposite. From Cole's point of view, he could even believe he was a good guy.

Remi blew out a breath.

"What is it?" Hawk asked.

"Sergei said something and I can't stop thinking about it. He'd been put between the proverbial rock and hard place and had no choice but to flee as he did. He said that his country would think of him as a traitor. They would believe he was taking their military secrets to America. But they wouldn't understand that he was preventing the device from getting into the hands of terrorists via their own government official. He'd tried to warn them, but the messenger had been silenced and, if Sergei stayed, he would be dead too. It was all in the perception his departure created, and the spin the Zarovian government would craft for the public."

"As it turned out, there was no hope of him surviving this." Hawk shook his head.

"It's all about perspective," she said.

And actually, Hawk had said the same thing earlier.

"What are you getting at?" he asked.

"When I was on the boat with Cole and he was speeding away, trying to take me to—I don't know—his secret lair and torture me? He said these words exactly . . . 'Remember before it's too late.'"

Oh . . .

"You're too quiet. What is it?" he asked.

Then she looked at Hawk. "Just hear me out."

"I will as soon as you tell me."

"Cole must be the one who sent the message. He needed me to remember, before it's too late."

"Those words are generic, why would you think he was the one?" Hawk asked.

"I'm not sure, but I think we're missing something important. I just don't know what it is."

"Even if he was, that doesn't mean anything more than he needs the information you have. It doesn't change anything."

"Fine. Maybe you're right. Let's go see John." But she wasn't all that sure she was going to share the location of the Tempest device with anyone until she talked to the top brass in charge.

Lord, open the doors. Close the doors. Lead us and guide us. Reveal the truth. Show me who I need to give this information to. In the hands of the wrong party, it could tilt the balance of power and change the future.

Finally, Hawk steered them into the hospital parking garage.

She wiped her palms on her jeans. Her nerves were getting the best of her. She'd already met this man and looked forward to seeing him in better health, but she was getting closer to sharing a lot of delicate intelligence she was never supposed to have. And . . . maybe John wasn't the right guy after all.

Hawk opened the doors to the main lobby for her, then together they headed to the north tower elevators. She suspected that Hawk was more than anxious to see his friend. In the hospital, familiar sensations bombarded her, reminding her of Germany.

I'm being watched.

We're being watched.

She shouldn't have expected anything less. While it could be a good thing that John had a protection detail—and, by extension, Remi and Hawk while there—that fact made her uneasy. Next to her, the tension rolling off Hawk increased.

They shared an elevator with an elderly woman in a wheelchair and someone—her daughter, maybe?—in her sixties pushing the chair.

"We'll be there soon, Mom."

Hawk and Remi stood behind them, giving them the right-of-way to exit the elevator first. She risked a glance at him. His jaw was working. What was he thinking? Was he second-guessing this plan to talk to John? Hawk had maintained this was their best option—tell the man everything and let him take it from here.

The elevator stopped. The doors slid open, and the daughter pushed her mother out. The doors whooshed closed again. These could be the last moments they would be alone before seeing John.

"What does the company he works for do, even as a front?" she asked.

"Conclave Assets. That was the name. He told me it's an import-export business but a front for an intelligence firm."

"And he didn't mean a private investigation company. Did you verify that information? Do we know anything at all about it other than what he said?"

"I already knew he worked at the company, but I didn't know it was a front. It has a website, I checked. This is what we know. We know that John is our best contact right now, and for no other reason than he already knows about the operation, and we can learn more from him. We've been over this." Hawk shot her a sideways glance.

"You didn't even know he was involved before. You can't—"

The door whooshed open, and Remi said nothing more as they stepped out into the hall. She was letting her doubts take over. Cole was the bad guy here. Cole had abducted her.

He'd abducted Jo. She needed to remember that. But there could be numerous parties after the information she had.

After studying the room-number signs, they headed toward a hallway that should take them to John's room. Two men stood outside his door, deep in conversation using hushed tones. A man stepped out in front of them from a side hall and smiled. He wore an official-looking suit and had the air and haircut of a federal agent. "Mr. Beckett. Ms. Grant. Mr. Marshall would like to speak with you. He thought you might have gotten lost." He gestured behind them. "I can show you the way."

They allowed the man to accompany them to the room.

Looked like they were doing this. How much, or how little, should she tell John that she'd remembered? Very little. Nothing vital. She only needed one thing from him—to contact the person in authority over Operation Blackout.

32

Hawk's situational awareness spiked. This was a hospital. Nothing could happen here. Scratch that. Nothing *would* happen here. John had a security detail protecting him. Cole wasn't going to show up here to finish him off or to try again to get his hands on Remi.

He and Remi stepped into John's hospital room, ushered there by a bodyguard.

Hawk's heart pounded. He thought he'd prepared himself to see his friend again. Tubes were hooked up to him and monitors beeped away, and the sight slammed Hawk in the gut. He kept his composure. Made sure Remi was close by his side. Close enough to protect.

The wounded man's eyes were closed. Was he sleeping after sending his bodyguard to get them? He suddenly opened his lids and looked around the room, his gaze finally settling on Hawk.

"John." Hawk stepped closer and forced a smile. "You're looking better than expected."

"I'm feeling better than I thought I would too. If it wasn't for you, I'd be dead. You got there just in time."

His thoughts racing, Hawk said nothing. John nodded at his bodyguard, and the man stepped out of the room and shut the door.

"Who is that guy, John?"

"You don't think I need a security detail after being shot by an assassin?"

An assassin who had missed the mark. "I didn't say that. But I get the feeling you already had a security detail ready." Except they hadn't been present at his home to protect him then.

"What's going on? Who do you really work for?" Hawk tried to keep accusation out of his voice.

"How long have we known each other?" John hadn't missed Hawk's less-than-trusting tone.

"Long enough," Hawk said. "That's why I don't understand why you've kept all this from me."

"Intelligence work, Hawk, means secrets. It's a balancing act of loyalties to my country, my job, and those who trust me. So please, trust me to keep you safe."

"So, you're not going to tell me."

"I might have said too much when I was injured." Lines deepened around his mouth and eyes.

"You didn't say enough. What's this operation about? Why is Cole after Remi?" Might as well play ignorant.

The door promptly opened, and the security dude stepped inside.

"It's okay, Banks," John said. "I'm good."

The man stepped back out into the hall.

"I can't tell you," John said. "Knowing more will put you in that much more danger."

If only you understood. "How much more danger can Remi be in? She's a target, man. Cole snatched her right out of your home."

"I get it. You don't know what to do next. I'll help you

with that, but I need to know, Remi . . ." John shifted his gaze to her. "What have you remembered?"

She shared a look with Hawk, and he nodded, trusting her to share what she felt comfortable with.

"I fell out of a helicopter. There was an explosion and I think the helicopter crashed."

"Do you remember why you were on the helicopter?"

"While I don't remember much, I feel uncomfortable talking about this."

John fisted his hands and pounded the sheet. "Your life is in danger, girl. If you remember something, I need to know."

"Hawk seems to think you can help us connect with . . . um . . ."

"Connect with who?"

"I don't know," she said. "That's why we're here."

Girl? Hawk had enough. "John, you know she's right. You seem to know something about what's going on. What Remi and I need is to know who was in charge of Operation Blackout. Remi will talk to that person only."

John closed his eyes and leaned against his pillow. Were they overtaxing him? Or was it just an act? He put on a strong front despite the fact that he was still recovering from a gunshot wound that almost took his life.

He opened his eyes. "I'm in communication with the high-ranking official you need. I'll make the necessary arrangements for you to meet. I'm sure he'll be anxious to learn what you've remembered. I have a feeling there's more, but you're not telling me, and that's understandable. You're doing the right thing." John leveled his gaze on Remi. He'd been trained in how to read people.

Hawk was torn between his fierce loyalty to John and trusting his instincts about this situation. He stepped forward. "John, I—"

Cutting him off, John held up his hand, his expression one of understanding. "Please, Hawk. She is to be commended for her diligence in insisting on only speaking to those authorized to hear what she has to say."

A nurse entered, and the bodyguard stepped inside and held the door open as if he had some read on John's desire for them to leave now. They were of no use to him if Remi wasn't going to share.

"I'll be in touch, Hawk. Until then, keep her safe."

"And you trust me to do that? Why aren't you insisting that Remi go to a safe house, a secure location, if you believe she is holding on to highly sensitive information?"

"Remi trusts *you* to do it. You have the necessary skills and training. You haven't failed her yet. You won't fail me either."

Way to put the pressure on while also making Hawk feel a little guilty for doubting his friend.

"I know that because Cole is in custody," John said.

Feeling the sucker punch to his core, Hawk released a surprised exhale. "What? When did this happen?" Myriad emotions charged through his heart and mind and clamped down on his chest, squeezing. Hawk had to work to remain composed, but John had to know how much this news affected him.

"I was informed right before you arrived. I don't have details yet. But he won't threaten her anymore." To Remi, he said, "Take your time. Give yourself the space to fully recall the facts and the incident in question. Once I've secured a meeting, I'll contact you."

"What about whoever hired Cole? Was it the man you mentioned, Charles Whitman? He could send someone else for Remi."

"We'll find out what we need to know and cut that snake off at the head." John sounded confident, determined. The former chief warrant officer Hawk remembered. "I can arrange a security detail for Remi, to assist you in protecting her, if you need it."

"I would appreciate that. I'll let you know once I have her situated."

Remi was giving them both looks. They were talking about her like she wasn't there, but she said nothing.

"Sounds like a plan," John said.

"Will do. Just get better and make it quick." Hawk's words elicited a familiar smile from John, then he and Remi exited the room.

Hawk felt better about the meeting and more than ashamed of his initial confrontational attitude. But he and Remi had accomplished something. Arrangements were being made to meet with the powers that be. That's what they had hoped to accomplish.

And the news that Cole had been caught left him reeling inside. A fist squeezed his heart. He needed to process what this meant for his brother on every level, but much later.

Making their way down the corridor, he walked close to Remi, his hand hovering at her back as they moved down the quiet but busy hallway. Nurses sat at their stations, staring at computer screens. A few aides entered or exited patient rooms. All the normal hospital stuff he would expect. So why was he feeling that keen sense of impending danger, especially now that he had learned that Cole was in custody? Even if he wasn't, Cole wanted Remi alive. He hadn't killed her before. Instead, he'd shot John. He could have killed him with one shot, but he hadn't.

My brother isn't much of an assassin. Oddly, that should have comforted him, except Cole was in custody for serious crimes. Hawk had hoped to confront him under different circumstances and help him turn away from this path. He would be turned away all right. And Hawk would face him and try to reconcile their relationship.

Finally they stepped onto the elevator, and he was surprised they were alone. He would take that moment to breathe before they stepped off. Then he had to get Remi somewhere safe until she handed off this burden to the right person, whose name John had never actually given them.

Hawk wanted to say something, but he wasn't sure where to start so he remained silent.

"I hate to say this out loud," she said, "but I'm scared, Hawk. I'm terrified. Sergei told me everything in case something happened to him, and maybe I should tell you in case something happens to *me*. The closer we get to this finally being over, the more terrified I am." Unshed tears brimmed in her eyes, but she lifted her chin and shoulders and shifted to stare forward.

She might have been terrified, but she had fortitude. Hawk was equally tormented, and he would be right beside her through this. He wouldn't forgive himself if anything happened to her.

"You're going to be okay." If only he could believe that, feel it to his core.

"You don't know that, so I'm going to tell you where to find the Tempest device."

33

She blurted it out to him before it was too late. Before he could respond, the doors opened. Was he upset with her for telling him? She and Hawk stared out into the hallway, but neither of them spoke. Neither of them moved to exit the elevator.

Hawk leaned in close to her ear. "You're going to live to share this information yourself."

A white-coated physician and a nurse in purple scrubs rushed to catch the elevator, and Hawk and Remi stepped off. As she walked next to Hawk in silence, he picked up the pace. Easy for him with such long strides, but she had to work to keep up with him. They exited the hospital into the parking garage.

Hawk suddenly moved behind a column and pulled her with him.

"What are we doing?" she whispered.

"Someone was looking at our ride."

"What?"

"I recognized him."

Remi had been too preoccupied to notice. "John's security detail?"

"I assumed he was. I saw him talking to two men standing outside John's door, including Banks. But I could have gotten it all wrong."

"What do you think he was doing?"

"If he's with John's team, then he could have been trying to make sure it was safe and no one had bothered it."

"Or if he wasn't with John's team, he could have tampered with it." She wouldn't say the word *bomb*.

John wanted her alive for the intelligence he suspected was hidden away in her brain. But someone *else* wanted her silenced for that same reason. Her pulse kicked into overdrive. "What are we going to do?"

"I'll look it over."

After making sure the guy was gone and no one else was lurking and watching, they rushed forward to the vehicle. Hawk checked beneath it—looking for a bomb or a tracker? She wasn't sure. He gave her a thumbs-up.

What did that mean? He found something or he hadn't found anything?

But when he opened the door for her, she knew it was all clear. She climbed in and Hawk shut the door. While he moved around to the driver's side, she glanced at her cell to read a text that had just come through. Earlier, she'd texted Jo the burner phone number. Jo would receive it whenever she got a bar. Hawk wouldn't be happy, but Remi couldn't remain unreachable to her staff. She managed the lodge, after all. They hadn't prepared for her sudden disappearance during the height of storm-watching season. So, she'd asked Jo to give her updates, and finally Remi got one. She quickly read the text.

What could it mean?

Hawk opened the door and climbed into the driver's seat. "I sent Gordo a text letting him know we're on our way."

He started the vehicle and adjusted the temperature,

then just stared at the rearview mirror. No shifting gears into reverse. No backing up.

"What are we waiting for?"

"I'm thinking."

And he was watching. What would she do if she didn't have Hawk with her in this? She shuddered to think of going through this alone. But she'd been followed before and had disappeared on her own, or so she had thought. Maybe being alone would make it easier to go completely off-grid. Then again, she would not choose that for herself. Besides, she really liked Hawk more than she should, and maybe she was getting much too close to him for her own good. But this involved his brother. She owed it to him to let him make that decision, that call, for them to go their separate ways whenever that needed to happen.

With the thought, she realized how much time she'd given up and the relationships she'd avoided. She'd avoided romance, declined invitations to dinner because she couldn't afford to get too involved. Her proximity to Hawk screamed that reminder every day she was with him. And she'd given up much more than relationships all because she'd taken a picture of Sergei.

That her need to see the world and expand her horizons—write a travel blog—had landed her in Hidden Bay, hiding from the world, was pure irony.

But if she had to hide, she couldn't think of a better place.

The one thing she had going for her was that no one except Hawk knew what she knew, but evidently it was enough to *suspect* she held on to those secrets. Still, she could keep playing dumb about the events until the time was right to share.

She stared out of the parking garage at the constant rain.

Finally, Hawk backed out of the slot and steered slowly through the busy garage. Hospital staff both exited and entered the facility. Afternoon shift-change time. Patients and their caregivers walked slowly to their cars or entered the hospital. Had he simply been waiting for the activity in the garage to pick up before they exited? Behind a line of departing cars, Hawk turned out of the parking garage onto the street, went through a light, and then merged onto the freeway choked with heavy traffic. They hadn't discussed where they would go so she could be safe while waiting to hear from John, but she had an idea.

He swerved out of the way of a vehicle switching lanes. "I never liked the traffic here."

"How about we get lost in the rainforest?" She chuckled. *I sound hysterical.*

"Funny. I think I've had enough of traipsing through the cold woods during this storm system. Let's not do it again."

Yeah, she didn't want to land there either. She was so tired of running and hiding. "Hawk, I know what to do."

"I'm listening."

"You're not going to like it," she said.

"We'll never know until you tell me."

"I need to go back to Hidden Bay."

He jerked the wheel. "You're kidding."

Had he swerved to avoid another vehicle, or was that just a physical knee-jerk reaction to her statement?

"I'm not, actually. John said I need to relax and take my time to recall details. I'm not going to feel comfortable until I'm back there on the rugged coast. I keep going back to what Sergei said, thinking about it. He thought he was a good guy doing the right thing, but he would be labeled a traitor."

"And?"

"I need perspective. So much about this isn't making sense to me. Isn't adding up in my head. I just have this gnawing feeling in the back of my mind."

"I understand needing perspective. But the lodge isn't exactly the safest place for you right now."

"You heard John. Cole is in custody. You can let him know where we're going, and he can have people waiting when we get there. How about that?"

He grunted.

"Look. I know my way around better than anyone. It's my home turf—at least it has been for two years." And she might call it home forever if given the chance. "You saw the photographs of the waves that I took. The ones with the faces?"

"Yep. I'd love to ask you more about them. Like how in the world did you get them. But more importantly at this moment—what do they have to do with our situation?"

"Patience. And perspective. Do you know the difference between an amazing photograph and just a boring image?"

"Other than one is amazing and the other is boring, not really."

She laughed. "To capture an image that stirs emotion, you can't look at things at just eye level. You have to move around and look at things from different angles."

"I get what you're saying. But *why* do you think we need to look at things from a different angle? There's nothing more to figure out here. You've remembered. Now you just have to tell the right person."

"Do you really think it's that simple?"

He sighed. "There's more going on here, but I'm not sure it's for us to worry about. Regardless, *how* will going back to the lodge give you a new perspective?"

Yeah. About that. "Jo texted me with an update."

"Wait. We got burner phones, and you passed that number to someone else? Brilliant."

"I'm responsible for that place," she said. "Jo isn't going to share the number with anyone."

"You're not responsible to manage the lodge when your life is threatened." He practically growled. "Your friends and employees can pick up the slack."

"And I appreciate that. But just listen, will you? I'm glad she got my text and was able to respond."

"Get to the point."

Right. He was right. She dreaded telling him the rest. "I got another one of those packages."

"Package with the puzzle piece?" His jaw working, Hawk stared straight ahead. "All the more reason you shouldn't go back."

"That's what I thought you'd say."

"If you really believe Cole sent the package and is asking you to remember, then it's just a strategy to lure you back to the lodge."

"How do you know? Okay, maybe I'm wrong and Cole isn't the one behind it. That was just a working theory. Whoever sent it might not even realize that I'm not there at the moment. So we need to go back. If it'll make you feel better, you can let John know so he can send assistance. I understand why you trust him, and I don't blame you. I'm not asking you not to trust him, but whatever we do, let's just be careful."

Let's. As if they were a team. Because they had been working together. Hawk had saved her and helped her. Part of her kind of hoped he would remain with her now even though his brother was incarcerated. Weird to admit that was true. But she might be fooling herself believing that Hawk thought of her as more than a means to an end.

34

areful? She thought she had to tell him to be careful? What did it take to truly trust another person? Did Remi even completely trust Hawk? Humans made mistakes. Big mistakes. Hawk had once trusted Cole, and now look at his brother. He shoved away the distracting thoughts. This was no time to think about everything that had gone wrong and everything that *could* go wrong, though Hawk was doing his best.

For fifteen miles, in and out of traffic, he watched the mirrors.

Hawk had expected they would be followed, and he wasn't disappointed. John had said he trusted Hawk to protect her, but he would have a backup plan too, unless this was someone else following them. Someone had hired Cole, after all. Someone else besides John Marshall and the US government wanted what was in Remi's head.

"Is someone following us?" Remi asked.

"Yes."

"Well, can we lose them? I'm hungry and tired and I'd like to sleep in my own bed tonight."

"You aren't letting this lodge thing go, are you?"

"No. And after all, your friend John told me to relax and try to remember the details, and I need to be there in case there's more to remember."

"You said that."

"And I thought we agreed that's where we're going."

Actually, he'd never agreed to anything. "To see what's in that box, no doubt. Maybe it's puzzle pieces. Maybe it's something else. Have you ever thought of that?"

"What, like a bomb? No. Aren't you curious?"

"You've remembered most of what happened. You said so yourself. You also said whatever image the puzzle pieces create doesn't matter anymore."

"I don't need you to remind me of what I said."

"So, why is the box supposedly containing more of the puzzle suddenly important?"

Remi huffed, her agitation growing. "Because Jo found it in the garbage."

He shrugged, unconvinced. "Someone thought it was junk mail."

"Possibly."

Hawk tried to lose his tail, but they were staying on him, four cars back. Seattleites loved their full-size SUVs or else this tail would have been a cliché straight from the movies—a big, black Suburban. The vehicle closed the distance, and Hawk shifted in his seat.

He called John, who picked up quickly. "Hawk. I didn't think I'd hear from you so soon."

"We have a tail. Is that you?"

"No."

"Because you put a tracker on the vehicle so you didn't need to tail us?"

"What? No."

"I'll call you back." He ended the call.

Then maneuvered around an eighteen-wheeler and a wolf pack of cars before speeding up.

She reached for the grab handle above the door as he weaved through traffic on the slick highway. "What's the point of any of this if we don't make it out alive?"

"You don't like my driving?"

"I'm not a fan, no."

"You want me to lose them or not? Because this isn't a protective detail, compliments of John."

Remi said nothing, and Hawk focused on the road. The traffic behind him looked snarled and had come to a complete stop. Good. He accelerated and left the freeway, driving until he made it to Gordo's warehouse, leaving the followers stuck in the gridlock. He steered toward the gate and then stopped. The gate was closed, so he got out to open it, but it was locked up tight. Hawk pursed his lips. What was going on? He got back into the vehicle and called Gordo but got no answer. Not good. Not good at all. Gordo practically lived here. Hawk had texted they were coming.

Even if he hadn't, Gordo wouldn't have locked the gates in the middle of the day.

"Why is the gate locked?" Remi asked.

"I'm not sure. Wait here." He jumped out and then opened up the back and searched the small toolbox inside the storage compartment. He found heavy-duty pliers he could use for cutting the chains. Remi watched him from inside the cab of the truck.

Cole was supposedly in custody.

John had assured them the danger had passed.

But he was wrong. Dead wrong. And Hawk had a feeling things were about to get even more interesting. After cutting the chain loose and opening the gate, Hawk got back into the vehicle and steered them into the parking lot. He closed the gate again but didn't lock it. Hawk figured

Gordo had some security cameras and alarms, and maybe somewhere they were going off, but it was nothing Hawk could hear, and his unease inched up. Regardless, he needed his helicopter back.

"Just stay here, okay?" He parked and got out to look at the helicopter a few yards away. Had his bird been tampered with? Because right now, it kind of felt like someone didn't want him flying out of here. His cell buzzed in his pocket, and he pulled it out to read a text from Gordo.

Get out of there now! Come to the old Transnational building in the industrial section of Port of Seattle. I've got you a ride.

Hawk hurried back to the vehicle and got inside. He trusted Gordo and didn't need to question him. But why hadn't the guy texted sooner? Hawk backed up and steered toward the gate.

Two men rushed around the corner of the building and aimed their handguns at Hawk's vehicle. He flew through the gate without stopping to open it again, knocking it from the hinges and scratching Gordo's vehicle, but it couldn't be helped. Bullets pinged off the back end.

Remi hunkered down in the seat. "*What* is happening?"

"It's obvious they wanted us grounded."

"Who are *they*?" she asked.

"And that's the kazillion-dollar question." Hawk floored it, accelerating to get away from Gordo's warehouse. He had no intention of getting back on the freeway where he'd left behind the black SUV in gridlocked traffic, and the guys from Gordo's warehouse hadn't pursued them that he could tell. He could easily make it to the port area via the backstreets.

"They? You mean Charles Whitman? Or your brother?"

she asked. "There's no way for us to know who else is involved."

"The country of Zarovia, for all we know, or the terrorist group who wanted the Tempest from Whitman." Hawk added to her list. Had she thought of that? Because if she hadn't, she should.

"I feel so much better now—sarcasm intended," she said.

"You wanted me to make you feel better?"

"I don't know why I said that. So, what are we going to do now? We could just *drive* to the lodge, which honestly is what I thought we were going to do."

"We could. But Gordo told me to meet him. He said he had a ride for us."

Hawk hated that they had to drive slow on the backstreets and stop for the red lights and stop signs. He was eager to meet Gordo and see the ride and get in the air and out of Seattle.

"You mentioned you're hungry," he said. "You want McDonald's or Wendy's?"

"I love McDonald's fries."

"McDonald's it is."

As they sat in the line at the drive-through, Hawk second-guessed his decision to stop. But they both needed sustenance to keep their energy up, and who knew where this day was heading.

"Thank you, Hawk."

"For what?"

"For being thoughtful. You remembered that I said I was hungry, and you stopped. I know you didn't want to stop because we're in the middle of escaping bad guys yet again."

"Stopping might not have been the best idea, but I wouldn't have done it if I didn't think it was safe at the moment."

"I'm still going to enjoy the fries. I mean heroes have to

eat too. Whatever happened before in your job, you're a hero. Don't ever let anyone tell you otherwise."

He didn't care if anyone thought he was a hero. He wasn't seeking that title, but the words coming from Remi meant the world to him. He wished he could somehow tell her, show her.

After getting their food, he hit the road again and ate with one hand. It didn't take him long to devour a Quarter Pounder with Cheese and large fries. Finally, he entered the Port of Seattle and crept along the street until he found the older industrial section. And there it was, the abandoned Transnational building. Hawk steered into the parking lot, apprehension building in his chest.

What would he find? More gunmen waiting to meet them? Had Gordo really sent him the message?

Hawk parked and stepped out of the vehicle to look around. His friend rushed forward from the stairwell. Relieved, Hawk grabbed Gordo up in a bear hug. Remi strolled around the vehicle and stood back, watching.

Hawk released Gordo and motioned Remi to come closer.

"Man, what happened?" Hawk asked.

"A couple of gunmen were out there looking at your bird. I grabbed my pistol and went out to question them and get them off my property. They opened fire, and I took cover. I called the police. The men were gone by the time the police got there."

"Well, they were there just now."

"I know. I got the video feed. I would have warned you sooner, except I didn't see your text until I got here. I decided to get out of there. Figured this was about whatever business you're wrapped up in. Man, it's always something with you." He grinned, though the gravity of the situation remained behind his eyes.

"Thanks for having my back," Hawk said. "Oh, and I'm

sorry about your vehicle." Hawk angled toward the back
end.

Gordo looked at the bullet holes, his frown deepening.
"This can be fixed. I'm just glad you weren't hurt."

"Yeah, me too. But the damage here makes it hard for
me to bring this up. You mentioned you have another ride
for me."

Gordo chuckled. "Yeah, I can understand that. But desperate times, right? It's on the roof. A Bell 206B-3 helicopter."

A Jet Ranger. Hawk was more than familiar. This Bell was
what he'd flown for King County. He gave a low whistle.
"How did you get your hands on that?"

"It had some issues. Let's just say a guy owed me and I
got it for a steal. Been working my magic."

Hawk wasn't sure about this. "You sure you want me in
the cockpit?" Because the last time he'd been in this bird,
he'd crashed.

"I'm sure."

"I don't know."

"I've got your bird back at the warehouse for collateral."

"It's not an even trade."

"Who said anything about trading. Just bring it back to
me in one piece. I trust you. You got me out of a lot of
messes, so I'm here for you."

His words touched Hawk to the core. He couldn't repay
him if anything happened to this bird. He squeezed Gordo's
shoulder. "I don't know what to say."

"You don't have to say anything. Just get out of here. You
can go anywhere you want."

He could think of a few hundred places he'd like to go,
but then he glanced at Remi. She blinked at him, then
looked away. Yeah. She'd wanted to travel the world, so
she told him, but now she was gunning for the lodge. She

might not have told him everything because right now, that didn't seem like the best place to go. But she was at the center. The main reason he should keep her safe and maybe ignore her demands, and on the other side of that same scale, he needed to listen to her needs, her direction, her intuition that had kept her safe and alive before Hawk even showed up.

What her brain had hidden away was at the heart of this mission.

35

Gordo told them he'd catch up. Hawk and Remi took an elevator to the fourth floor of the abandoned building, then had to take the stairwell the rest of the way to the roof. They stepped off the elevator into a workshop of sorts. At least it was covered. She peered out the window with Hawk to watch the rain beating the rooftop.

She didn't have to step closer to the helicopter to see it was newer and more solid than Hawk's older bird. But she wouldn't mention it and risk hurting his feelings. He loved the helicopter he'd worked on.

Hawk opened the door of the building to head to the helicopter.

"Hawk, wait."

He stepped back inside. "What's wrong?"

"I don't know if this is necessary." She hadn't wanted to say anything in front of his friend. "It's only a three-hour drive back to the lodge." Four or five depending on weather and traffic.

"And we'll get there in half the time or less. The faster

we get there, the faster that . . ." A slight frown creased his forehead as he let his words trail off.

She flinched. "What? This can be over, and you can be rid of me?" The look in his eyes had sent a sliver of insecurity through her and suddenly, out of nowhere, the thought had popped into her head. "I shouldn't have said that. But since I did, if that's how you feel, it's fine. You don't owe me anything, Hawk. You can step away at any time."

"What?" His face darkened and he huffed. Pursed his lips. Glanced around as if expecting sudden danger. Then his eyes swiveled back to her, his gaze so intense she struggled to breathe.

"I didn't say that," he said.

Took him long enough to respond. "But you were going to say it. And that's okay. I don't know why I even reacted."

She twisted away, but he gently caught her arm and turned her to face him. Then he stepped closer. Her back was to the wall now, and she couldn't escape.

Even if she wanted to.

And right now, she wanted to stay here with him—a red flag that meant she wasn't thinking clearly. But it was kind of hard to with this man—the lumberjack pilot with blue eyes—who, from the moment she'd met him, had literally held her life in his hands.

His attention was fully on her, his gaze penetrating. "Yes. I want this to be over so *you* can be safe." His words came out breathy and he seemed to struggle to speak. Then he frowned. "I want this to be over so . . . so that . . ."

He shook his head, then leaned closer. He was so close. She couldn't move. Couldn't breathe.

Just kiss me already.

Then Hawk pressed his lips against hers, gentle and caring, flooding her with tenderness. Without hesitation, she wrapped her hands around his neck and pulled him closer.

His arms enveloped her body, holding her tight against his sturdy chest, while his mouth took hers, caressing, exploring . . . cherishing.

Hawk kissed her.

Deeply.

He kissed her senseless.

The stairwell door banged open. Remi startled, but Hawk remained close, softening his lips against hers, drawing her attention back to this small private moment with him, far from the troubles that chased them.

That . . . was beyond anything she could have imagined or expected. And she felt a little dizzy, in a good way.

He eased back enough to look at her, and she couldn't tell if she saw regret in his eyes. On his face. She wasn't sure how she felt about what just happened between them. On the one hand, it felt right and almost inevitable. On the other hand, what was she thinking? Her heart had definitely overruled her mind.

"Hawk . . . I . . ."

"Look, if you didn't want that, I'm sorry."

"I wanted it. You know I did. But maybe it wasn't such a good idea."

A throat cleared. "I hate to break up the fun, but we've got company. A couple of men are making their way up."

"We have to go." Hawk grabbed her hand. "Gordo, you coming?"

"Nah. I'll hold them off."

"You sure, man? You've already put yourself on the line for us. You could get away with us now."

"What are friends for? Go. I already called the cops, so help is on the way."

"We could stay to help you," Remi offered.

Hawk squeezed her hand.

"Hawk, get her out of here." Gordo then bolted the stairwell shut. He waved.

Following Hawk, Remi raced out into the rain. The icy cold drops slapped her, breaking her out of the weird trance she'd been in after that kiss. She jumped into the fancy helicopter, glad to be out of the elements. But she wasn't looking forward to flying in this wind. Still, she trusted Hawk, more than anyone, to get them where they needed to go.

And she might be preoccupied by that toe-curling kiss when she absolutely needed to focus. Figuring out what she was missing in all this could make the difference between life and death.

36

This day had started ridiculously early and had held promise and hope. Now they were once again racing for their lives against an unknown foe.

Inside this bird, Hawk could almost imagine he was back working at the county as a deputy, and that was a bad thing. All he could see was that crash. Now wasn't the time to berate himself again, so he pushed those dangerous thoughts out of the way to forge a new path.

He relied on the instrument panel as he navigated around the heaviest wind and rain.

"You really love flying, don't you?" Remi asked.

"Let's just say it's a love-hate relationship."

He could say that about his brother too. When this was over and Remi was out of dangerous waters, then he would pay Cole a visit in whatever facility housed him. Maybe with Cole in prison, Hawk would have the chance to talk to him, brother to brother, and try to reach through and crack the wall around his heart. Hawk hoped that Cole wasn't completely gone. He wasn't truly a stone-cold killer. At the end of the day, where a person's heart leaned—toward God or away—was what mattered. Right now, it looked like Cole had tipped far away from God and had turned away from doing what was true, good, and right, and that crushed Hawk.

He hadn't seen that drastic change coming in Cole.

And that ate him up inside. But he did see something else—they were being followed. Again. Only this time, in the air.

He couldn't lose this jerk, not in this weather. He wouldn't risk Remi's life. Chances were that with the direction Hawk was flying, his destination was already known. In this weather he couldn't risk disabling tracking. He wouldn't risk crashing into another helicopter if someone else dared to fly in this, and apparently someone had.

He ground his molars. It didn't matter if they'd driven or flown, danger was closing in. It was time to face the threat head-on. If he didn't know that Cole was in custody, he would suspect his brother was in that bird following. He was the most relentless, stubborn, and capable person Hawk had ever met.

Except for maybe Remi, and the thought could make him smile in the middle of this disaster.

Sheets of rain came at them sideways in the gusting winds. The storm was building. He'd hoped to land at the lodge before the brunt of this last of the series of storms—a true monster and the harshest one yet, so meteorologists warned them.

He might be the only living soul who felt more confident in the air in this weather than he did on the road. Sometimes he regretted his decision to leave the Night Stalkers. SOAR was the perfect drug for thrill seekers who wanted to make a difference in this world.

That was okay because he had a new mission—a double mission. Protect Remi. Face Cole.

But one thing at a time.

"How long before we land?"

"A few more minutes." Adrenaline pumped through him as he focused all his attention on the path ahead.

The other bird was closing in without concern for keeping a safe distance. Just like Andre Aslam, the terrorist in the pursuit that had ended two lives and Hawk's career. What was going on? Did the pilot want to bring him down or just stay on him, fearing he might lose him?

Hawk owed Gordo for his help, and the last thing he wanted was to damage this bird. Maybe he should have refused, but he was desperate to get Remi out of there. And do what? Take her back to the place where this had started?

Hawk used the radio frequency for air-to-air communication and expressed his displeasure with the pilot.

Cole responded in a threatening tone. "I'll see you soon."

Hawk's blood turned to ice.

"It's your brother?" Remi's voice shook with incredulity. "So, your longtime friend and mentor who saved your life lied to us, and Cole isn't incarcerated at all?"

The man had assured them that Cole was out of the equation. "He could have escaped."

Remi said nothing more. She had to be terrified. Furious.

He was all that and more. "Listen, Remi. We can go anywhere right now. Just say the word. I can take you somewhere and make sure that he never finds you."

"You mean hide."

"Until this is over, yes."

"It's not going to be over if I hide. Don't you get it? We have to face him today."

Yeah, unfortunately. He got it. But he didn't like where this scenario was taking them. He didn't have a good feeling about this. "You could die. Have you ever thought of that?"

"Every day."

"Do me a favor and contact John. Use my SAT phone. His direct line is in there. Let him know that we're being tailed. Ask him if his security detail is already in place at the lodge. I might need some help sooner than expected."

Hawk increased speed and pushed the helicopter to its limits in this storm. Maybe the bird behind him couldn't keep up.

Remi made the call. "It's not going through."

"Keep trying."

"If I don't get him," she said, "I'll leave a message."

"You can text him too, and then try again."

"Done texting. I'll try calling again. But I don't think I can take any more of this. I mean your flying is brilliant, but I need to put my feet on the ground. Oh, hey, you got a message from Gordo. He says he's good. Police came and scared the men off."

"That's a relief." He didn't know what he'd do without his friend. "I think I lost our tail. I'm not landing at my house this time but closer to the lodge."

"As long as you land, I don't care where it is."

"I've already scouted out a few additional spots." He'd done that early on when he was thinking about the tour business.

"So, how far is this from the lodge? How do we get there? I'm guessing you don't have a vehicle waiting, and I know you said you didn't want to be stuck in the rainforest during the storm again."

"I said that, yeah. It's not far, but we might have to fight the storm in the woods."

"Oh, I got something. I'm leaving a voicemail." She left a few details. "The call dropped before I finished."

"I'm sure it was enough." Chances were that he and Remi would be at the lodge before John's security people. They probably drove.

"Why do I feel like we're just going in circles," she said. "That we aren't getting anywhere?"

"Do you mean that metaphorically or literally?"

She laughed. Actually laughed. In the middle of this horrible flight.

Remi Grant might be the woman of his dreams, and he had never let himself envision a happily-ever-after future. But if he was going to dream—Remi was the one.

"I mean literally."

"Good, because I assure you, we aren't flying in circles." Not quite.

The wind buffeted the helicopter more than he liked, but he focused and maneuvered and worked with this beautiful bird. Man, he wished he could afford one for himself. "Metaphorically speaking, we're definitely getting somewhere. We know much more than we did the last time we fought the storm in these same woods."

"Where'd you say we were landing?"

"You know the old military camp near the bunkers? There's the remnant of a helicopter pad there. Think about the best way to the lodge from there. You're in charge of that."

"Do you have permission to land there?"

Do I need permission? "I don't think anyone is going to care right now." He certainly didn't. He just needed to land somewhere. "This bird is big, and I need some extra space."

"There's not a direct path from the camp to the lodge. Not by a long shot."

"Then use the SAT phone and call someone to meet us and pick us up."

"Good idea. I think the last of the storms is moving in. It sure feels like the roughest ride yet. Are you sure we're not going to blow away?"

"The wind is picking up." He wouldn't mention that

it was quickly becoming too much for him to fly. "We're landing just in time." He glanced at her, though maybe he shouldn't have. He had trouble enough concentrating on flying after he'd kissed her—but he hadn't been able to resist that look, her ever-changing eyes filled with longing.

He landed and powered down the rotors. Then took a deep breath. Remi watched him, and he looked at her. He had so much to say, and yet he had no idea what to say. He'd come to care deeply for her in a short period of time, and for the first time in years, he'd met someone that drew his attention—partially because she was involved in his personal drama and so he was naturally drawn to her. Couldn't look away or ignore that she stirred up his insides. And he was at the end of his search for Cole. So maybe now he would give himself permission to pursue a real life. A relationship. Still, he ran the risk that Remi might want nothing to do with him because he would always remind her of what she'd gone through. His brother was an assassin, after all.

And they weren't out of danger yet.

"Jo should be here soon."

He wasn't looking forward to facing the storm again, especially since he knew things were about to ramp up. That other helicopter brought a menace that was his brother and would land somewhere near and fast. He had to get Remi out of here.

He had to prepare to face evil head-on.

37

Coat snug, hood tight, Remi jumped out of the fancy flying machine. While it was cushier than Hawk's personal bird, she hadn't enjoyed that trip. Planting her feet on the ground, she relished the feeling of the earth beneath her.

Bracing against the wind and rain, she started to walk toward the trees. Hawk rushed around the helicopter and gripped her arms, his eyes wide.

Another helicopter buzzed over them. She and Hawk both reflexively ducked. "You couldn't lose him?"

"He's determined." Frown lines deepened in his forehead. He shoved his wet hair back out of his face and searched the woods. "But I'm more determined."

With those words, he ushered her away from the old helipad and into the cover of the forest. Releasing her arm, he hovered near, protective, on high alert. The blue-eyed pilot sent a thrill through her even as dread engulfed her. This was absolutely the wrong time to be into this guy.

Hawk appeared fierce and ready to battle it out, but he wouldn't want Remi anywhere near the confrontation with Cole.

Frenetic waves crashed nearby. She drew in a deep breath to clear her head and squashed the urge to go find the cliff-side view. She hadn't realized how much she'd missed the sounds and smells of the tumultuous Pacific Ocean. The scent of salt water was stronger here than in the city, where the pungent scents of exhaust and oil and the dense population near Puget Sound overshadowed nature. She'd been a farm girl and maybe she was still a nature girl, at the very least.

Under the thick greenery, the rain and wind lessened but only a little. She hugged herself, drops sliding down her face. "Well, here we are again. In the woods, waiting out a storm. What do you think your brother is going to do? Can he land here?"

Hawk drew close, fear and dread apparent in the contours of his face. "I don't intend to wait around to find out. Let's get to the road so we can head Jo off." He tugged Remi closer and held her hand as they weaved their way between the trees and sword ferns, stepping over gnarly roots that jutted out.

A rutted vehicle path came into view and Remi started forward, but Hawk pulled her back. "We need to keep to the trees."

"Like he can't figure out where we're going?" she asked.

Around the curve in the road, the grille of a truck emerged from the forest, and the engine rumbled when the driver accelerated. Hawk stepped out of the woods with Remi, and Jo slammed on the brakes. The truck slid in the mud.

She opened the door. "What's wrong?"

No time to explain, Remi rushed around to the passenger

side and got in. She slid over to the middle of the bench seat, but Hawk remained standing outside and shut the door. She lowered the window. "Get in. What are you doing?"

He leveled his gaze on Jo. "Get her out of here. I need to deal with this."

"No, wait!" Remi shouted.

But Hawk had already taken off, bolting into the woods, cutting through them in the direction they'd just come.

"What's he going to do?" Jo maneuvered the truck to turn around in a tight space.

"He's going to face the guy who abducted you and attacked me. His name is Cole, not Collin Barclay. He followed us. This can't end well, and I don't want Hawk to do it."

"Remi, wait." Jo held her arm so she couldn't get out. "I have a lot to tell you. It's important and has to do with everything. Let Hawk take care of this."

When they'd started for the lodge earlier this afternoon, she had imagined a much different arrival. *God, please keep Hawk safe.* Fear gripped her chest and squeezed. She couldn't hide her feelings. Didn't care if Jo saw.

"I know you're worried about him, but what can you do, Remi?"

Jo was right. "End this, that's what." She buckled up. "Let's go."

After skillfully turning the truck around, Jo sped south to the lodge. Remi stared out the window at the lush mossy greenery of the Olympic National Forest.

"There's something else. Cole . . . Cole is Hawk's brother," Remi said.

"His *brother*?" Jo sounded incredulous.

Remi shared with Jo about Cole, what little she knew. "Yeah, it's complicated."

"Have you remembered?"

"Some of it." She didn't want to put Jo in more danger than she already had. "You said you had a lot to tell me."

Jo swerved into the parking lot at Cedar Trails Lodge. "Better yet, I'll show you."

They jumped out of her truck and then rushed across the lot until they were at the entrance to Remi's office. Jo fumbled with the keys but got the door open, and Remi followed her into her office. "Please tell me everything has been running smoothly here."

"Everything's fine," Jo said. "But you've been missed, even if it was only a few days. It's good to have you back. I wish I could say you're safe, but sounds like this isn't over yet."

Remi was beginning to doubt it would ever be. "I'm so sorry about everything that's happened to you, Jo, because of me. Are you okay?"

"I scheduled an appointment with someone. She's booked out, of course. It is what it is. I'll be fine." Jo sent her a smile. "I've been through stuff before. I'm good."

Jo unlocked the desk drawer and pulled out the package. "I found this in the trash."

The packaging was the same size, and Remi could feel a box inside like the two other boxes.

"I'd say someone thought it was junk mail," Jo said. "But I don't think that's what's going on here."

Remi would question Jo more on that response, but right now she focused on the package. She tore into the paper and found the same box as before. Then she opened the box to find more pieces of the puzzle. *All* the rest of the pieces of the puzzle. She counted twenty in total. She grabbed the two pieces she kept in the drawer.

Her pulse raced. "Hurry, help me with this."

But she had a feeling she knew what the picture would

show. "You probably shouldn't be here to see it." Though it would mean nothing to Jo if it was simply the cathedral, but Remi sensed there was more to see. Something she'd missed.

"I'm in this, Remi. I'm in it already. Just . . . let's do this."

38

awk had waited under the cover of trees for Cole to find a place to land, which wasn't easy with the wind and the limited space to maneuver the bird. Catching a tree in a rotor would end in disaster. Maybe that was a better outcome than facing his brother.

No. He couldn't think like that.

But really, what did he hope to accomplish?

Ending this.

Saving Remi.

And he had no idea how to approach his brother. Aim his gun and tie him up? Make a citizen's arrest? Hawk had so much more he wanted to say and do, and the last thing he wanted was to be forced to kill his own brother.

God, why does it have to come down to this?

He raced through the trees and found the opening where Cole was trying to land. Hawk watched his brother set the bird down in a precarious spot. Cole was a skilled pilot. Admittedly, it surprised Hawk just how skilled he was. He didn't know his brother as well as he thought. He'd missed some things. Cole didn't wait for the rotors to slow as he hopped out of the bird and raced toward the trees in the direction of Cedar Trails Lodge.

God, help me stop him!

"Cole! Stop!" Hawk chased after him. He meant to stand between his brother and Remi.

He stepped out in front of Cole, who instantly lifted his weapon, aiming at Hawk. His chest squeezed tight. What was he doing standing here vulnerable? A target for his brother. Hawk lifted his hands. "Are you really going to shoot me?"

He'd shot *at* him before.

He lowered the gun and stomped forward. "I don't want to, but I will if I have to, so get out of my way. You're a traitor to your country." The words seethed from Cole as he bumped past Hawk, hitting his shoulder.

Oh yeah? Cole was asking for a fight. Hawk had dreamed of the moment when he could beat some sense into his brother. He grabbed his shoulder to yank him around. And Cole responded. Instincts kicked in as he fought Cole.

Boiling anger rose in Hawk's throat. "*I'm* the traitor? I have no idea what you mean, man. What are you talking about? Explain it to me. You're the assassin. You turned rogue. Why, Cole?"

"You're wasting my time. What have you done with her?" Cole lifted his weapon as if he was going to finish Hawk. "If only Dad could see you now. He was *so* proud of you, his *favorite* son, but you've turned your back on all that's good and right."

Cole's words were like a shot in the dark, except they didn't miss their mark, cutting Hawk right in the heart. "You've got me mixed up with someone else."

Facing Cole wasn't going down like Hawk had imagined—that he would be able to reason with his brother. Nope. He was going for the throat.

"Let's finish this once and for all." Hawk fisted his hands.

"Fine by me." Cole stomped forward and punched Hawk in the face.

Men suddenly became boys again. Brothers. Wrestling. Punching. Grunting.

Mom tried to pull them apart. Dad wanted to let them finish . . . but apparently, they never had.

But they would today.

On the ground now, slowing through the wet earth, their wrestling days as brothers fresh on his mind, Hawk held Cole in a choke hold. Cole would pass out if he couldn't break out of this. His brother tapped his leg, signaling he was giving up. "Are you sure you're done? Because I could keep going."

Slamming his fist into Hawk, he let him know it was now or never. Hawk released him and he rolled away. They both lay in the muck, gasping for breath, rain lashing them.

Cole scrambled to his feet, ready to pounce again. "Enough games, Hawk. What have you done with her?"

"Like I would tell you."

"I'm taking her." Cole readied his weapon. "Don't stand in my way."

"You'd shoot your own brother? What happened to you, Cole? You were a hero, and now you're a gun for hire? How does that even happen?" Anger and shock fueling him, Hawk barely noticed the pain Cole had inflicted on him, but the look that Cole was giving Hawk left him confused. "I've got news for you. I'm standing in your way. In case you haven't figured it out yet, I'm protecting her from you."

Hawk braced against a strong gust of wind. Prepared for Cole's reaction.

Still gasping for breath, Cole swiped the rain from his eyes. "From *me*? What are you talking about?"

A gunshot rang out. Hawk jolted at the sound. Grimacing, Cole grabbed his shoulder. Hawk yanked Cole with him as they dove behind a boulder for cover. Gunfire ricocheted against the rock. Leaning against the cold, wet stone, Cole's face twisted as he looked at his shoulder, then pressed a hand against it.

"Keep your hand pressed there. Stop the bleeding."

"I know how to do it!"

"It must be John's men," Hawk said. "They're supposed to be here to protect Remi. They saw you, so took a shot. That was a wrong move, but I understand. You tried to kill John, so they're out for revenge."

Blood leaked between Cole's fingers, and Hawk added his hand. He couldn't watch his brother bleed out. "I'll fix this. I'll get us help and keep them from shooting you. But you're going to have to come in. I don't know how you escaped."

Hawk started to move, but Cole gripped him. "I don't know what that conspirator John told you, but I didn't shoot him. I didn't try to kill him." Cole spat the words at him.

"I saw him with my own eyes."

"You saw him. Already shot? The first time you saw *me* at John's, that was the first moment I stepped into that house. You didn't see me shoot him, did you?"

"No, but . . ."

"He told you that, didn't he? Like he told you I was an assassin."

Was Cole just trying to get in his head and twist things all around in a weird psychological game? "Well, yes, but . . ."

"And you're part of this. Working for him, so who's the traitor here?" Cole asked.

"I'm not working for John! He was helping me keep Remi safe. He sent me to the lodge, knowing I'd find you. I've

298

been looking for you." Hawk had already gotten a very bad feeling about it.

Cole pulled Hawk close and ground the words through clenched teeth. "You're telling me, brother to brother, that you're not after the device."

"No. I didn't even know about it." And Hawk's reply meant he'd confessed to knowing something. In fact, he shouldn't have said that much, but he wasn't going to lie to his brother. They were already in too deep for it to matter. Either of them could die today. They might not make it out of this.

"Guess what?" Cole asked. "John is trying to get it so he can sell to the highest bidder. He was all set to sell to Andre Aslam when you tangled with him."

"What? How do you know this? You can't believe that. I *won't* believe it."

"Then you're naive."

"I've known him for years. He saved my life."

"And he's counting on that loyalty. He's using it to turn you against me, and by the way, you've known me longer. When this is all over, he'll blame whatever happens on me. Don't you see?"

No. Hawk didn't see. Or maybe he didn't want to see. But this was Cole. How could he have been so willing to believe the worst?

"Remi said you were there on the helicopter that crashed. Tell me what happened to bring you to this point." Hawk needed to hear this story. He was torn between believing his brother and his longtime mentor and friend.

Cole winced in pain and drew in a few quick breaths. "Someone took out my team. I made it my mission to find out who was behind it, and in the process, I discovered your buddy was working with an arms trafficker but double-crossed him. They wanted to sell what Sergei developed to the highest bidder, which just happened to be a very bad dude who ran a very bad terrorist group."

"Aslam."

"Yes. My team got caught in the crossfire. And then their most valuable asset—Sergei Petrov—was dead. It's all been a race to wait."

"A race to wait. What do you mean?" Then Hawk thought he understood.

"For Remi Grant to remember. She was inadvertently drawn into keeping Sergei safe. My intel connections suggested that both Whitman and Marshall believed Sergei must have told her something. But I suspected it to begin with. I saw him push her out of the helicopter. We were over water, and he had to suspect what was coming next. He was self-sacrificial in that way. But she couldn't survive on her own, or at least I thought. Our bird had been sabotaged from the inside out. I jumped to save Remi, and I thought the rest would follow. They would have. I know they were going to, but a rocket launcher took it out."

Cole closed his eyes.

"Bro. You still with me? You okay?" Hawk had to get him out of this position. He fired his weapon, keeping the men after them at bay, but he could only hold them for so long.

"I didn't find her. I was rescued and later learned that she had been too, but she was off-limits. Untouchable. But I got close, and I saw John Marshall there."

"Are you sure you're right about him?" Hawk hated himself for asking the question.

"I'm positive. I've been working with a cyber operations specialist—a hacker in the Army, basically—who lost someone on that mission gone wrong. She's been helping me. She intercepted communications between John Marshall and Charles Whitman, and we've sent this to the appropriate authorities. It's only a matter of time before John is arrested. I'm relieved that you're not working with him."

"I can't believe you thought I was," Hawk said.

"And I can't believe you thought I was a rogue agent, a gun for hire."

"What was I supposed to think?"

Hawk thought about John's words.

"... the difference between the good guys and the bad guys was often a matter of point of view."

John must have been using that philosophy as his justification to go after the Tempest device.

He peered around the rock, trying to find their egress. Shadows crept between the trees. Time was running out.

"It doesn't matter right now. Let's just say that they know that two different parties want what she knows, and someone *else* wants her dead. I tried to encourage her to remember. Jar her memory before it was too late."

"With the puzzle pieces? That was you, wasn't it?"

"Yeah. I showed up to watch out for her and found you here. I thought you were *working* for him, man. I couldn't seem to get a break and get her away from you. You had her fooled into believing I was on the wrong side of this."

"Why would you think I'd betray my own country?"

"You were close to John. You were here. Remi was here."

"That makes sense. But we need to trust each other. I'm sorry that I believed John. But I was trying to find you so I could talk to you. Why didn't you just come to tell me?"

"I did . . ."

"What? When?"

"I followed you. You were meeting with John, and it was too late. He'd already turned you against me. I thought *you* were the traitor," Cole grunted out. "But that's his men out there. And they're not just trying to kill me. They're going to kill you, too, because by now they know that John's game is up."

His brother's words left Hawk grasping for something solid. The storm system was building to a crescendo around them—it was almost a metaphor for this situation. How would they escape? Hawk spotted two men on either side of them, hiding in the woods, signaling each other and creeping forward, so he kept shooting.

"I'm running out of ammo."

If Cole was telling him the truth, then they were both in trouble.

"They're making their way around," Cole said. "We need an escape. You know this place better than me."

Hawk doubted that. "The cliff. We can get close to the edge in those trees, and then make our way over to the bunkers. You remember those, don't you? You abducted Jo and chained her to a wall."

"Dude, I don't know about the bunkers, and I didn't chain anyone to the wall." Cole grimaced in pain.

They crawled through the underbrush, making their way close to the edge. "Not too close." He didn't want this to be one of those rare moments when erosion tried to dump them in the ocean.

Hawk and Cole pressed forward until they found the entryway to the bunker built in the cliffside. The ocean boiled below, pounding the rocks and soaking them to the bone with cold sea spray.

Hawk and Cole scrambled toward the entrance.

"It's a maze down there." Hawk shook his head as they entered the corridor built into the cliff. "This was a bad idea. We should have found another way. Remi needs protection. We need to get back to her."

He should never have left her to stop Cole, who wasn't even his enemy here.

Well played, John. Well played.

"They'll follow us," Cole said. "They aren't going after Remi until they've taken us both out. They need us out of the way."

"Unless more of John's men are at the lodge."

"Doesn't matter. We can't help her until we get out of this," Cole said.

Hawk pressed forward. "We can draw them in here and take them down." Hawk moved to the door but found it bolted shut. "What?"

He pounded on the door. Jo must have come back and made sure no one could be locked up inside again. He didn't blame her.

But now we're trapped.

39

Remi stared at the picture. The completed puzzle was an image Remi had taken. The church. Sergei. But other people were in the background. Why send her this image and think it would trigger her memory?

"Look at this." Jo tugged a face mask from the bottom drawer.

"What's that?"

"This was in the garbage too." Jo turned the combination face mask and hat inside out.

Remi looked closely at two blue hairs. "What are you thinking?"

Jo sighed. "Hawk's brother didn't abduct me. Erika did."

"Erika? How do you know? How's that possible?"

"Think about the guy who attacked you in the woods. Really, think about it. Did you see him? It could have been Erika. Did you ever hear him speak? My abductor never said a word."

"How did she get you to the bunker?"

"I don't know. I'm small, she's big. A fireman's carry. A

wheelbarrow. She had help? I'm telling you . . . I think it was her."

Remi closed her eyes and thought back to that moment on the road. The guy approached with a knife. But he was covered in a thick raincoat and a mask. She fought him in the woods. Could she have fought Erika instead? The guy had dark eyes. Erika had blue eyes. But sometimes she had green eyes or purple eyes. She loved her colors. Hair and contacts.

Remi eased into the chair at the desk. Erika had been the one to tell her about Paco. Erika had suggested Jo's ladder over the radio. In the woods, she and Hawk had been running to hide from someone. Then he'd gone back and run into Cole. No mask, the guy had made himself known.

At gunpoint, Cole had abducted Remi at John Marshall's secure island home. He was a medium-height guy. Muscular. Smaller than Hawk, who was more like a lumberjack in her mind. Erika was bigger than Remi, bigger than the average woman, and she was strong. Chopped wood and carried it in like it was nothing.

Still, Remi struggled to wrap her mind around this.

"Nothing is as it seems. I don't get why someone would send this picture and tell me to remember. This doesn't seem important."

Jo looked at the image closely. She pressed her fingertip near a woman walking on the sidewalk. "Who is that?"

Remi peered closer. *How could it be?* Her heart rate kicked up. "I'm not sure, but . . . she definitely resembles Erika."

"I didn't want to say anything until you said it," Jo said. "But I agree. That's Erika. She was there and now she's here. How does Erika tie into this?"

Remi took a step back and drew in a breath, her head spinning. She hadn't remembered this part because she hadn't even noticed.

"She was working here before I even got here." Remi didn't understand.

"For like a week. Maybe you coming here had been the grand plan all along."

"To wait for me to remember something? And if I did . . ." Erika had tried to kill her. "And what was Cole's role?"

"I don't know, but I'm thinking that Cole never rented that cabin. Erika was in charge of the rentals, remember? She put Collin Barclay's name, an alias, but it was her. She changed into her scary-man-in-a-mask outfit there in the cabin. I walked in on her, and she pulled the mask on so I couldn't tell it was her. She could have killed me."

"How do you know it was her if she had the mask on?"

"Because I'm the one taking out the garbage from the cabins, and I noticed the mask inside the plastic. It made me shudder. Reminded me, and I dug it out. That was a mistake on her part. It's not like people don't wear them around here in the winter, but she has blue hair." Jo lifted a shoulder.

Right. That danger was always so close sickened her. "Where is she?"

"She's gone. Left right after you did."

Remi sank onto the sofa and pressed her head into her hands. "I need to warn Hawk of the additional players."

"So, there's Erika, and what about this Cole guy?"

"Cole wasn't wearing a mask when he abducted me and put me on a boat," Remi said. "He was trying to escape. He told me that I needed to remember before it was too late. Those exact words here. I believe he sent this picture." She hadn't thought of this, even after her memories had rushed back, but . . . "When he helped me up into the helicopter, he'd taken my rucksack, which had my camera inside. It was waterproof, so it could have survived if he went into the water with it."

"That would make sense," Jo said.

"I wanted to come back to the lodge for perspective, and I think I have a new one."

"What is it? If you don't mind my asking. Erika bad. Cole . . . good?"

A knock came at the door. Remi yanked her handgun from her holster. "Who is it?"

"It's Dylan."

She lowered it to her side. Jo opened the door and Dylan entered, leading another guy into her office.

Remi squeezed the grip of her gun. "Dylan? What is this?"

"You mean who?" the stranger asked.

To Dylan, she said, "I mean what are you thinking, bringing this guy in here?"

"He says he's part of your security detail, compliments of John Marshall," Dylan said.

She didn't recognize him, but that didn't mean he wasn't John's security. She'd test that. Remi lifted her gun anyway.

The man aimed a handgun at Dylan's head. "Lower your weapon, Ms. Grant."

"You aren't security detail for John. Who are you?"

Two men stepped in behind him and entered the office. "These men *are* the security detail that John sent you. Now they work for me. It's a buyer's market. John Marshall has double-crossed me."

Her insides buckled.

"Are you . . . Charles Whitman?"

"One and the same, only my friends call me Chuck."

"And Erika?" Jo asked.

"You mean Latasha Pascoe. She was an operative for Zarovia, protecting their interests. You don't have to worry about her anymore."

Was?

"She's been eliminated." Whitman signaled to the security detail and gestured at Jo, Dylan, and Remi. "They're all coming with us."

"Wait a minute," Jo said. "Someone needs to stay behind and take care of the guests."

Like he would care about that, but Remi was thinking the same thing.

He glanced at one of his men. "Take care of it."

Remi screamed, "Wait! What are you going to do? You can't harm innocent families and children."

"Relax. I'm not a barbarian, for goodness' sake. Inform them there's a gas leak and they should all pack up and head home. The lodge is shutting down for now."

He wanted them to go out in this storm? But the storm was safer than being in Whitman's path of destruction. While that meant people would be safer, horror filled her that it was all coming down to this.

"It's okay, Remi," Jo whispered. "They'll be okay."

No. No, it's not. Jo and Dylan aren't part of this. But if she said something, this guy might kill them in her office. Except he'd said he wasn't a barbarian. Still, Jo and Dylan already knew too much. And Hawk. He was out there somewhere, and maybe he could get here in time to help them out of this nightmare before it was too late. He was good at that, after all.

A radio squawked and Whitman answered. "Speak."

"We got 'em. They're trapped."

"Kill them." Whitman looked at them. "Your hero and his brother aren't coming to save you."

You're a barbarian after all.

40

awk and Cole. Brothers to the end.

"Listen, bro," Hawk said. "I'm sorry I doubted you. That I so easily believed that you'd gone rogue. In my defense, I wanted to find you. I've been looking for you for months. I wanted to make you see reason. I couldn't understand why you'd be working as a hired gunman. I blamed myself."

Cole scoffed. "You give yourself too much credit."

Hawk laughed. "You're right. You can hold your own without my interference." For good or bad.

"What's the plan?" Cole asked.

Hawk fired his gun at the lock and the chains broke away.

"So, you really want to hide in there?" Cole arched a brow. "Won't we be trapped? Let's wait out here in the shadows. Let *them* go into the bunker."

"And we'll lock them in," Hawk said. "I like it."

"After we take them out we'll take their radios and guns. We need to know what they're planning." Cole grimaced slightly. Trying to hide his pain?

Hawk nodded. "You came up with that while bleeding from a gunshot wound. Impressive."

"I aim to please. Now quiet."

Hawk left the door partially open so it was easy to see they'd shot off the lock. This way, the men would think Hawk and Cole had gone into the bunker to hide.

He joined Cole in a shadowed alcove beyond the bunker entrance, pressing back against it, squeezing into the too-small space. He gripped his locked and loaded gun, ready to use it. The raging storm echoed against the concrete walls, making it hard to know if the men had even found the bunker yet. Had they made a mistake?

Because he couldn't exactly wait here forever.

Movement in the tunnel triggered him to press back as far as he could, pushing against his brother. Cole grunted, breathing hard. The pressure was hurting his wound.

Four men argued about going inside the bunker, and one of them came up with the bright idea to simply lock Cole and Hawk inside. Wonderful. Not really what he and Cole had planned, but they would roll with it. If they rushed forward with their guns out, they were going to get a belly full of bullets. They had no egress here. Their armed pursuers hadn't been as stupid as they had counted on. Lesson learned.

Then one of the men opened the door and went into the tunnel after all. One of the other three followed him inside. Yes! The two remaining men paced near the bunker doors.

"Divide and conquer?" Cole asked.

"What about your wound?"

"I'm running on adrenaline, man. Let's do this."

Hawk nodded. They wouldn't escape without taking these men out. It was now or never. "I'll take the cave dwellers."

When the two who had remained outside shifted toward

the rail overlooking the fierce Pacific, Cole and Hawk crept forward, pressing into the wind. Cole rushed the two men near the rail and Hawk slipped into the bunker, stealthily approaching the other two from behind, then disarmed them both quickly. Kicking their weapons, flashlights, and radios toward the entrance, he backed out. Once he'd tossed their stuff out, he slammed the bunker doors, leaving them standing in the dark. Using the damaged chain, he quickly secured the door again, preventing the men from escaping the bunker. He'd send someone back for them later. They pounded and shouted their disapproval with colorful language.

"You're scared of the dark? Get over it." But the storm's rage reverberated off the concrete recess leading up to the bunker doors, and he doubted they heard him.

He turned to assist Cole if needed. At the sight, shock waves rolled through him. Wrestling with the last of the gunmen, Cole fell over the rail, along with the man he battled. Anguish squeezed Hawk's chest. He couldn't lose Cole . . .

"No!" Hawk sprinted to the rail. *God, no! Help us!*

Cole clung to the rail with his one good arm. Below him, Hawk caught a glimpse of a body on the rocks before the ocean swept it away. That would be Cole's fate if Hawk didn't help.

Hawk grabbed Cole's arm and reached for the other one. "Give it to me. I know it'll hurt, but you can do this."

The rail leaned with the weight, metal twisting and straining. Waves boiled and slammed the rocks below. Unbidden, an image flashed in his mind.

Hawk holding Remi's life in his hands. And now he held Cole's life in his hands.

"Just go!" Cole shouted. "You'll die too. Let me go!"

"No way." He wouldn't leave Cole.

His brother's face twisted in pain. "I'm only going to slow you down."

"I'm not giving up on you."

"And you never did, even when you thought I was an assassin. You need to save the girl, man. If they get to her, you'll never see her again. She's gone." The moisture impeded his grip on Cole's arm, his hand was slowly slipping from Hawk's grasp.

Groaning, Hawk strained to pull harder. The rail bent forward, threatening to topple completely into the ocean and take them both with it.

God, please help me! Hawk's hope that he would bring his brother to safety was slipping away along with his grip. But he wouldn't let go or give up.

Night Stalkers never quit. The motto burned through him even though he was no longer part of that elite team.

"That rock." Cole gestured, angling his head to the right. "That outcropping right there. Swing me over to it. If I can land on that, I can make my way out of here."

"You can't."

"It's either that or drop me. I'd prefer a controlled drop. The last guy fell to his death."

"I mean the king tide is coming in again. You'll never make it off the beach."

"Then I guess you'd better hurry."

41

Charles Whitman and his henchmen, John's former security detail, rushed Dylan, Jo, and Remi out of her office and into the inclement weather without their coats. The wind terrified her. She couldn't remember it ever blowing so hard.

"Should we really be out in this?" She wouldn't stop arguing or confronting them. Using delay tactics where possible. She'd keep trying to reason with them until the end. "Should you be making these people get out in this?"

"Shut up," one of the jerks said.

Whitman remained under the awning. Planning to come out once they were all tucked forcibly inside the vehicle? Or maybe he had his own, because Remi didn't recognize the red sports car next to a utility van. Sure enough, the three of them were ushered to the van. One of the men pushed the side door open and gestured for Dylan to get into the back seat. The gunman waved his gun at Jo to follow. "Get in and I won't shoot you."

"Have you met Little Jo?" she asked.

"Who?" He scowled.

Oh no. Say hello to Jo's little friend.

Jo whipped her wrench out of her back pocket and slammed it against the man's temple. Remi grabbed his gun and dove behind the red sports car. She opened fire on the remaining security guard. Whitman disappeared inside the lodge.

Oh, great. That's all they needed was for him to take a hostage. Dylan climbed out of the vehicle.

"Call the sheriff," Remi said. "Tell him we're under attack at the lodge."

"On it," Dylan said.

"We make a good team," Jo said. "But now what? How do we get this Whitman guy before he hurts anyone else?"

A figure emerged from the woods. Hawk.

I don't believe it.

Her heart jumped to her throat. Relief blew through her harder than the violent gusts. But he looked beaten and barely hanging on. She wanted to rush to him, but she was still dealing with a volatile situation.

"As for Whitman," Remi said to Jo, "wait for the sheriff. Don't go in there and try to face him."

"He'll probably try to take a hostage," Jo said. "Maybe I shouldn't have used Little Jo."

"You did the right thing. If we got in that van, we were riding to our death." And Remi would have likely faced torture until she gave up the location of the Tempest device. Someone wanted it badly, and it scared her to think of what would happen if it were delivered to the terrorist group.

An armed man suddenly stepped from the woods and started for Remi, aiming a gun at her.

Hawk grabbed him from behind and disarmed him, kicked him in the groin so hard the man fell over. Hawk grabbed a zip tie—one of several hanging out of the man's pockets—and tied him up, then stood over him and waited for Remi and Jo to join him.

"Hawk . . . I thought . . . Whitman ordered his men to kill you."

"Whitman?"

"Yeah. He's here inside the lodge. From what I gather John was working with him to begin with, but now John is competing with him . . . planning to sell the device to terrorists too." Had she made a mistake believing Whitman's words? He was a criminal, after all.

She knew how Hawk felt about his friend and that her statement would hurt him.

"I know," he said.

Wow. Okay. What happened? How did he find out? "And . . . Cole? Is he. . . ?" She couldn't bring herself to say the word. He could be incapacitated or tied up. She had to tell Hawk the truth about his brother, though she wasn't entirely sure herself what that was.

"Cole is going to die if I don't get down on the beach and get him out."

"What? How did he end up on the beach?"

"It's a long story. I need you to get somewhere safe, though, or this is all for nothing. Then I can go help Cole. He's been shot, and he won't be able to make it off the beach without help, especially with the rising tide."

"I'll get him. You stay and help Remi." Jo didn't wait for Hawk's agreement and ran toward the stairs down to the shore.

"Be careful," Hawk shouted after her. "I can't be positive other gunmen aren't out there or those in the bunker didn't escape."

Jo slowed and turned to walk backward.

"Haven't you heard? I'm a survivor." She whirled around and took off.

"Whitman's in the lodge," Remi said. "Dylan's watching to make sure he doesn't escape. We're waiting on the sheriff. Hawk, Erika was behind the attacks. Jo's abduction. She was probably the driver that took out the sheriff's vehicle. Cole wasn't behind any of that."

"I know it wasn't Cole."

The air whooshed from her lungs. "What? How?"

"Cole and I came to terms. John"—Hawk gasped in pain—of the heart or physical?—"lied to me. Told me Cole was an assassin. Had gone rogue. He wanted to come between us so he could stop Cole. And Cole thought I was someone to protect you from. That I was working with John to get the information. John pitted us against each other."

"If you were, then I'm an idiot. I gave the information to you willingly."

Hawk pressed closer and hugged her to him. She drew in his masculine scent mixed with salt, mud, rain, and sweat.

"I'm just glad Whitman didn't get you or take you," he whispered against her cheek, then released her. "I left Cole behind to come and find you. Now I need you to stay safe while I go face Whitman and end this."

The red sports car raced away.

"He's getting away!" Remi started toward the parking lot.

They'd been distracted for only a few moments, during which he'd made his move. The sports car headed north past the cabins.

"He's going for the choppers," Hawk said. "I need a ride." He looked around the parking lot.

"Here, take my truck." Dylan jogged from the lodge over

to them and tossed Hawk keys. "Mine's the old junker there. I'm sorry. I couldn't stop Whitman. He slipped by me and was in the car, speeding away before I knew it."

"Thanks, Dylan. We're not going to let him get away to try to kill us on another day," she said.

Hawk hiked toward the truck. "You're right. *We're* not. You're not coming."

"You're not stopping me."

She climbed in on the passenger side while Hawk got into the driver's seat of the old beat-up truck. The engine rumbled to life, then he raced down the road, steering toward one of two helicopters.

"Jo said Cole didn't abduct her. That it was all Erika. Anytime someone had that mask, that was her. And Hawk, get this, Erika was there in Zarovia. I put all the puzzle pieces together, and the image was one I took of the church, Sergei, and Erika. I hadn't remembered that. I think Cole sent that to me to help me remember. To help me to realize that I was working with someone who was watching me every moment."

"Because he knew that danger was closing in. He said he didn't shoot John, so I'm not sure who did. I'm sorry he abducted you and took you away on the boat. It's hard to swallow all of it."

"He thought I was in danger," Remi said. "He was trying to protect me, to get me away from you, knowing I would fight him because I didn't understand the danger I was in trusting you. That's why it seemed so weird that he was concerned that I was cold. He seemed caring and it didn't fit with his actions. But I get it now."

Hawk filled her in on what happened to the special ops extraction team and that someone had shot the helicopter down with a rocket launcher. The covert operation had been doomed from the start.

What was happening to John? Was he secretly escaping the hospital and getting away? Going into hiding with all his intelligence connections? These thoughts filled her mind as Hawk steered the truck along the rutted two-lane road through the dense forest. The thrum of helicopter rotors resounded through the trees, letting them know that Charles Whitman was getting away.

Hawk accelerated, but the old truck wasn't going much faster. Besides, the road was so bumpy she was going to get knocked out if he kept this up. Finally, the helipad where he'd landed earlier came into view.

The truck slid across the mud when he stopped.

"Oh no!" Hawk growled. He pounded the steering wheel. "Gordo's going to kill me. Does Whitman even have the skills to fly in this storm?"

Gordo's helicopter lifted above them and started moving away over the trees and then out over the ocean. The wind was blowing so hard, and even Remi could see the chopper was struggling.

She and Hawk got out and ran toward the cliff to watch, rain and wind thrashing them where they stood. A sound drew her attention around in time to see a rocket racing toward the helicopter.

Remi screamed as that day from her past collided with this catastrophic moment.

Instantly, the bird exploded. Flashes of orange and yellow flames filled the sky. The blast boomed over the roar of the storm. The wind drove debris and the body of the broken helicopter toward the cliffside.

Instinctively, Remi ducked as though her action could have protected her, but what remained of the destroyed chopper crashed into the ocean, swallowed up as if it never happened. The jagged edge of a rotor lodged into a sea stack as if to stake a claim, but violent breakers snatched it away. All of it happening within a few seconds, leaving her stunned. Heart pounding, she glanced toward the woods from where the rocket had been launched. Remi caught a glimpse of a masked figure watching.

"Erika? Is that her?" Just because the person had on a mask didn't mean it was Erika, or Latasha.

Then the mask came off. Erika-Latasha saluted Remi, then disappeared into the woods.

Remi sucked in a gulp of air. "I thought she wanted me dead."

"Looks like she had it out for Whitman more."

"Could she have learned that he had made a deal with someone within her own government?" Remi shrugged, confused. "He made it sound like he'd ended her. So obviously he tried but got it wrong. She escaped."

Remi didn't know if she was safe or not since Erika had tried to kill her while pretending to be part of the staff at the lodge, her cover and her alibi working to keep her from suspicion. "Whitman said she was an operative for Zarovia. I guess her mission was to watch me, and if she thought I was starting to remember, then she was supposed to take me out."

"Except just now, she took out someone else," Hawk said.

"Erika could have been the one to take out the helicopter with Sergei and the special forces team. I was supposed to die. So was Cole."

The storm picked up with gusts fiercer than she'd ever experienced, as if it had been holding back the last few days. Gale-force winds were upon them. They raced to the truck and got in. The forces of nature buffeted the old truck, pushing it across the mud. Hawk gained control again and steered down the mucky path, then floored it.

"You're a speed demon, aren't you? Anything with wheels or wings or rotors."

"I like that you know that about me."

I do too, Hawk. I do too.

42

Guests had left the lodge, warned away with the non-existent threat of a gas leak by bad men who'd come to abduct Remi, and so it was eerily quiet except for the storm. Dylan and Hawk had gotten a fire blazing in the fireplace, then they'd moved the sofa, positioning it to face the window. Hawk sat next to Remi, with Cole and Jo on the other side of him. Together they watched the storm before darkness stole the view within the next few minutes. Hawk suspected they all dreaded time spent staring at four walls during the investigation into the events. Behind them at the coffee bar, in desperate need of caffeine, Dylan messed with Shawna's espresso machine.

Cole's wound had been doctored and the bleeding had stopped, but he still needed a surgeon.

So they waited.

Someone from the sheriff's department would arrive soon. An ambulance too, as soon as one became available. Hawk's entire body throbbed. He felt every bruise, every cut. His head had started aching again.

But his heart was warm and full. Cole was here with

them, alive, and he would be well. His only real crime was taking Remi, but he'd thought he was rescuing her, protecting her, even from herself, when he put the plastic ties on her. She wouldn't be pressing charges. Almost every occasion where they had thought Cole was to blame, Erika had fooled them all.

Hawk, Cole, and Remi concluded that she'd been planted to watch Remi and neutralize her if she became a threat. Then Hawk showed up and stood in her way at every turn. But she hadn't killed Remi in the end and instead had chosen to take out Charles Whitman—he was the bigger threat.

Remi was safe for the moment, but Hawk would remain cautious. She had a lot of information in her head to share with important people who could take the burden from her. Hawk had spoken directly with Sheriff Thatcher and requested he work through his channels to contact the Department of Homeland Security—because Remi's information had everything to do with national security—and they could then forward it to the DOD, the powers that be. It would take time to learn the truth and find the evidence necessary to charge John. It might even be his word against Cole's, but Cole claimed the evidence of John's connections and dealings with Charles Whitman would take him down.

All they could do was pray and trust that the device would land in the hands of the right people and that they would be left alone. Remi would be free to stay here at the lodge and never run again. Or travel like she'd always wanted.

He would give her time to figure out what she wanted, and then, if it made sense, he might ask her out on a real date. He was old-fashioned that way, and maybe he had moved too fast and jumped the gun a little with that kiss. But pressure cookers had a way of quickly bringing all the emotions to the surface.

"I don't believe it." She stood and moved to the window.

He instantly missed her warmth. He frowned, unwilling to move just yet.

She touched the window. "Don't you see it?"

"The storm? What?" Jo asked.

"I could swear it was there," Remi said. "One minute."

"Gone the next. The ghost ship," Jo said. "Maybe one day someone will actually get their hands on it."

"Not likely," Remi said. "That thing has been floating around for decades."

Hawk couldn't care less at the moment. Didn't they realize that government agents were about to descend on this place? How were they going to explain everything? And what would happen to Remi? As much as he wanted this to end and was relieved that Cole wasn't an assassin, he didn't know what the future held for any of them.

Remi returned to sit next to him, and he put his arm around her shoulder like it was the most natural thing to do. She leaned against him, settling into it. They'd been running on fumes for too long now, and he didn't have the energy to keep the walls up around his heart. Besides, there was no need. He would savor every moment.

Soon he'd be whisked away to a room to answer questions. They all would. Remi would be ripped from his arms, and even after only four days, he felt as if she had always belonged there. But he had to accept the fact that she wasn't his and he didn't know her that well. He didn't know what life would be like getting to know her under normal circumstances.

But the date. A good old-fashioned date. Then they'd see where it took them. That is, *if* she said yes to a date.

Incredibly, sirens screamed through the lodge over the raging monster winter storm.

Remi stood again. "And it begins." She eyed Hawk, a little fear in her eyes.

Cole remained where he was, looking pale. He blinked up at Hawk. "I'm okay."

"I know." He wasn't letting Cole out of his sight until he was better, and frankly, he needed time with his brother. They needed to reconnect, and he would never let Cole get too far out of reach again if it was up to him.

Jo had doctored Cole's wound and brought him broth. Nurtured him. The woman had single-handedly rescued his brother. He owed her, big-time. But he had a feeling that Cole would be the one to repay that debt. The way he looked at her, he might be smitten.

Hawk finally stood. "I'll get the door."

He opened it and Sheriff Thatcher limped inside, leaning on a cane. He wasn't taking time to recover from his injury, despite what the county rules might say. "I brought the cavalry. I hope you got your facts straight."

He wasn't sure he had. Where did he begin? Working with John to protect Remi, misunderstanding the entire situation? John's men. Whitman's men. The guys in the bunker? The dead guy that got washed away? The other guy gunning for Remi that he'd taken out in the woods and zip-tied had escaped but then fallen down the newly formed gully to his death. A couple of Whitman's henchmen had escaped, though.

Thatcher squeezed his shoulder. "You're a hero in all this. It's going to be okay."

But heroes didn't always come out unscathed. Experience told him that.

43

The heavy marine fog hadn't burned off yet as Remi walked the disconcertingly quiet beach. At least it was peaceful now that the series of big storms had passed. Normally, the wind would still blow hard and cold on these rocky shores. But maybe nature had run out of fuel after the last fierce display.

So Remi would savor walking on the beach while no one else had ventured out. All manner of seashells littered the shore, along with a few sea creatures.

The lodge had weathered the series of monster storms and remained strong and sturdy as it had for a century. Remi had contacted the geologist specialists to come and evaluate the new gulley created by the unexpected collapse near the Bluff Cabin, and depending on their assessment, decisions needed to be made. The Bluff Cabin was off-limits until then.

Guests had already started returning to the lodge to continue watching the rough seas and the crashing waves and to walk on the beach to look at tide pools during low tides. Watch from the window during high tides. King tide season was almost behind them.

She wished that was all she had to worry or think about, but it would take her a good long while to forget all that occurred, except she didn't want to forget. She would always remember. Forgetting was overrated.

She'd shared all she knew about the device with the two men from the DIA—Defense Intelligence Agency, part of the DOD. She relayed the information Sergei had shared, including where to find the device. While he had been speaking at a university in Europe, he was able to hand the Tempest off under the guise of a research project to a trusted friend who then shipped it to the Pacific Northwest National Laboratory, where it was stored until Sergei himself could retrieve it. The friend had no knowledge the package she'd sent contained the Tempest device, leaving Remi as the only one to know its location. Remi could only assume that responsible parties within the US Government had recovered it because no one had come back to question her about the location. She'd been tasked with not sharing what happened with anyone else or she would be charged with treason. She wasn't sure about that, but she didn't intend to test that threat.

At least the danger surrounding the device had been neutralized and the Blackfire cell of terrorists would never get their hands on it. Andre Aslam—the same man Hawk had pursued and who'd died in the helicopter collision— had belonged to that same cell. John Marshall had been arrested for his efforts in coordinating international espionage and working with a now-deceased arms dealer. John had double-crossed his partner, Charles Whitman, who had cut him a deal to retrieve the device for him. In fact, he'd gone as far as shooting himself to perpetuate

Cole's role so he could be framed when the device went missing and Remi was ultimately killed. Cole and his military hacker friend had provided evidence against John, and it sounded like Cole was coming out of this with job offers. State and federal agencies wanted his investigative skills.

And Erika . . .

Remi shook her head and almost smiled. The woman had tried to kill her on multiple occasions. A week after Erika had shot Gordo's helicopter down, killing Charles Whitman, she'd appeared in Remi's room in the middle of the night. Remi thought back to that moment.

Heart pounding, she'd reached for the gun she now slept with under her pillow. But it was too late. Erika stood over her with a knife. Always a knife with this one. A sliver of light filtered through the window. Erika was a redhead now. Remi couldn't see her eye color. She remained a shape-shifter.

"What do you want?" Remi asked.

"Relax. I'm not here to kill you," Erika whispered.

"Why the change of heart?"

"You're no threat, Remi. I'm Zarovian intelligence, and my job was to prevent our star scientist, Sergei Petrov, from delivering the Tempest device into the wrong hands. We thought you were a spy sent to learn from Sergei and that you were working with Charles Whitman, who planned to sell the device to a group called Blackfire. We couldn't allow that. Whitman thought he'd killed me and left me for dead, but I completed my mission and neutralized him. As long as he was alive, he would always be a threat to not just my country but yours."

"So, you don't consider me a threat?"

"I learned directly from him that you weren't working with him. And our countries are allies, and besides . . . I think of you as a friend. Yeah, I was a deadly threat right in your midst, and I'm sorry about that. Sorry I tried to kill you." Erika smirked.

Before Remi could say more, she slipped out the window. Remi ran to look, but Erika was nowhere to be seen. Remi could breathe a little easier for the time being. She believed Erika because she could have killed her while she slept, then been well on her way to her own country before anyone would have discovered Remi's body.

Jolting her back to the present, a wave rushed up and soaked her to the ankles. The cold sent a rush through her, and she gasped. If she ever again ended up with the choice to help someone running from bullets, would she avoid getting involved next time? She hoped not.

But the biggest pain in her chest was Hawk.

He'd saved her. They'd been running from danger together and he'd been there to help her. She'd helped him. But she had a feeling that he was like that ghost ship . . . in and out of sight . . . always just out of reach.

After walking as far as she could before she'd have to get wet to maneuver around that obtrusive but beautiful sea stack, Remi turned around to head back to the steps to the lodge.

The heavy marine fog cleared, revealing more sea stacks. Crashing breakers soothed her soul, and yes, maybe she could make this place her permanent home. Remi had been surprised that Mrs. Monroe hadn't wanted to dismiss her after the guests had been endangered because of Remi.

The woman had pished. And she'd poshed. Evelyn Monroe was as eccentric as they came, and she lived in an old Gothic-style mansion to prove it. Remi smiled at the thought.

In the distance, a lone figure emerged from the fog, walking toward her. She was still a little shell-shocked after the events that had knocked her over and into Hawk Beckett's arms. Now that she remembered and the danger was over, she was free to fall for someone. Build a life together. But where was Hawk now? Not here. He'd just disappeared.

The figure had a gait about him. Shoulders like a lumberjack.

Hawk? "Hawk!" She was an idiot to run, but she couldn't help it. She didn't care. She picked up her pace, stumbling over rocks here and there. Was it her imagination or was he hurrying toward her too? She wanted to run right into him. Imagined him picking her up and swinging her around. Yeah, she was an idiot.

Instead, when she approached him, she stopped a couple of feet away and squinted up at him. Took in his kind eyes, his thick hair, and strong jaw. His protective demeanor. Warmth swept through her, then settled in her heart. She had it for this guy worse than she'd thought, after only four days. What would happen if she spent more time with him? She might be in trouble.

"Come here." Hawk stepped forward and pulled her to him. He squeezed her long and hard.

When he finally released her, it was much too soon. Remi could have stayed in his arms forever. Waves rushed in and soaked through her shoes, the cold shocking her again.

"I'm surprised to get that kind of welcome." His grin told her he liked that she'd rushed toward him.

"I was afraid I wouldn't see you again."

"I thought we had an agreement," he said. "I was going to give you the grand tour in my helicopter and then you might consider letting me run a tour package out of this lodge." He cocked his head. "You *are* staying, aren't you?"

"Whatever gave you that idea?"

He shrugged and gazed off into the distance. "I don't know. Just a guess."

"Yes, I'm staying. And for your information, I ran this by Mrs. Monroe just in case you ever came back, and she's in agreement. You can run your tour package if we keep it quiet and low-key. No advertising, per se. Nothing to draw too many visitors. The place is already booked from word of mouth and decades of families visiting."

Hawk's smile warmed her to her cold, wet toes. The shoes weren't as waterproof as advertised.

"I'm good with that," he said. "But I'd still like to give you a personal tour. You made the decision before I got to show you around during good weather."

"And *I'm* good with that. But what about you? Won't you be bored? Seems like there's an opening at the sheriff's office since Deputy Hunter retired."

"I don't know what the future holds, Remi, but I hope you're in it. If you want to be. Do you?"

"What do you think?" She smiled.

"Then how about a date tomorrow night." He angled his head and quirked his brows like he feared she might reject him.

"What about right now?" She smiled again. "We can start making new memories."

Hawk's grin sent warmth racing through her. He tilted her chin up and kissed her gently, then stepped back.

She took his hand and walked with him on the beach. Someone stood on top of the cliff and watched them.

Evelyn Monroe.

To Evelyn, Remi and Hawk probably looked like they had disappeared into the fog.

Turn the page for a sneak peek at the next installment in the thrilling Hidden Bay series from **ELIZABETH GODDARD!**

1

Three may keep a secret, if two of them are dead.

Benjamin Franklin

*Y**ou won't see danger coming . . . until it's too late."*
Those words shared by her mother moments before her death had defined Jo Cattrel's life for the last three years. And maybe the life of every dead or missing person whose case she'd ever worked as a forensic artist. As for suspects, she lived to take them down with nothing more than a pencil. But there was a downside to it. A morbidity.

So much time spent with the dead, the missing, or drawing criminal faces meant that she couldn't trust people. It meant that she glanced over her shoulder more than the average person. Like right now. If anyone cared to notice, she might appear downright paranoid.

Was someone watching? Following?

She couldn't escape the fear that she'd made a mistake in leaving her hiding place in Hidden Bay.

But Pop had sent her a cryptic message.

Don't worry about me, Jo. I didn't mean to
lead trouble to you. Please forgive me.

One cryptic message had compelled her across Puget Sound to the city, of all places, to search for her father. She'd only just found him three years ago. She wasn't about to lose him now.

And this note felt like . . . *goodbye*.

No way would she let him disappear on her. Was she a fool to chase after him? Yet another person to leave her? Didn't matter. She was here.

I'm doing this.

After living in the misty rainforest near the Washington coast, she was overwhelmed by the city sights and sounds. Nothing like a lungful of concentrated exhaust. The towering skyscrapers impeded fresh air. Having parked two blocks away, she dragged in too many breaths of pollution as she ascended the slick uphill sidewalk on a cold, rainy day, hiking toward the tallest building in Seattle.

If Pop hadn't wanted her to follow, he should have responded to her many texts demanding an explanation. So she'd used a locator app they shared. Fortunately for her, he'd probably forgotten about it.

She couldn't picture Pop in the big city. Back in Hidden Bay, he owned and operated the R&D Body Shop, got his hands dirty, and was always in his coveralls, fiddling with tools and covered in grime. He called himself a grease monkey, so what was he doing in downtown Seattle at the Columbia Center building?

Finally arriving at her destination, she peered up at the seventy-six-story building. Dizziness swept over her, so she stared at her feet instead. Got her bearings. Then pushed through the glass door.

The sleek lobby intimidated, but she pressed forward. She needed to act like she belonged. The locator app told her that Pop was here. Or at least he *had* been. But now when she looked at the app, she got nothing. Was he still here?

She started toward the bank and nodded with a friendly smile at the security guard, though she feared her smile and the clear I-don't-belong-here look on her face would give her away. Jo's sling bag snagged on a brass stanchion, and she knocked the whole thing over. Of course, it banged on the floor and echoed. A few people glanced her way.

Her heart pounded as the security guard approached. He set the stanchion back in place.

"I'm so sorry. I'm just clumsy. I'm just . . ." She pointed. "I'm going now."

She hurried toward the directory. How in the world would she find Pop? He could be literally anywhere. Numerous businesses took up space. Tenants too. She could take the elevator and look around the Sky View Observatory. But she'd need to purchase a ticket first. Jo retrieved her cell and texted Pop again.

> I'm at the Columbia Center. Where are you?

Then she took a picture of the directory. Jo should really get out more often because right now, she couldn't feel more out of place.

I just want to go home. But . . . Pop.

"Can I help you, ma'am?" The security guard stood next to her at the directory.

Yeah, she had a feeling she was giving off the wrong vibes.

"Actually, maybe. I'm looking for this man." She pulled

up an image of her father on her cell and showed it to the guy. "He's my father. I was supposed to meet him here."

A little white lie. But he didn't need to know everything.

"A lot of people come and go, but you're lucky. I remember seeing him. He left about an hour ago."

What? "Weird. Okay, I'll just wait at the Starbucks. I can text him that I'll be there." Now that she thought about it, the security guard might wonder why she hadn't texted Pop to begin with. Well, she had but never got a response. "Thanks."

Acid rose in her throat. Jo rushed through the exit without looking back. She didn't know whether to be concerned or cry over his hurtful actions, or just be plain furious. But there was nothing more she could do.

I never should have come.

She stepped out into the rain and hurried down the hill. Glancing over her shoulder, she happened to catch someone leaving the building . . . and stopping to watch her. She turned to get a better look. The watcher ducked out of sight. Frowning, Jo blew out a shaky breath. She was just seeing things.

Jo rushed forward, speed-walking her way around the pedestrian traffic until she got to the corner.

Another glance back confirmed that no one followed her. Still, the sounds, the rush of people would give her an anxiety attack. She didn't wait for the light to signal, but dashed across the street, receiving honks and a few choice words. At the parking garage, she raced to her vehicle over in the corner. Another glance over her shoulder—because there could never be too many—told her others entered the garage, heading to their vehicles, oblivious to her.

Sayonara, Seattle.

Jo scrambled into her red Land Rover Defender that Pop had customized. Starting it, she appreciated the deep rumble. Nobody was going to mess with her while she was in this beast. She paid at the gate and sped out of the parking lot.

Jo was done with the city. And . . . done with her father? The thought sent a pang through her heart. She wasn't done with him. This couldn't be the end.

Downtown traffic was maddening, and Jo didn't relax until she was on the ferry, crossing Puget Sound to Bremerton, where she could drive the rest of the way to Hidden Bay. Sitting in cold silence, Jo remained in her beast where it was safe, fighting the nausea erupting from the rocking motion of the ferry. The water was surprisingly rough today.

Jo glanced up from her cell and she couldn't believe her eyes.

Waves crashed onto the deck with the cars, moving them around a little too much for comfort. She couldn't imagine this was a normal happening. Maybe she should get out. Another wave, and then the Toyota Camry in front of her nearly knocked into the Lexus next to it. Getting out now might be dangerous.

I should have stayed in Hidden Bay. She'd been hiding away for the last three years, and now venturing out into the world was giving her a panic attack.

The waves calmed. If she was getting out of her vehicle, now was her chance. She'd head up to the top deck. Grab some vending machine food. Jo weaved between the parked cars, noticing that she'd been the only one to remain inside her vehicle.

"What are you doing?" A muffled, fear-filled voice drew her attention.

The question hadn't been for her. She glanced around the shadowed car deck filled with vehicles. Hearing nothing more, she headed toward the steps where she could make her way up. Pressing forward between the cars, she couldn't ignore the grunts that came with a struggle, and in the reflection of a truck window she watched as someone slid down the side of a car. Someone else holding a knife appeared in the reflection and looked down at the body, then slinked away. The killer wore a heavy overcoat with the hood pulled forward.

Jo should scream.

But she couldn't breathe.

He hadn't looked in her direction, but he was aware she was there and watching—she knew that to her bones. Looking at her would send him to prison—whoever he was—because then she would see his face. She hoped security cameras caught him.

Jo hurried toward the stairs. She had to get out of here. Get away. He was still here somewhere, hiding behind or in a vehicle, she didn't know. Another wave crashed, sending water onto the loading deck. Jo held back her cry for help. The intrusive waves rushed around her ankles, soaking her shoes in ice-cold water. The cars were moving with the waves again, and she could end up crushed.

She eyed the stairwell. Where were the two ferry crew members she'd seen earlier? Maybe someone would come down to check on the vehicles and see what was happening. She had no choice, really. Jo rushed between the cars and sloshed through the water, slipping a few times as another wave crashed.

A chill crawled over her. The tiny hairs on the back of her neck lifted. Her breaths quickened.

She sensed someone near and—

A hand covered her mouth as a strong arm seized her. She fought and kicked, but he treated her as if she was as weightless as a small plastic toy. He dragged her between the vehicles, then, at the last car, opened the door. Horror filled her when she saw a body in the back seat. The man he'd killed? A scream erupted in her throat, but he punched her in the face, stunning her. Pain shot through her head as it lolled. Stunned, she struggled to find her way out of the growing darkness and failed.

Blinking, she suddenly realized she was in the driver's seat of a sedan. He'd knocked her out, but she was awake now. She scrambled to get out, but the car was already in motion, rolling over the edge. He must have removed the net barriers and forced the vehicle over.

Heart hammering, Jo screamed as the sedan plunged into the water. The man stared down at her from the deck, his face shrouded in darkness.

Except his eyes.

She'd never forget them.

And that's why he was killing her now, destroying the only witness.

I'm going to die.

The car slammed into the water, jolting her head forward, then bobbing and rocking forward on the rough, stormy waters. Icy cold seawater filled the cab as it sank faster than she would have thought. But she could escape. She could do this. She tried to open the door, but it wouldn't budge against the pressure of the water, so she tried the window button.

Hope filled her. She could swim through the opening.

Except the window stopped. What? Why had it stopped? No way could she make it through that small gap. "No, no, no!"

"God help me!" Jo cried out.

She just needed to break the glass.

The force of the water pushed her up to the roof, and it was then she realized her foot was tied to the accelerator. Even if she could get the window open, she was trapped. She yanked and pulled on her ankle, tried to undo the zip tie, but she couldn't free herself.

A knife, she needed a knife.

The vehicle was completely submerged now, and cold seawater poured in. Her entire body shook as she held up her face to breathe from the remaining air pocket. Her last lifeline.

She fought the window and the door. Taking what could be her last gulp of air, she opened the glove compartment to search for a gun or a hammer, anything to help her break the glass, or a knife to cut herself free. Papers floated out of the compartment.

A lump of terror squeezed her throat.

Panic engulfed her as fast as the rising water.

God, I'm going to die. All this hiding from one killer, and another one got me anyway.

Mom had been right.

Jo hadn't seen danger coming . . .

Acknowledgments

I am so blessed to be writing yet another series for Revell. This first novel in my brand-new Hidden Bay series has been such a joy to write. As always, I couldn't have done it without the continued encouragement and support of many people.

To my writing buddies near and dear—Susan, Lisa, Shannon, Sharon, Chawna, Michelle, and Lynette, as well as so many others—thank you from the bottom of my heart!

To my family—my children and grandchildren and husband—you guys keep me going.

To my Revell team—Rachel McRae, Brianne Dekker, Karen Steele, and the art team—you are the absolute best publishing team.

To Steve Laube—I'm so grateful you believed in me all those years ago.

To Jesus—you gave me the dream and opened the doors. I give you all the glory!

Elizabeth Goddard is the *USA Today* bestselling and Christy Award–winning author of more than sixty novels, including *Cold Light of Day* and *Shadows at Dusk*, as well as the Rocky Mountain Courage and Uncommon Justice series. Her books have sold more than 1.5 million copies. She is a Carol Award and Reader's Choice Award winner and a Daphne du Maurier Award and HOLT Medallion finalist. When she's not writing, she loves spending time with her family, traveling to find inspiration for her next book, and serving with her husband in ministry. Learn more at Eliza bethGoddard.com.

A Note from the Publisher

Dear Reader,

Thank you for selecting a Revell novel! We're so happy to be part of your reading life through this work. Our mission here at Revell is to publish stories that reach the heart. Through friendship, romance, suspense, or a travel back in time, we bring stories that will entertain, inspire, and encourage you. We believe in the power of stories to change our lives and are grateful for the privilege of sharing these stories with you.

We believe in building lasting relationships with readers, and we'd love to get to know you better. If you have any feedback, questions, or just want to chat about your experience reading this book, please email us directly at publisher@revellbooks.com. Your insights are incredibly important to us, and it would be our pleasure to hear how we can better serve you.

We look forward to hearing from you and having the chance to enhance your experience with Revell Books.

The Publishing Team at Revell Books
A Division of Baker Publishing Group
publisher@revellbooks.com